"Bring your hurt to me," she told the snake, "and I will heal you."

The snake shifted, her scales rippling as she pressed her head and the coil containing the lump against the bars.

Khorii dipped her head to touch the lump with her horn. She felt the snake's head swaying above her and was startled momentarily when a drop of something wet fell past her nose and sizzled on the street just beside her foot. Glancing up, she saw the fangs protruding slightly from the snake's mouth, venom dripping. Khorii knew the secretion had been involuntary, and the snake rippled with what could have been an apology.

She touched the tumor with her horn. She felt the tumor begin to uncoil its wadded cells inside the snake's body as it began to disintegrate, then realized why the serpent looked so sad. This was not a real tumor, but the calcified bodies of the snake's young that she had ingested before she was captured. Instead of reabsorbing into her body normally, they had congealed in a lump, then grew hard and putrid inside her and sickened her.

The snake wound its long body in a tight coil and regarded Khorii with those beautiful eyes again. Then it slowly dipped its head, as if bowing in appreciation of what the young Linyaari had done for it.

And all during this time, the man who was supposed to be tending the snake watched the entire event with his mouth hanging open. Then, when the snake belched, he fainted dead away.

THE WORLD OF ACORNA

By Anne McCaffrey and Elizabeth Ann Scarborough

By Anne McCaffrey and Margaret Ball

See also

THIRD WATCH

ACORNA'S CHILDREN

ANNE McCAFFREY
and ELIZABETH ANN SCARBOROUGH

An Imprint of HarperCollinsPublishers

This book is a work of fiction. The characters, incidents, and dialogue are drawn from the author's imagination and are not to be construed as real. Any resemblance to actual events or persons, living or dead, is entirely coincidental.

EOS
An Imprint of HarperCollins*Publishers*
10 East 53rd Street
New York, New York 10022-5299

Copyright © 2007 by Anne McCaffrey and Elizabeth Ann Scarborough
Cover art by Chris McGrath
ISBN 978-0-06-052543-9
www.eosbooks.com

First Eos paperback printing: August 2008
First Eos hardcover printing: August 2007

HarperCollins® and Eos® are registered trademarks of HarperCollins Publishers.

Printed in the U.S.A.

10 9 8 7 6 5 4 3 2 1

To Liz O'Connell and Frieda Bates
with thanks and affection

Acknowledgments

We'd like to thank Richard Reaser, our science and salvage consultant for these books. We'd also like to thank Denise Little of Teknobooks and Diana Gill at HarperCollins for their editing and inspiration throughout this series. Finally, we'd especially like to thank Anne McCaffrey's collaborator in the first two books, Margaret Ball, for her brilliant contributions to the characters and cultures in this series.

THIRD ACORNA'S CHILDREN WATCH

chapter 1

Now and Then

Now

Elviiz,

With all of the time changes we've been through during our journey and the disappointment of not being
able to get Mother and Father out of quarantine, we
cannot sleep a wink. So we decided to go visit the
LoiLoiKuans and see how they're settling in to their
new home in our ocean with the *sii*-Linyaari. Please
tell everyone so they won't worry. We'll be back before you know it.

Love,
Khorii, Ariin, and Khiindi, too. (You know how he is
    about fish.)

Khorii left the message on Elviiz's portable com—the
one he needed now that he was fully organic and missing his
critical android modifications.

Then, with the moons shining down on them, she and her
twin walked down to the pearl-crested sea, Ariin carrying
Khiindi.

"He'll walk if you want to put him down," Khorii told her

twin. "We could stop to graze on the way. It would make our story more believable."

Ariin frowned. "He really does need to come with us, and he's so unpredictable."

Khiindi took matters into his own paws by hopping down, waving his tail as if beckoning them to graze. The girls assumed grazing posture and bent to taste the tantalizing grasses growing in the meadows sloping down to the sea. Their horns, a single shining pearly gold one in the center of each of their foreheads, glowed softly in the silver moonlight.

When they were done, Khiindi dodged Ariin's questing hands and trotted ahead, just out of reach. The cat was not about to let the young Linyaari use his crono to spirit Khorii off to the distant past and get her into who knew what kind of trouble without him there to protect her. Nor, for that matter, was he going to miss a chance to escape the little kitty form into which he'd been frozen by his fellow shape shifters, all because of a very slight miscalculation during a mission with which they'd once entrusted him. If they insisted on continuing to hold their grudge, he would be better able to act freely back in the time before the monstrous Khleevi had destroyed the large time-traveling device. The buglike aliens wrecked everything they touched, and they had wreaked havoc not just with the time machine, but with the whole planet. The ecological damage had been repaired, but the time machine was no longer functional.

And, of course, the fish were lovely, too. The LoiLoiKuans saw the three of them approach. The younger ones, well trained by Khiindi back in the days when they were pool pupils, or poopuus, at the school on Maganos Moonbase, flipped a sleek, fat fish out of the water directly into his mouth. Good. Delicious. They had not forgotten the tribute due to their patron cat.

He barely had time to devour it and no time at all for a good wash and brushup before the twins stepped into the water. Khiindi jumped in after them. Makahomian Temple Cats, his lineage in more ways than one, did not mind a nice swim now and then. However, he remembered the first time he had met the aquatic dwellers, after suffering at the hands of that brat Marl Fidd, who had hurt him badly, then thrown him into the pool back at Maganos. The large brown LoiLoi-Kuans with their fused legs and flippered feet swam up to surround them. They were joined by their watery hosts, the *sii*-Linyaari, who were as indigenous to Vhiliinyar as anybody was.

Aari, the twins' father, had transplanted the *sii*-Linyaari to the current time from a previous one in which they were about to become extinct. They were not an attractive species, at least, not to anyone except others of their kind. They were examples of a failed attempt on the part of Khiindi's people, known to the Linyaari and the Ancestors as the Friends, to create the Linyaari race. Like Khorii and the rest of her race, the *sii*-Linyaari also had horns—many little ones growing all over their heads. Some had long, waving hair, some had none. They had fish tails instead of legs, and glistening scales, and spoke only in a bubble-accented thought-talk.

Although they had a reputation for being difficult and even hostile back in their original time, Khiindi figured it probably had a lot to do with their rejection by their parent creators. These days, they were quite happy to see him. If they knew that Khiindi was one of the Friends who had made them, they apparently thought his being a permanent pussycat was punishment enough because they were as friendly to him as they were to the girls and their new guests, the LoiLoiKuans.

"Greetings, everyone," Khorii said. *"We thought you*

*might like your waters freshened up a bit. Fancy a race to
the island?"*

All of the sea people were a bit overstimulated from the
events of the previous day, when two tanks of LoiLoiKuans
had been decanted into the surface-connected inland sea of
Vhiliinyar. A nice sea race was apparently just their idea of
a good time.

Popping bubbles and other expressions of assent rose
from the water as bodies dipped, tails flipped, and the sea
peoples left the twins and Khiindi wallowing in their wake.

"Now!" Ariin said. Khorii held on to her arm and took the
liberty of grabbing Khiindi's tail. And suddenly, they were
then.

Then

One moment they were in the water, the next they were
inside a room bursting with fancy flowing robes framing a
huge mirror and a chest brimming with jewels and cosmetics. Ariin looked around and nodded.

"Where are we?" Khorii asked.

"Akasa's wardrobe. That's where I found this," Ariin
said, holding up her wrist to show off the crono, which dan-
gled loosely on her small arm. *"No more questions now. It's
complicated. I need to get us back to an earlier time, before
we were born."*

"This is before I was born?" Khorii asked.

*"Right. This thing seems to default to the time and place
it was before starting the next time sequence, but we're not
ready to be here yet. I have something to show you a little
farther back."*

She gave Khiindi a look that was remarkable for its wick-
edness in one so young. He knew what she intended then, but

it fit in well with his own wishes so he sent her the desired information. He could, of course, still converse without resorting to Linyaari, Standard, Makahomian, or even Cat. Nor did he require the cruder forms of thought-talk. He simply formed a picture of the time they needed to go back to. Back before he had brought Ariin's egg to his people. Back before he had first befriended her father, Aari. Back when he could walk on two legs. Ariin recklessly tapped the crono without even looking at it, allowing his image to flow from her to the device. He picked the time, but she picked the place.

They stepped out of the water again, onto the grassy banks. Behind them the *sii*-Linyaari dived and fished, or sunned on the island just offshore. Before them, a meadow full of wildflowers, insects, and small animals stretched up to the mountains. Over the mountain peaks shone Vhiliinyar's two moons, one of which was to become the Moon of Opportunity. It glowed with the fullness and benevolence of Hafiz Harakamian's face gazing fondly at the profit balance on his ledger. The other moon was a mere crescent-shaped sliver of light.

Reflecting the light of both moons were the white and shining coats of the creatures hunted on their homeworld for the healing, purifying, and supposedly aphrodisiacal properties of their spiraling, golden, opalescent horns. There they were called unicorns, for obvious reasons. Here they were simply the Others, who were not the same as the Friends, although their kind varied. The Others were beautiful, useful, and innocent beings with whom the habitually self-centered Friends had become uncharacteristically enchanted. Usually, the Friends were the ones who did the enchanting, chiefly of themselves, when they beheld their own reflections. If they didn't like what they saw, they simply changed it to something more pleasing.

Most had a bipedal and humanoid form that generally alternated with a dominant alter form. Khiindi's own dominant alter form had always been feline, though not always or even usually a mere moggy.

"We must hide Khiindi here until we need him," Ariin told Khorii. "He has enemies in this time, and even more enemies later on, when we're going. We'll have a use for him soon, but we have to lay some groundwork first."

Khorii bent and picked the cat up, laying his head against her neck, his front paws on her shoulder, his magnificent, fluffy tail curled around her forearm. "Khiindi-cat, you know the Ancestors in our time. These are their ancestors. They are very good creatures and as you know, they like cats. You'll be safe here with them. There are fish in the sea and other creatures for you to eat in the meadows. We'll return for you before you know it, if I understand this timing thing correctly."

Khiindi clung to her with every available claw. He knew Khorii would not abandon him willingly, but he had no idea what Ariin was up to. That one had a positively *ka*-Linyaari ability to conceal her thoughts. He also knew she meant to repay him for bringing her to be studied by his kind as their experiments in creating the Linyaari race continued. They knew they had created the Linyaari. They just didn't know how or when. Of all of them, Grimalkin was, if not the only empath, certainly the one in whom the quality was best developed. He had imagined he would be around during Ariin's youth to see that she was treated well and reasonably happy. Instead, his people, who were angry because he had brought only one of Acorna's embryonic twins instead of both, took away his crono and froze him in little cat form for all time, the first part of which he was to serve as Khorii's guardian and friend. This had left Ariin out in the cold, an object of pity and even scorn.

She hadn't taken it well at all.

Khorii unhooked him and tried to set him down, but he clung to her arm. When she shook him off and tried to step back, he clung to her leg, even wrapping his tail around her ankle. Finally, Ariin grabbed him around his sizeable girth and threw him into the middle of the unicorn herd, to be surrounded by white-bearded muzzles and long, slender white legs. The unicorns parted enough that he zipped out from among them to catch up with the girls, but they had already vanished.

He meowed his frustration, and one of the ancestresses touched him gently with her horn. "Poor little fellow. Stay with us. They'll be back. You're welcome here. You're sort of cute. What are you anyway?"

The horn touch made Khiindi feel even warmer and fuzzier than he actually was, which was saying something. He purred and gazed up at her with wide, adoring kitty cat eyes, his specialty. *Oh well, gather ye allies while ye may.*

Khorii and Ariin were back in the closet again. *"I hope you had a good reason for that, Ariin,"* Khorii said. *"That was kind of mean. Poor Khiindi was really upset and he doesn't like to be tossed around."*

"We can't have him tagging along while we're going undercover," Ariin replied. *"You do want to get to the bottom of this alien threat, don't you? And release Mother and Father from quarantine?"*

"Of course, but I don't understand the plan or what Khiindi has to do with it," Khorii replied. *"You insisted we bring him along and then the first thing you do is abandon him."*

"The first part of the plan depends on us being interchangeable, so that the Friends think we're both me," Ariin explained. *"That way, while you are doing what they expect me to do, I can try to get people to tell me what we need to know."*

"What is it that we need to know? And what makes you think I can't gather information as well as you can?" Khorii demanded.

"I know this time better than you do," Ariin said. *"I know these people and how they act and what they want. I know what we're looking for and—be patient, I'll tell you— and I know where to look and how to ask. You're much too polite."*

"No, I'm not! I can be very rude if it helps my family. Our family. I can be—"

"That's not what I mean," Ariin said, trying to be patient.

"Well, what do you mean?"

"I don't like to say."

"Then I don't like this plan," Khorii said. *"I want to go home. I haven't seen Mother and Father in months, and I'm worried about Elviiz."*

"You needn't be. We'll be back before they know we've gone. We can be back before Elviiz wakes up and reads your note even. It will be fine. Trust me."

"Why should I?" Khorii asked. *"You don't even trust me enough to let me help find out the information we came for."*

"Yes, I do. But I'm better at it than you. If you keep the Friends busy, I can move around more freely and probe a little. If we're clever, they'll never find out there are two of us."

"Why shouldn't they know that?" Khorii asked. *"These are the Friends who saved the Ancestors. They're not evil or anything."*

"If they know we're both here, they'll want to interrogate and experiment on both of us," Ariin told her.

"We could just tell them we can't do that right now, but will be back later to answer their questions."

Ariin gave an internal groan. *"Look, Khorii, you know how you can see plague indicators? It's your special talent?*

Well, I can—persuade—people to think about something I want them to without them realizing I'm doing it. That's my special talent."

"That's not very nice. It's kind of sneaky, isn't it?"

"I was afraid you'd feel that way," Ariin said. "That's why I didn't want to tell you. You grew up among our people, but everybody isn't so nice. Like that Captain Coco."

"I thought you were pushing him, but I was surprised when it worked," Khorii said, remembering how unexpectedly reasonable the pirate chieftain had been. "*I gave him credit for seeing how sensible Mikaaye's solution was."*

"*People like that rarely care about how sensible things are. They just care about getting what they want. Speaking of which, Akasa is awake now. I'm going to hide. You be me."*

"But won't they know?"

"*It's not like we can't thought-talk,"* Ariin replied, dismissing her fears. "*If they wonder why I'm so slow all of a sudden, tell them you're getting in touch with your inner self. They like anything that refers back to themselves, so they'll think it's perfectly natural that you do, too."*

The door of the wardrobe opened and a beautiful, human-looking female with long rainbow-colored curling hair stood in the opening. She had large, gemlike eyes that glittered from amethyst to sapphire blue as she looked at Khorii. "Narhii, you stupid child, what have you been doing in here? You've washed off all of the cosmetics I helped you with. I thought you wanted to wear some of my robes and jewels?"

Khorii stammered, having no idea what the radiant being was talking about. Ariin told her, "*Oh, yes, they call me Narhii, and I was loaded with robes and jewels when I left. Sorry. Her name is Akasa. Tell her you didn't want to take them."*

"I'm sorry, Akasa. I thought you were just letting me play; I did not know I could wear them outside of this room."

"You really are rather backward, you know. I cannot imagine where you found that rag you're wearing. I must have left some old coverall in my closet long enough for the fabric to deteriorate to lose its color and shape, and you put that on." She flipped Khorii's beaded braid between her fingers. "This shows some promise, though the effect is more *sauvage* than *soignée*. Still, I suppose it shows you are making an effort. Ah, well, if you're good, we can do this again later. No time now. You must return to your quarters or to the field with the Others if you like. There is a ball tonight, and I must find something to wear."

"Oh, no! If she starts searching through her clothes she'll find me," Ariin said. *"Tell her since it's the first time you've been in her house, you'll get lost."*

Khorii said, "I understand, except I have never been here in your rooms before, Akasa. Can you not take me back to my home yourself?"

Akasa shrugged, then grabbed her by the arm and dragged her out the door and to the front of the house. The house reminded Khorii a little of the mansion where the cruel and untrustworthy Marl Fidd had tried to hold her captive.

Looking over her shoulder, she was startled to see that the door through which she and Akasa had emerged was an eye that looked very like one of her hostess's, set in a wall-size depiction of the upper half of the female's face.

Akasa's grip loosened and her mouth softened when she saw that Khorii was staring seemingly awestricken at her countenance. "It is rather good, if I do say so myself. Self-portrait. I wanted to make my home look like me."

"You—certainly succeeded," Khorii said, rather stunned at the vanity of it all.

"Ask her about her other artwork in the house," Ariin, monitoring Khorii's thoughts, suggested. *"That should keep her occupied until I can escape."*

Khorii did as her sister suggested. Admiring Akasa's decor did indeed turn out to be a good move. Akasa unhooked her hand from Khorii's arm so she could use both hands to make grand, sweeping gestures as she indicated her various sculptures, frescoes, mosaics, and some more striking but rather gaudy self-portraits of herself in various outfits painted against a black velvet background and embellished with shiny beads and—what were those called?—oh, yes, sequins.

"There are an awfully lot of rooms here that don't seem to have any function except to be cleaned," Ariin remarked, seeing the tour through Khorii's eyes.

"It's a huge gallery!" Khorii said aloud.

"Why, yes, it is, child. As you can see, the depth and breadth of my creativity are well represented here, although my home is far too small to include my public artworks and various other contributions to this city."

"I had no idea," Khorii said, quite truthfully.

"Naturally. A mere child lacks the aesthetic experience to appreciate my work. But don't despair. Your attitude clearly demonstrates that you are maturing into a young adult with excellent taste and a discerning eye. Many of the gowns and robes in my wardrobe are also my creations, you know."

"No! Really? I am truly impressed. It was so good of you to allow me to handle your precious things. I would be overjoyed if you would do so again someday."

"Another time, when there is not a ball for which I must prepare. Perhaps if your development continues to be so pleasing, I will help you gown and bejewel yourself in earnest next time, so you may attend."

"Oh, goody!" Khorii said, clapping her hands and borrowing an expression she'd heard Sesseli use. She said it loudly enough, she hoped, to mask her insincerity.

"After all, it's high time you learned to attract suitors," Akasa continued.

"Oh, yuck!" Ariin said. *"There's nobody here but more of her kind, and even though most of them can manage to be fairly good-looking—as humans go—they are very old, and none of them have ever really been nice to me."*

"Obviously they aren't familiar with our customs. Choosing a lifemate is serious—and it's almost like my people don't even choose. Lifemates just recognize each other."

"These people do a lot of mating, but never bear young," Ariin said. *"They don't seem to stay with each other for any longer than it takes to mate. In fact, I don't think any of them will ever find a lifemate the way you think of it, outside of a mirror. The only thing they seem to love is themselves."*

"That is very sad. But now that you mention it, I have noticed quite a lot of mirrors in this dwelling," Khorii said thoughtfully.

"I've found an exit now," Ariin told her. *"You can go whenever you want. I'll check in when I've gotten what I need."*

"What do you need?" Khorii said. But she got no answer. Left alone in this strange time and place, she could only hope that Ariin wasn't up to her horn in trouble. And that she hadn't dragged her twin with her straight into even more trouble.

chapter 2

Khorii bid farewell to Akasa, who pointed out the way back to Ariin's tiny quarters.

While on a field trip with a teacher and twenty other Linyaari younglings, Khorii had once seen Kubiilikaan as the ruined underground city it was in her time. She was curious to see what it had been like before it was a ruin. She also thought she'd go see the original Ancestors and visit with Khiindi if he was still there. The poor cat would be very upset at being abandoned. Really, she had to put her foot down with Ariin about being so rough with him. Though she had never seen any evidence of his being so, she was sure he was a very sensitive cat.

On the street outside Akasa's house, she perceived a familiar movement in the cityscape around her. Building facades shifted colors and shapes, though not their actual sizes, with a frequency that was fascinating in its variety, baffling as to what was causing it, and slightly nauseating in that she could get motion sick without moving a step, in the same way she had done entering the wormhole.

Doorways changed from round to rectangular, arched to irised, and windows changed similarly or disappeared altogether. Colors shifted constantly, and sometimes during the shift a wall could be blue on one side, green in the middle, and yellow on the other end. The ornamental patterns on what looked like tiles wriggled like worms as they rearranged themselves. A cold, wet wind blew up from the sea, but instead of going into the towering building Akasa had pointed her toward, Khorii walked down the street to the shoreline.

"Where are you going?" Ariin demanded.

"Why are you monitoring my thoughts if I'm not being questioned or sending you questions?" Khorii countered. *"I know you're new to our customs, but that is considered rude."*

"I have to keep you from making silly mistakes, and this is one. You're supposed to return to my cell and stay there until they come and get you. If they come for you and find you— me—gone, they'll be very cross."

"No worries on that account. I got the impression from Akasa that all of the Friends would be at the ball."

"In our dreams! Besides, what if you get lost?"

Khorii sighed. *"It hasn't changed all that much, in spite of everything. The reconstruction and the terraforming on Vhiliinyar have been extensively based on historical records and the memories of survivors of the Khleevi invasion. The research teams who traveled back to pre-Khleevi eras have also consulted extensively with the terraforming crews to en-sure the authenticity of the planet's re-creation. So I've lived here as long as you have. Just not in this city surrounded by these particular humanoids."*

"Go ahead then, Miss Stubborn, and do what you want, but don't ask for my help if you get in over your head tonight. I have a mission to carry out."

"And I don't?" Khorii asked. *"I'm beginning to get the picture now. The only reason you wanted me to come is so that I have to live like you lived all those years till you escaped."*

She could feel Ariin's chagrin. Her silly sister had actually thought she was being devious.

"I don't mind being the decoy when it's necessary, Ariin," Khorii told her. *"But this is my mission, too. After all, I've been involved with the alien plague and the creatures it turns into longer than you have. I care about the people they're threatening. And while I know you want to show me the misery I escaped all those years by not being you, two horns are better than one at sorting this thing out, right?"*

Ariin didn't answer but Khorii felt her seething, thinking to herself that Khorii, who everybody thought was so perfect, was going to hog all the glory from this mission, which was Ariin's idea, too.

"Ariin, honest," she told her sister, *"you can take all the credit when your brilliant plan saves the universe as we know it ought to be, but I am not going to vegetate in your cell when I could be helping. For one thing, I'm going to go see how Khiindi is doing."*

"How do you know he's even still there?" Ariin demanded, adding nastily, *"He might be dead by now. One of the Others might have stepped on him, or something from the woods could have eaten him."*

"Khiindi can take care of himself. Makahomian Temple Cats can be very fierce, and they live almost as long as we do, longer lots of times. And he's with the Ancestors. If anything happened to him, they'd cure him in a heartbeat. You shouldn't be so mean to him. He's just a little cat."

"No, he's not," Ariin said, then closed down and refused to say any more. Khorii wondered what she meant by that, but soon forgot about it as she began exploring the ancient city.

Khiindi made the best of his situation. After twining through the legs of his new hosts, including those of the sympathetic female, he trotted off to the woods bristling on the hills above the meadow. He wasn't sure when exactly he was, but he thought it ought to be before the time when he'd been form-frozen. If so, the situation was laden with possibilities. Once among the trees, he attempted an easy transformation first, trying to morph into another of his feline forms, a larger cat. After a few false starts—his tail length at one point exceeding twice his body length, then his ears sprouting so that each was larger than his entire head while his paws grew as big as galoshes on thin little cat legs— long eons of practice came back into play to make up for six *ghaanyi* frozen into one form. Of course, he'd have had to check his reflection in a pool to make certain, but every part of him he could look at or lick had become a quite presentable and apparently ferocious tiger.

Could he also change to something two-legged? He tried his humanoid form, and although a certain cattiness remained in his countenance—the long whiskers above his eyebrows and on his cheeks, a certain pointiness and furriness of the upper ear—on the whole he thought it a good try. Perhaps he should try a more recent incarnation? He had traveled with Aari and managed to impersonate him to his nearest and dearest for quite some time. He wished Khorii was still nearby. He would have loved to see if he could make her think he was her daddy and not her kitty.

As for Ariin, her nature led him to believe that perhaps his presence around her mother just before her conception must have had some influence on the girl. She was so devious and manipulative, albeit in a rather obvious way, that she seemed to be a chip off his own block rather than Aari's or Acorna's.

Taking Aari's form again, the erstwhile cat grew a horn and lost the whiskers, though he did grow the little wispy beard under his chin that some Linyaari continued to sport

in honor of the Ancestors. Now for the next step. He would
turn himself into an Ancestor and go out and join his fellows.
From Aari to Ancestor was an easier transition than it would
have been from cat to unicorn. Once he had all of the unicorn
parts in their proper places, he trotted out and began grazing,
allowing the others to seek him out.

"*Hello. I haven't seen you before,*" said the female who
had been sympathetic to him in cat form. She seemed slightly
startled by his presence, interested in him but not suspicious.

"*I was left behind on Terra when the ship picked up the
rest of you. I was born on a big boat during a terrible flood,
and both my parents were lost. I was crying for them when
a passing patrol ship of Friends heard my heartbroken cries
and whisked me away to grow up on their ship. They dropped
me off near here only a few minutes ago.*"

He gave her a soulful look meant to inspire pity, and it
did, sort of.

"*Some younglings dropped off a frightened little felinoid
thing just before you came. He ran away, but I fear he will be
eaten or get lost and cold. He seemed so lonely.*"

"*Why, yes, I believe I saw such a creature. He was going
off into the deep woods. Come, and I'll show you where I
saw him last.*"

He hadn't lost his touch. Batting her ivory lashes over her
beautiful golden eyes, the female trotted beside him, touching shoulders now and then.

Khiindi/Grimalkin's attitude toward Ariin softened considerably.

Now

Mating," Thariinye said wisely when the girls did not
return from their nocturnal walk. "*No getting around it,*

they're that age. They've gone off looking for mates, or to prepare to look for mates, or to make themselves more attractive to mates."

"They're too young!" his own mate Maati protested.

"You weren't much older when you pointed your horn at me," Thariinye reminded her, unwisely.

"I did no such thing. I thought you were the most conceited, deceitful Linyaari male ever born."

"But I grew on you," he insisted with a wink.

"Not exactly. Once I realized that you were much more trouble to yourself than to any of the females you fancied, I felt someone had to keep you from an early demise. It was the linyaari *thing to do."*

"My hero!" he said, snorting.

Khornya, as Acorna was known among her own people, interrupted in a pleading tone. *"Whatever you think, Thariinye, would you and Maati please go ask the sii-Linyaari and the LoiLoiKuans if they saw the girls?"* She felt so helpless being stuck in quarantine.

Aari tried to soothe her. *"They can't be in worse trouble than they've been in while they were off-world, love. There's no trouble to get into now, since we eradicated the Khleev—"* He stopped and looked at her, the same idea dawning on both of them at the same time.

"They've got a time device, haven't they?" Khornya said, though she needed no answer. *"Ariin had to have something to come forward to this time. Why didn't we think of it before and confiscate the wretched thing?"*

"Ariin probably masked it so we didn't even think about it," Maati said. *"She's very clever at thought-misdirection, you know."*

"She didn't have to have a device, did she?" Thariinye asked. *"She could have used the big machine before it got broken, and found a way to get herself sent here even though*

it's broken on this end. She did come out of the water, after all, and that's the way the big device worked."

"I hope you're right, Thariinye," Aari said. *"Because if that's the case, then the girls are still in the here and now. It will be easier to find them elsewhere than elsewhen."*

Joh Becker emerged from the *Condor,* his shoulders and mustache drooping. "Damn kids," he complained. "They should all be implanted with personal locator chips at birth."

"If they timed it, a chip wouldn't help, Joh," Aari told them. "But, on the bright side, if they timed it, they will literally be back before we know it and we will not retain even the memory of worry on their behalf."

Khornya didn't bother to point out the holes in her mate's logic. They already knew the girls were gone. And she was already very worried.

Khiindi!" Khorii called. "Khiindi cat." By now she was far enough away from the city that she felt her calling would not arouse undue interest on the part of the Friends. Ariin's comment that Khiindi might have died by now did worry her. She didn't have control of time-travel devices. She had no idea how long ago in the past he had been left. He might be so old he'd lost his hearing by now. Not that he ever came when she called, unless food was involved.

In the meadows ahead, a small group of Ancestors looked up from their grazing and gazed quizzically in her direction.

"Narhii?" One of them, a female by the thought-voice, asked.

"Not Narhii!" a male voice told the female emphatically. *"Who are you, youngling?"*

"I'm Khorii, her sister."

"Ah, Narhii's sister," several in the herd murmured to themselves.

"Yes, only her name is Ariin now. It's a proper name, like mine, a combination of our parents' names. We're twins."

"We know that, Khorii. We told her about you."

"How could you? I've never met you before."

"No, but we know of you. Because he did not bring you back with him and brought only your twin, Grimalkin was form-frozen and stripped of his powers."

"I heard something about that, but I don't know any Grimalkin. I'm looking for my cat. Do you remember him?"

The Ancestors broke into what could only be described as horse laughter.

"It's not funny! He's gray and fluffy and has been with me since I was a baby. We've never been separated before. If you ask me, my sister's upbringing here has made her kind of cruel for a Linyaari."

"There's no cat here now, youngling," another female said. "But if we see one, we'll tell him you're looking for him. But why are you here?"

"My sister has a plan, and I'm supposed to be helping her with it." Khorii sighed. "Although I think she really just wanted to bring me here to suffer like she did."

"We did not think she would ever return once she left this time," a gruff older male said, with a snort. "The last thing we expected was that she'd return with you. Why are you not both back with your family? You're both just foals."

Khorii shrugged, feeling much wearier than she had realized. "It's a long story."

"Scoot over, Hruffli, and make room for her to graze too," said the female. "Tell us all about it."

Khorii did, starting with the quarantine, working forward to how her parents became ill and she recognized her special talent, and forward again until she met Ariin, they witnessed the plague's mutations, and returned once more to their parents. "I thought the plague would be gone, but

Mum and Dad are still affected. Ariin seems to think there's a clue of some sort back here that will help us unravel the source of the disease or infestation or invasion or whatever the wretched thing is."

"That was very brave. How is it going for you?"

"So far, it doesn't seem to me to be going at all. Ariin's idea is that I take her place as the lab rat for the Friends while she pursues the investigation. She's a bit angry with me at the moment because I want to see what I can find out, too—at least when I'm not supposed to be pretending to be her."

"And this cat of yours—why did you bring him?" one of the friends asked with a little sly sideways look through a veil of forelock hair.

"I told you, didn't I? Ariin doesn't like him, and she somehow seems to blame him for something—which is just silly. How could a little cat have anything to do with an interplanetary plague? I mean, he's a very clever cat, don't get me wrong, but really!"

The friends nickered and chuckled among themselves, and Khorii got the distinct impression that everyone here knew something she didn't.

chapter 3

*T*here *he is!"* Grimalkin in unicorn guise cried, galloping away from his new friend. *"Some large beast has frightened the poor little kitty!"*

"Truly? Your senses must be very acute. I don't feel anything."

"There! There! Stop, you bully!" he cried to the woods in general. *"Leave that little cat alone! I will trample a mudhole in you and stomp it dry!"*

He tore through the trees until he felt that he had lost his lovely companion for the moment. Then he made a noisy show of rearing, neighing, trampling, and issuing threatening curses at the nonexistent attacker of the currently nonexistent, or at least temporarily de-felinated, feline. *"Take that! And that!"*

By the time the female arrived, he was breathing heavily, lathered with foam and scratched bloody from his exertions. He poked at shrubbery with his horn as he called sweetly, *"Here, kitty, kitty, come out now, little one. You are safe. I have saved you from the evil beast. Come out and purr for this nice female and assure her that you are unhurt."* Although he actually could be in two places at once with the help of his crono, without the crono it was impossible, so the cat in question did not appear.

"Look at you!" the female cried solicitously, rubbing her horn across a bloody scratch on his flank. *"You've been hurt. Did it bite you?"*

"What?" he asked, luxuriating in her horn touch so that he forgot the imaginary attacker he had just created. *"Oh, that! No, no, it did not bite me. It couldn't touch me actually. I'm very fast, very agile, you know. But it may be some time before we see your little friend again. Whom shall I say is inquiring if I meet him?"*

"I am Halili," she told him. *"What are you called?"*

"Alkhiin," he replied, having given some thought to this while he was trouncing the grass. He had, of course, had many names on many worlds, but he gave her one that sounded a bit like the end of his real name and a bit like his cat name, Khiindi. *"We'd best get back. Your mate will be missing you, Halili."*

"Mate? I don't have a mate? But if you think yours—"

"Tragically, my mate was killed when hunters tricked her into attempting to rescue a youngling. It was very sad. She was a noble female. She was carrying our young when she died." A large crystal tear, still quite easy to manufacture in other than cat form, trickled down the side of his nose. As he had hoped, Halili comforted him with a prolonged nuzzle. All those years of being an adorable little pussycat had certainly paid off. He had learned that females liked to feel sympathy for those who were hurt or in need. At least, most females did. He had always considered himself a godlike being in cat form. He had once taken it for granted that ladies would respond in a suitably impressed and cooperative fashion when the pitiful furry friend turned into a proud handsome humanoid with, if he did say so himself, quite startling powers in many areas. Those who were not impressed, he frankly had had no opportunity to notice as they were trampled, at least figuratively, by those who considered him the—ha ha—cat's

meow. It was a bit like the Terran fable of the frog prince.
It was only since he had been Khiindi that it had occurred
to him that some females, among them perhaps those who
would make superior mates and mothers, preferred the frog.
They found princes overbearing and insufficiently cuddly.

With his amazing empathic powers, he had divined that
Halili would be one of that sort of female and intuitively set
about making himself as cuddly a unicorn as he had been a
cat while in Khiindi form. Perhaps more so. Halili was the
most appealing of her race he ever recalled meeting. Even as
a cat, he had felt an instant connection. He must remember,
once the girls came back for him and they were again shipping out together to save the universe, to delay his revenge—
peeing in Ariin's shipsuit—for three or four days, since she
had done him a good turn, however unintentionally.

If he decided to go back with them, of course. As Halili
and he touched horns, the probability of his wishing to do
that decreased greatly.

□nce her sister had gone out to search for the wretched
cat, Ariin sought the technicians' quarters on the far side of
the city. Many of the technicians lived in spaces similar to
her own laboratory cell, near their work areas so they could
be easily called upon when their superiors required their services, even if they were sleeping, eating, or otherwise engaged in their own frivolous pursuits.

But only the higher-level technicians, who maintained
the time device, the space fleet and flitters, and other critical
equipment, lived in the cells. Those who specialized in domestic devices, the sort that every one of the Friends had in
numbers, and which did not require daily maintenance, had
their own area of the city.

Ariin had never been there before, but toward the end of
her previous time in Kubiilikaan after her telepathic powers

had developed, she had learned of the area from their conversations. Disguised by a plain black, hooded cloak she'd discovered at the back of Akasa's wardrobe, she walked briskly through the constantly changing city. She knew at once when she had reached her goal. The technicians' quarters were, as she expected, less grand and pretentious, being essentially a large flat hive of rooms connected by corridors, much like the time device building or the interior of a spacecraft. Unlike a spacecraft, the complex had no engine, and unlike the time device building and all of the other areas of the city she had seen to date, its appearance, size, color, and the placement of the windows and doors remained constant and unchanging.

On Vhiliinyar and MOO, even on Rushima, being still was the normal thing for dwellings and buildings. When Ariin saw the shifting alien sea undulating through the docking bay of the *Blanca*, she was reminded of the houses of the Friends and had wondered if there might be some connection. Other than the shapeshifting, the houses appeared to be made of the sorts of things human houses were made of—wood, stone, metal and plas, both crete and glas and other inert building materials. But after seeing the alien thing created when ghost-processed inorganic material mingled with the stuff that animated the ghosts themselves, she was not so sure. She reached out and touched the shifting facade of a food store, wondering if it would be soft, spongy, or squishy, but it was none of the above.

Of course, it could hardly be exactly the same, or the aliens would have destroyed things the way they had elsewhere in the universe.

Maybe the Friends had domesticated the aliens here? Probably not. Probably the moving houses of the Friends and the big, lumpy, galumphing alien forms had nothing to do with each other, but she thought they did. She thought the cat had thought so, too. She'd felt it inside his furry little devious mind.

If anyone would know whether or not the houses were organisms or merely dwelling places for other organisms, the technicians who worked on them would. Only, how should she get them to talk about it? The Friends did not have children and did not die, as far as she could tell. She had seen no signs of new houses or buildings under construction and no signs that the old ones were in need of replacing. But that might be due to nothing more exotic than good maintenance.

Maintenance didn't explain the constant and seemingly random changes the buildings made. Random. Hmm. What about when the Friends wanted a building to change in a particular way? Did the technicians do certain specific things to get an office to become a ballroom? Was that possible?

She stopped in her tracks and looked ahead into the still, motionless dwellings of the technicians. They were mostly empty. She felt that now. That would have something to do with the ball, of course. If she hadn't been so busy arguing with her spoiled sister about the accursed cat, she would have figured that out to begin with. Like it or not, she was going to have to return to the central complex the overlords occupied if she was to learn anything.

Back she sailed, her cloak billowing behind her, across the rolling waves of windows morphing from small diamond-shaped panes to large single ones, roofs flattening and peaking, trim sprouting around the edges of things, then receding. Surely this organized and even artistic domiciliary activity could not be caused by the same thing as the ugly alien ambulation?

The Friends were already arriving at the front of the ballroom when Ariin slipped in through the back and found herself a handy shadow to melt into. The ballroom ceiling was faceted crystal tonight, but a delicately hued gossamer tent ballooned from a central, starlike chandelier, the draperies trailing down the sides of the room, where they gained opacity from other more substantial fabric behind the veiled panels.

Behind these, the technicians busied themselves with lights and holos, music and the sound of an invisible crowd cheering the arrival of each guest. When all attendees had been ushered in, the lighting changed.

Ariin pulled the curtain aside to peek into the ballroom. Before her, the cosmos yawned in the sort of vast grandeur she had not witnessed even in space.

The central star was not one star but a galaxy of them, blooming and fading like flowers in bursts of multicolored lights. The gauzy curtain was no longer visible. Instead, planets, suns, and moons revolved slowly around one another in an intricate weave echoed by the dancers themselves as the females whirled, skirts flaring, around the males, and the males pranced around other couples.

They seemed to be doing all of this in midair, up among the stars, or far below Ariin's position. She was afraid to step forward for fear she would fall into nothingness.

It looked so much like space that she was amazed people weren't dressed in shipsuits, but no, their clothing was as elaborate as the setting. So were their bodies. Many of them had assumed at least portions of their nonhumanoid aspects—Odus half flew on giant wings studded with gems in honor of the occasion. Akasa's dress bore a long, spined train like the tail of a great lizard. The tall, fanned comb at the crown of her head did not look detachable to Ariin.

She did not even have to look very hard to find them among the other fantastic figures, because those two always had to be the center of attention, a remarkable accomplishment among their flashy and pompous kind.

However, perhaps the ball is not the best place to find

out about the shapeshifting properties of the buildings, she thought. Many of the effects were achieved by bringing in things like the holos enhanced by the draperies, crystals, and special lighting. But she thought the space within the ball-room appeared far larger than usual. It couldn't have achieved that depth without some structural changes, could it?

The music stopped and another, louder strain, rose dra-matically as another couple flew into the room. One soared on the beating wings of a great roc. The other streamed a spray of brilliant pink/orange/red/gold plumes ending in flames. Because of the flames, Ariin could see them clear across the expanse, up to the entrance and down, down, until they were swooping together far beneath where she stood. How did they do that? Was it an illusion? Cautiously, she ex-tended her foot and brought it down where the floor should be. Fortunately, she was hanging on to the drapery, or she might have lost her balance and plummeted beyond the fan-tastic flying couple without the benefit of wings.

Behind her one of the techs said, "Very well, their Excel-lencies have made their entrance. Reextend the staircase."

The exotic airborne dancers had distracted her from see-ing that the staircase had disappeared, replaced by a steep drop from the entrance. Now, extending from the curtained and crystal-lit portal, a red expanse rolled itself forward like an uncurling tongue. No sooner had it unfurled than it crimped itself into the long, sweeping stairs, pinched in to form a comparatively narrow waist at the top before belling out at the bottom.

"Good. Cue the floor up again," another one said into a mouthpiece. Ariin realized she could only hear them because she was listening with her mind more than with her ears. They all wore headsets such as the humans wore around noisy equipment. "Gently," the tech cautioned, as the couples beneath her seemed to soar upward.

This was all very interesting, but Ariin wondered once more if the floor rose because of machinery or because it moved of its own accord. Why would technicians be needed to maintain and repair an organism that could change its shape at will?

"Beauty!" the head tech said as the floor rose, the heavenly bodies shrinking as they swirled, appearing to recede. When Ariin extended her toe again, it touched what seemed to be solid marble.

"This place has really come along, I tell you," the tech whispered to his companion. "A few years ago we'd never have got it to do all this. I remember when it was nothing but a starter blob. Most unpromising thing you'd ever hope to see."

"Except another starter blob," mumbled a lower-echelon tech who was less impressed than his superior with the fluctuating environment under their—care? Tutelage? What was their role here? Obliging Ariin's mental nudge, the fellow said, "It's about time we started some more. It's getting quite boring, isn't it, coddling these as they go through their paces, correcting their corners, getting them to resculpt their windows. There's no challenge with a structure as skillful as this one."

"You're just more interested in the raw modeling than the nuances of refined sculptural training," one of the other fellows said haughtily.

"You have to tame them first, or they'll sculpt you. Don't forget, I was on that last collection mission. I saw them in their native habitat, before the modifications."

"The way I hear it, they are their native habitat."

"In the last stage, yes, because they've processed everything else, one way or another. Pircifir discovered them by chance and was intrigued. We tracked them to their original planet. Once there, we experimented until we coaxed them into some of the more popular shapes you see throughout the city today."

That was it! Ariin wanted to go out onto the dance floor and twirl around a few times herself, she was so excited. The stuff the Friends used for houses had to be the same thing as the aliens that had caused the plague. They fit the description exactly. Now all she had to do was find Pircifir and get him to tell her what modifications he'd made to render the aliens harmless, even helpful. She would be even more of a heroine than Khorii, more than her mother and father, loved and revered not only by their own people but by all people everywhere for subduing the menace. Everybody talked about the bug monster Khleevi her parents had finally caused to destroy each other, but this would be even better.

The only problem was that she didn't know this Pircifir, had not met him or even heard of him before, which was odd because if he modified a life-form, he had to have some interest in genetics. Her old quarters were in the genetics lab. Never mind. She would simply use the timer thing and be there when he did it. Then she'd go back to her parents with the solution.

She dampened her own enthusiasm and tried to draw out the technician who'd actually been on the mission, but he was preoccupied with the stupid ball. She would have to wait and follow him home and work on him there, where the distractions were fewer.

Khorii reluctantly left the herd behind and walked back to the city. It looked very different than it had when she left. It was dressed for the ball, she thought, with twinkling lights outlining graceful domes and curves and sparkling on softly glowing walls and windows. It looked beautiful. One especially elegant structure overlooked the sea, its reflection doubling its grandeur. As Khorii approached, gaudily dressed beings strolled or flew, even swam away from the building, laughing and talking, some continuing their dance steps in the streets. They were incredibly giddy, and she couldn't imagine why until she was close enough to detect the fragrance of their collective breath. At first she thought they might all have been afflicted with the same happy illness, but then she saw some waving and occasionally drinking from delicate globes filled with something soft green and sloshing.

So that's what intoxication was. Her people didn't have that sort of thing, since their touch turned any beverage to water. She'd heard the human plague survivors talk about it—among the older ones, especially, who spoke of wishing they could get drunk. They could not, of course, because in order for supplies to be safe for consumption, a Linyaari had to decontaminate them with horn touch, which meant that the intoxicants lost their ability to intoxicate.

The fancily garbed celebrants danced and sang and whirled each other around. Some walked with an odd gait, indicating that their equilibriums had been compromised. Others spoke or sang with strange accents so pronounced she felt a LAANYE would be helpful at understanding them. Their numbers had dwindled by the time she turned from the waterfront road onto the one leading from the ballroom up the hill and past the building where the time device and her sister's former quarters were located. Music still poured from the ballroom, and some of the revelers sang or hummed snatches of tunes. One of these jumped into her head and onto her tongue before she realized it, and she twirled and skipped up the hill. Though Linyaari vocal cords did not lend themselves to humming, she made noises that approximated the tune and thought it sounded lovely.

"Narhii?" a voice said behind her. She thought the woman was calling a friend until she said more sharply,

"Narhii! What are you doing out here at this hour, child?"

Khorii paused in midtwirl and faced Akasa, accompanied by a large male wearing a feathered cloak.

"I went to visit the Ances—the Others," she said. *"Ariin?"*

"I'm busy," her sister replied tersely.

"Where are you? I may need your help here. Akasa is right behind me."

"Stall her," Ariin said, and though she did not answer Khorii's question, Khorii could feel her sister ahead of her, places and numbers—dates?—occupying most of her thoughts.

"You're at the timing device, aren't you?" Khorii asked. *"What are you doing there?"*

"Researching. I found out something important, but I have to follow it up."

"Good. I'll come, too."

"You can't. You have to keep them busy. Ah! There it is. Don't worry. I'll be back before you know I'm gone."

And then she was gone—her thoughts and presence vanished out of Khorii's mind. All she had gleaned from Ariin's mind was a set of numbers, but they didn't mean anything to her.

"Don't scold her as if she were still a child, Akasa," the male said. "Our little Narhii is becoming quite the grown-up female these days. See how she likes to dance?"

Without asking, he grabbed her hands and spun her around and around in the middle of the road until she felt quite dizzy. He was dizzier than she was, however, and pulled her to a stop so he could lean on her. They both fell down, and, for a quite-alarming moment, he lay on top of her and leered down at her, his thoughts full of mating. It was far more straightforward than Marl Fidd's sadistic fantasies but no more appropriate. The drunken Friend was very strong and quite heavy. Bits of him pinned her arms and legs. She took a deep breath, ready to pull her knees up sharply in an attempt to dislodge him, when Akasa grabbed the feathered cape and jerked him upward. Khorii noted that the female was extremely strong.

"You're frightening her, Odus," was all Akasa said. Khorii was not so much frightened as she was disgusted. No wonder Ariin had wanted to escape this place and these people. Odus clearly had no moral qualms about forcing himself on her, not because he was actually cruel but because he was so conceited he believed he was doing her a favor, that she did not offer to mate with him because she was intimidated and made shy by his magnificence. Akasa intervened not because she was concerned about Khorii but because she was jealous. How could awful people like these have been partially responsible for her people?

Ariin had been absolutely right to leave when she did, but she was absolutely cracked if she thought Khorii was going back to that cell to wait to for Odus to try to convince her once more that she was good enough for him. Or almost. Her mane shook all the way down her spine. Odus? Odious was more like it. She'd heard her human friends use the word, and it fit. Odious Odus.

It wasn't very nice of Ariin to leave her here. Khorii decided that rather than returning to the cell, she was going to keep moving and try to learn what she could, The crono Ariin was wearing wasn't the only one. Akasa and Odus both had them, and Khorii figured a lot of the people here probably did as well.

Akasa's gaze pierced her back. Khorii turned around and wiggled her fingers as a parting gesture before entering the building containing the timing device. She wasn't going back to that cell, but she was going to see if she could figure out when Ariin had gone.

* * *

Grimalkin thoroughly enjoyed his unicorn disguise, but it was important to return to little cat form for two reasons. One was so that Halili would see him and know that unicorn-him, Alkhiin, really had saved kitty-cat-him, Khiindi. She would not worry, and she would continue thinking that Alkhiin was wonderful.

The other was that, as he had learned over the years, little cats could make themselves invisible, could overhear private conversations and thoughts unnoticed, and could steal small objects and be far away with the loot before anyone else noticed.

He found the company of the unicorns, especially Halili, most congenial, but if he stayed with them, it would be because he chose to do so, not because some inferior copy of his Khorii stuck him there.

With a lash of his tail, he leaped out of the grass, sprinted past the herd and toward Kubiilikaan. He had done so much traveling through time and space in his former life that he was not certain exactly where Grimalkin-he might be at this moment, but nevertheless, he had a mission. He had to find himself.

Ariin knew exactly where she was, which was where she had been before she touched the crono. She stood in the middle of the time lab in the same spot she had been, but according to the time signature on the illuminated wall display, it was three hundred *ghaanyi* before, though it looked the same, as far as she could tell.

According to the pictobase built into the time device's display, this was when Pircifir should be setting off on his mission. The display showed an ever-changing map of where each person on Vhiliinyar was located at any given time. Of course, it was coded, and you had to know the code to find the person. In Ariin's time, the Others were all represented by white dots. She didn't see them on this board, but maybe their dots had been added later. Each of the Friends had not only a specific color code but a shape code as well. Other creatures were also represented in the woods, meadows, ocean and streams, although the *sii*-Linyaari, who had aqua dots in Ariin's time, had no dots here at all. Maybe you had to know where to look to find them. At any rate, there was another shortcut. "Pircifir," she said, and a red-orange dot began blinking brightly near the spaceport.

She had timed it very close indeed. He must be about to set off on his mission, and she needed to be there, too, along with that technician she'd overheard talking about him in the ballroom.

What luck! Just as it had been in her own time, the time lab building seemed deserted, and she met no one as she bolted from it. The time of day she had chosen was just past sunset and as she left the building, she heard a babble of voices in the distance. But that was secondary to what she saw—or rather, did not see. The time building looked much as it always had, but outside it, everything was quite different. Instead of the fascinating ever-changing facades of businesses and homes, Kubiilikaan was surrounded by a hodge-podge of partially completed structures of stone, wood, mud, even steel. Within each there seemed to be a somewhat solid core, but all around it sprawled construction and destruction in various phases of completion or dilapidation. Whatever talents the godlike Friends had, building and the design of buildings was evidently not one of them at this point in their lives.

The voices congregated at the seaside, and she saw that there was a dancing platform erected down there, lit by many tiny lights of the same sort that were in the time wall. Their festive air was somewhat diminished by the fact that they blinked as if in alarm rather than twinkling. Twinkle technology must have developed later, she thought, since the lights in the ballroom she'd seen definitely twinkled.

She skirted the seashore and made her way to the spaceport. A half dozen ships stood in dock, but only one of them was loading supplies. A Friend she had never seen before supervised the technicians equipping the ship. She didn't see the one she'd overheard. Perhaps she simply didn't recognize his younger self.

How would she get Pircifir to take her along? Maybe she'd tell him Akasa and Odus had ordered her to go as part of her education—to see how she'd respond to alien environments or something.

She approached cautiously, and the supervisor glanced at her, then returned his attention to his work.

That was unexpected. In her time people were somewhat used to her, even though she had never been allowed out much, but here, would she not be a novelty? Perhaps other Linyaari had traveled back to this time? That would be disappointing. If she was going to go to all this trouble and brave alien dangers and that sort of thing, she wanted to be the first.

While she was deciding how to ask to go on Pircifir's mission, he glanced down at her again. "So, how'd you come up with that guise? It's certainly original. I can't even tell who you are."

Oho! So he thought she was one of the Friends in disguise? That would be handy. "It's something new I'm trying out," she said. "We're hoping it will be a handy shape for space travel. I need to go along with you and try it out."

He shrugged. He didn't care who she was. Theirs was a closed society, and he felt confident she would turn out to be someone he knew. Some of the Friends had political rivals, but their squabbles were short-lived. They had each lived a very long time, she knew that, and expected to live a lot longer, in good health and without perceptible aging. They didn't seem to have any children, but she didn't know if that was by choice or if they were sterile. She didn't think that was why, since they seemed to have everything they needed to create babies in the lab and had tried several combinations to create her own race. Odus had made advances and remarks about mating with her in order to jumpstart the Linyaari race. He certainly didn't seem to think he was sterile. She'd never thought to probe into the matter. Mating matters had not concerned her earlier because she was too young. Once Odus had tried to interest her in the subject, she avoided any natural inclination she might have had in that direction. It was just too—what did Jaya and Hap say? Yucky. That was it. It was too yucky to contemplate. It had become much more interesting when she was among her own kind, or even among human males close to her own age.

She certainly hoped Pircifir would not be as interested in that sort of thing, especially if she were going to embark on a space voyage with him. So it was handy that he thought she was a Friend. Their guises could cross genders, as their romantic interests often did, so if Pircifir made advances, she could say she was what he did not prefer or that she had a mate for the time being or—well, she could read him and find out what would dissuade him and make him think she was that. Simple enough, really.

chapter 4

To think she had imagined that having a sister would be a good thing! Khorii could not believe what Ariin had done—to her, to Khiindi, to their poor, plague-ridden parents, and to Elviiz, who might not be worried, or even concerned, strictly speaking, but would certainly be baffled without her around to bully, protect, teach, embarrass, and aggravate. She was, after all, his prime mission.

Angry tears welled in her eyes, blurring the colored lights blinking on the walls representing people going about their business. Most of the lights were clustered beside the sea, she noticed. That was odd. They should be fanning out from the ballroom. Then she realized that the lights were in a different place because the people were moving in a different time. So where were they then?

The lights flickered back and forth slightly but stayed within that small area on the beach. It was not, Khorii saw now, the shore near Kubiilikaan but was farther down the coast, near the field occupied by the Ancestors. A red circle blinked slowly on and off. One by one the dots moved within the circle's perimeter. Khorii watched, wondering what the circle could be. What had been there, on the way to the Ancestor's meadow? The spaceport?

Suddenly, the red circle turned to green, and the blinking stopped. The circle and all four of the smaller lights it contained blinked out.

"Ariin?" Khorii called, but she could not feel her sister, could not hear her. Ariin was gone, not only out of time but off the planet. Khorii's father had once done the same thing according to family lore, but he hadn't left her mother stranded in a time not her own, had he?

Since this was a time machine, maybe she could get it to take her to the time before Ariin actually left. The only problem was she had no idea how it worked. It couldn't be too hard, could it? And she could scarcely land herself in worse trouble than she was anyway. Anything would be better than being stuck here with Odus—anything except—when was it that the Khleevi invaded Vhiliinyar? When had they destroyed the timer for good? She certainly didn't want to make a mistake and take herself to that time. No, if she was going to stop Ariin, then she could wait until she could watch the time device in operation, see how it worked. Meanwhile, she looked around for some kind of signature that would tell her when Ariin had disappeared so that she could judge her own departure accurately.

The little gray tabby trotted back to Kubiilikaan, wishing he could have remained a unicorn until he was most of the way there. A cat's stride didn't begin to compare when it came to covering distance. However, shapeshifting in the middle of the meadow might draw unwanted attention. He did not wish Halili or his fellow "Friends" to recognize his true nature yet. In this time he was not yet frozen in cat shape, and he wanted to keep it that way.

Once inside the city, he bounded up the short steps between the street and the time building, then had to wait for someone to open the door.

No techs worked in the time room today, and the little dots shifted minutely around the screen with each passing second, so the thing was working perfectly. That was good. The device was large and clunky and did not guarantee his ability to return quickly to this time without the benefit of a stream or other watery conduit. He much preferred a crono, but it was harder for his little cat paws to manipulate than the big screen. If he could find his earlier self, the two-legged version, he could retrieve his own crono, find Khorii and her bratty sister, and they could return everything to normal. Of course, normal would do nothing to solve the problem of the morphing alien blob that would probably spread itself like a giant mutant slug all over the known universe, destroying life as they knew it, but he didn't see how that was any of his affair now. Even if it was, his girl should not be put at further risk to fix things. She was much too young to save universes yet. And someone needed to sit on that sister of hers until the wretched child was halfway socialized and safe to move among decent people and cats.

Elviiz now, Elviiz would be the ideal sort of fellow to help solve this glitch in the cosmic harmony to which Grimalkin was so uniquely and sensitively attuned. But Elviiz was incapacitated. A crono could fix that, too. All Grimalkin needed to do was fetch a future Elviiz, a fixed one, pull him back on a different time line and the two of them could go troubleshooting, with Elviiz doing the heavy lifting and the data compilation, analysis, and manipulation while Grimalkin operated on the more intuitive plane—or multiple intuitive planes, his particular area of expertise. It was vastly underrated and trivialized, but he was used to that. So few appreciated him. Tragic, but it seemed to be his lot. No matter. Once he saved the universe, he could return to the unicorn herd and Halili, for a while at least.

If he timed it right, he wouldn't even have to explain to her why he left without so much as a horn touch.

Paws and mind control were all he needed to operate the time device. Even tail brushes could shift the time lines of the sensitive machine. The best course of action would be to search for himself at an earlier time, use the time device to reunite his selves and acquire the crono, fetch Elviiz, save the universe, then collect the girls.

Of course, that was assuming there were no hitches in his plan, and even he had to admit that there always were. So, no, he really needed to secure the girls, get his crono back from Ariin, return the youngsters to safety, not that they'd stay there, then collect Elviiz, who would no doubt be more cooperative, knowing his sisters were safe.

Find Ariin and the crono, that was his first priority. Only, maybe it would be better to collect Khorii first, and they could both use the device to find Ariin and the crono. There was always the little problem that when he returned the girls and went to fetch Elviiz, the form-freeze would once more trap him in small cat form, which would be highly inconvenient.

Hmmm. Even if he found himself and his own crono, he wondered if he could outsmart himself long enough to get control of the device—or would his two forms meld? Ah, the much-vaunted time-space continuum conundrum. But, if anyone would understand his motives, he would.

He scanned the screen, searching for the deceptively insignificant dot that represented his own two-legged self. During this time period, his interests had included romantic dinners and long walks on the beach with any female he could interest in pursuing those activities and the ones he wished to follow them. His own kind were a bit indiscriminate that way, since all of the actual breeding they did was in the laboratory. No combination of themselves had actually produced offspring since he was born.

Perhaps the females of his species were sterile. He knew beyond a doubt that he was fully capable of reproduction. His activities in other times on other planets had proved that.

Where was he, anyway? He saw the avatar of his cat self sitting in front of the machine in the time building, blinking as the individual dots did when one sought them out. Was the machine refusing to acknowledge that there might be two of him during the same time? How limited!

He framed a protest to the technicians' guild in which he complained about the lack of individual freedom implied by such shortsightedness on the part of the device. Why should there not be two of someone as dynamic and large-spirited as he was? Who made up these silly rules anyway?

He lashed his tail in irritation and groomed his whiskers to calm himself. When he looked back up at the wall screen, he was gratified to see that his complaint had already been addressed. There were indeed two of him represented—both showing up as cat avatars inside the time device room.

At the same time that he saw this, he heard the growl. A low, menacing, ferocious growl, that of a powerfully fierce beast, almost made him jump out of his fur coat. He leaped three feet in the air, made a 180, and faced himself in the form of a magnificent, tawny tiger cat with a full, fluffy ruff and tail and a long lustrous coat sticking straight up over most of his body in a display of outrage. Unfortunately, Khiindi had little time to admire himself because he—the other he—seemed to be in an uncharacteristically nasty mood. Before he landed, his other cat met him in a midair clash of fangs, claws, and filthy feline language.

"No, wait!" Khiindi squalled. "Hurting me will only hurt yourself. Inhale! Sniff! Do I not smell intimately familiar?"

His other self ripped his poor little gray ear before the

thought sank in. "You smell like me and—and—the Others! Who are you?"

His other cat self wasn't thinking, but Khiindi was. The ear really hurt, but as the other cat's claws reached out to shred it, Khiindi had seen the gleam of metal among the hairs of the distended ruff. The crono! Quickly, and with great relief, Khiindi changed into his two-legged form, snatched up his feline self, and relieved the cat of the crono as gently as possible, considering that the cat self was filleting his hands. He tried to drop himself back onto the floor as he pulled the crono onto his bleeding wrist, but the other Grimalkin dragged claws all the way down his bare body.

"Stop it!" he commanded. "I'm only borrowing"—But suddenly, the claws gave way, and when he looked down, no fur or whisker of his other self remained.

Had he absorbed the other cat self into his two-legged form in the course of the fight? Had the cat recognized his own blood and retreated in embarrassment? He really didn't care. He'd had no intention of returning the crono anyway. It was his, after all.

Now to find Khorii and Ariin. From what the girls had said, he was fairly certain they would have returned to the building where he stood. Ariin wanted Khorii to take her place so she would return them to the time when she had lived among his own kind.

He could have used the crono, but it was easier to use the larger device to confirm the presence of the girls at the estimated time. He saw Khorii's dot, wavering uncertainly from within the time lab in the future. Ariin's dot did not wink at him from anywhere on the wall. He could backtrack to an earlier time, when presumably the girls would still be together, but then he decided that meeting Khorii alone would be easier. He wanted to explain his side of things to her without Ariin inserting her own interpretation.

He triggered the device, and there was Khorii, standing in front of him. He was in cat form again! She gasped as he leaped to her shoulder, crono around his neck again, and with a dextrous maneuver of his left hind paw returned them to the time he had just left. He preferred to be able to shift shapes at will while they finished what they had to do, and his unwilling transformation showed that the time Ariin had taken her to was within the boundaries of his banishment to permanent cat form.

Once the transition was made, he leaped from her shoulder and returned to two-legged form. He was naked, and naked humanoids were more naked somehow than naked Linyaari. Although he knew himself to be a beautiful male, he didn't want the appearance of all other males who might be appropriate mates for his young charge to pale by comparison with her memory of him forever after. He turned himself into a tiger, pawed open the panel where the techs hid their work robes, and held it in his teeth while he changed back again while she watched, puzzled, squeaking slightly at the tiger form, then rubbing her eyes while he pulled the robe around his two-legged form.

"Do not be afraid, Khorii," he told her.

She looked annoyed. "So Ariin was telling the truth. All this time you've actually been an alien shapeshifter, one of the demideities my people call the Friends. Some Friend! Bad cat, Khiindi! Very bad cat indeed."

"I'm not," he said, his lordly baritone carrying a hint of the plaintive mew that usually made her forgive him any trouble he'd caused. "Haven't I been your loyal friend all these years? It's very unkind of you to say otherwise. I pledged to help you through any troubles you encountered, and I always have. That's what I'm doing now, only I need my true form to do it. And I wanted to talk to you, face-to-nonfurry-face."

"I'm listening."

But at that point, a gaggle of female techs entered the time lab. "Lord Grimalkin, you've returned!" one of them said. "Why are you wearing that old thing?"

The speaker was clearly dazzled by him, and he gave her a kindly smile. "I fear I lost something in my translation," he said. "I don't suppose you'd be a dear and go to my quarters and collect my amber robes, would you? The matching slippers and headdress are packaged with it."

She nodded, he winked, and she danced out the doorway. Some days it took so little from him to bring happiness to others.

When he looked back at the other techs, they were whispering behind their hands, their eyes looking speculatively at Khorii.

"Ah," he said. "You're wondering about this youngling, I see. She's—mmm—the result of experiments I've been conducting in the future."

"Experiments?" the eldest of the techs chortled. "Is that what you call it now, you sly cat? Experimenting?"

He shook a finger at her. "You know me too well, Twexa. You're right, of course, she's a descendant we lords have been attempting to reverse-engineer."

"Bit young for that, isn't she, sir?" Twexa asked.

"You wrong me, Twexa. I am as serious a scientist in my own way as my colleagues are in theirs."

"Of course you are, dear. Your sense of fun can be misleading. I'm always telling the others that," she said.

"Thank you, Twexa. Your understanding means a lot to me."

The tech he'd sent to fetch his robes returned, and he allowed her to help him don them, leaving Khorii in the care of the others. At least she wouldn't have to answer any questions, since they were all asking them at once. He regretted the necessity for speed in his toilette. The tech—Polida—was touchingly appreciative. But her time would come as long as he had the crono. There was no reason for his sweet Halili to know about anything he did in his two-legged form.

With a hand in the middle of Polida's back, he shepherded her to the main time chamber, where Khorii was surrounded by techs, all gabbling together as they surveyed the time map spread before them.

He broadcast a burst of commands, and the techs scattered throughout the facility, leaving him alone with Khorii.

Turning from the time map to face him, she said in an accusatory tone, "Ariin isn't here!"

"I can't be held responsible for that!" Grimalkin replied. "If you recall, she was the one who got rid of me, not the other way around. I thought we two should stand together, as we have your entire life to solve this problem, so when I saw that she had abandoned you as well, I came to your rescue."

"You never told me you were a grown-up man," she said, unmollified. "Of course we stood together when you were my kitty."

"It makes no difference if we are standing together on four feet or six," he said, the wheedling mew underlying his voice again. "We are still a team. I may look like a grown-up, but many of my own kind claim that is a false assumption. Your sister dislikes me, and resents you because, when I was forced to bring back your mother's egg, I brought hers instead of yours. That is how I came to be frozen in the shape of a small cat. My people ganged up on me, took my crono, froze me, and sent me back to your parents as a birthing gift for you to punish me for not breaking your parents' hearts."

Khorii, arms crossed over her chest, snorted. "From what I hear, you didn't care about that when you ran away with my father, then tried to convince my mum that you were him."

"No, I didn't care particularly then. Even more than most of my kind, I am a curious and exploratory sort of fellow.

But your parents rescued me from the Khleevi—returned for me when they could have safely escaped. And although, as you suggest, my previous actions may have caused them alarm, even psychological pain, neither of them tried to hurt me. They were so happy once it was all over.

"I could not betray them so completely as to take both of their potential children. I knew you were twins and would be exactly the same for the purposes of science, so I simply took the nearest, your sister, and allowed the other, you, to be born in due time. Had I not been forced into small cat form to be your pet, I could have remained with Ariin and instructed her about her origins. I could also have shown my people how to treat a sensitive and impressionable child so she didn't grow up bitter and sneaky.

"I am the most empathic of my kind, which is one reason the females love me so, and I'd have had a softening influence on your sister's upbringing. It's not my fault that my people's idea of justice meant that you got the advantage of a loving family and an extremely talented, versatile and clever feline companion while your sister grew up surrounded with the tenderness commonly shown to laboratory animals."

Khorii thought that over, and finally said, "You have to admit you have caused a great deal of trouble for both of us, my parents, and even yourself."

"Yes, but see how that trouble has also made all of you learn and grow—even Ariin, who did find you after all. Now that we've resolved all of this, perhaps we can stop casting blame and get on with the mission?"

"First we have to find Ariin," Khorii said.

"I suppose we must," he agreed. "Now then, when could she have gone?"

Twexa reappeared as if they had summoned her. "Couldn't help overhearing you talk about some mission, sir?"

"Indeed, Twexa. There is an alien threat in my little

friend's time that may be the doom of the universe as we know it if it isn't addressed, and smartly. We have noticed certain similarities between the threat—"

"It involves great galumphing masses of matter-eating—er—matter," Khorii put in. "Organic."

"Yes," Grimalkin said. "It put my friend's sister and me in mind of the shapeshifting nature of our own fluid dwellings. You're a tech. Ring any bells with you?"

"Certainly, sir. Would the young lady have been using the time map or a crono?"

"She—uh—borrowed my crono from another time"—he supplied the signature—"but I don't know which she used. She will be raised right here in the time lab a few years hence and is familiar with the operation of the device."

"Ah well, I'll check the logs of both then."

"There are logs?" Khorii asked. "Why didn't you say?"

He shrugged. "I didn't know. Normally we leave these things to the techs."

Waving her palm across one of the wall panels, Twexa revealed a long, scrolling graph, then another. "Aha! There you are, you little minx. Gotcha."

"You found her?" Khorii asked.

"Indeed. After she left *then?* she went *then,*" Twexa said, pointing to Ariin's points of departure and arrival, respectively.

"What is significant about *then?* In particular?" Grimalkin asked.

"Ah, of course. That is when Pircifir launched his voyage of discovery and also when he returned with the organisms we've groomed into your lordships' dwellings. She arrived shortly before launch."

"Please arrange for us to join her, Twexa."

"If I may make a suggestion, sir?"

"Yes?"

"I—er—couldn't help overhearing what you and your young friend were saying about her sister. Perhaps if you arrive when she returns home from the voyage, she will have gained some maturity, a sense of personal accomplishment that will serve to alleviate part of her anger. If not, you can always return to the beginning of the journey. It was only a moment or two before the end, since Pircifir used his crono to return them just after they departed. Watch now. They should be arriving momentarily."

They waited for the egg shape indicating the space vessel to reappear on the time map, and for Ariin's and Pircifir's dots to emerge from it, but after several minutes, the map remained clear.

"Oh dear," Twexa said. "This is not how it's supposed to go at all. I'll do a forward search." The time map scrolled so rapidly Khorii felt slightly dizzy. Twexa turned to face them, looking worried. "They're not here, sir. Neither Pircifir nor Ariin. It's as if they never existed."

chapter 5

Grimalkin dismissed the puzzling disappearance of Pir-cifir and Ariin and had Twexa direct him and Khorii to the moment just before Pircifir and Ariin boarded.

As Twexa had suggested, Ariin was less than thrilled to see Khorii. *"How did you get here? Who's that with you?"*

Grimalkin nodded to Pircifir. "Greetings, brother."

Pircifir's stoic face warmed when he saw Grimalkin. "Brother!" He looked at Khorii and at Ariin and back again. "I see you have one, too."

"You're spoiling everything," Ariin told Khorii. *"Pircifir thinks I'm one of the Friends in disguise."*

Khorii hadn't ever been able to thought-talk with Khiindi, as far as she knew, but she quickly transmitted the idea to Grimalkin. She was relieved when he said smoothly, "Yes, this guise is all the rage among the ladies at the moment. You've had your nose in your schematics too much to notice the fashion, it seems."

"I can trust you to keep up enough for us both," Pircifir replied. "I don't suppose you would care to come along on this little jaunt, would you?"

Grimalkin grinned ingratiatingly. Pircifir seemed very fond of him. *Are they real brothers?* Khorii wondered. She didn't know any of the other Friends on what she considered a truly friendly basis, but presumably they had families, or at least relatives. She looked more closely. Pircifir and Grimalkin were around the same height and had the same tawny coloring, but Pircifir wore his mane quite short, whereas Grimalkin's flowing locks billowed in the breeze, and he sported a full beard as well, the total effect being that of a ruff surrounding his entire head and making it look four times its actual size. The complete effect was quite striking, even among the Friends.

Of course, with shapeshifters it was hard to say whether their resemblance was natural or assumed, but she hadn't heard any of the others address each other as kin.

"Exactly what I had in mind," Grimalkin replied. "We see each other so seldom these days."

"Come along then," Pircifir said. He turned to Ariin. "But—"

"I asked first!" she said belligerently. "And it's really important that you take me."

"Of course!" Pircifir said. "I was only going to say that you and my brother's friend will have to share a cabin. You seem to have a lot in common."

Ariin snorted with outrage, and for a moment Khorii thought she was going to throw a fit, but Ariin controlled herself and marched into the ship without so much as a glance at the rest of them.

This ought to be a fun trip, Khorii mused, shaking her head.

In his own way, Pircifir was as different from the other Friends as Grimalkin claimed to be. He was more polite, for one thing. Khorii thought it might be because his interests lay beyond Vhiliinyar, exploring new worlds and finding new cultures and their products just for the fun of it, apparently. Anywhere else he might have been a merchant, making his living by importing exotic fabrics, jewels, foods, spices, and furnishings. However, the Friends did not seem to have anything like an economy that she could see, at least among themselves.

"If people don't pay Pircifir for what he brings back, how does he pay for the items in the first place?" Khorii asked Ariin, who had spent a lot of the time in their cabin sulking.

"How should I know?"

"You grew up with them. Didn't you learn anything about them?"

"No, I was too busy being studied," Ariin snapped.

"You didn't notice where the meals were produced, or the clothing?" Khorii persisted. "I didn't see anything that looked like industry there, yet they have spacecraft and the time lab, all of these scientific things."

"Why don't you go ask your cat?" Ariin asked. "Not that he's very truthful."

"Maybe I will," Khorii said.

But when she asked Grimalkin, he just smiled in the same way he had when he was a cat and had caught something particularly tasty in a particularly clever way. "If you have an asset that's important enough, you don't need to have a lot of others, youngling," he told her. "When we dock at the next port, you'll see. But don't interfere. Remember the larger mission."

That aggravated her so much she forgot how irritated she was with Ariin. "He was such a *nice* kitty," she said, mourning the loss of her pet who, now that he walked on two legs, acted more like Elviiz than Khiindi, all superior and lording over her.

"I tried to warn you not to let him loose," Ariin said.

"I didn't. He found me. You took him back to before his friends made him stay a cat all the time."

Ariin repeated a word that Captain Bates sometimes used when she was mad, after which the captain usually mumbled an apology. Ariin didn't bother, however.

"For once you could have let me handle this on my own, you know," she groused. "You don't have to hog all the credit for everything all the time."

"We were going to," Khorii told her. "But once you got on board, the ship didn't come back like it was supposed to, so we came early enough to join you. Look, I don't really care about credit at this point. I'll be glad to tell everybody that everything was your idea—then they can look sad and disappointed at you because we ran away and scared them . . ."

"We'll use the crono and be back before they miss us," Ariin said in her own superior way, as if Khorii was being tedious.

"We'll still have to let them know about the mission," Khorii replied. "If we find the origin of the aliens invading everything, we'll probably still need help stopping them."

"Maybe. Maybe not," Ariin said.

Khorii privately thought the Friends relied on their cronos and the time device too much. If it wasn't for the time map, they wouldn't know whether they were coming or going.

She didn't know the half of it.

When they docked on a green planet paisleyed with deep blue oceans, Pircifir and his crew trooped out on foot to a nearby marketplace that reminded Khorii of the nanobug market on Kezdet.

They heard and smelled the market four blocks before they actually entered it. Vendors either cried their wares or broadcast prerecorded advertisements and jingles. Strange music blared, accompanying every variety of entertainment and many of the sales pitches. Engines drove both the machinery on display and the machinery used to transport and display it. Animals roared, brayed, growled, and chattered. Intertwined, over and under and all around these noises, were voices babbling in many tongues, bartering, admiring, disparaging, or just trying to make themselves heard in shouts and sometimes screams.

The medley of conflicting aromas, scents, fragrances, and stenches was exciting, but slightly sickening, too. Spicy foods, sweat, cooking meats, baking sweets, more sweat, excrement, pungent incense, animal odors, fresh, exotic flowers, and rotting vegetation assaulted their nostrils.

Awnings covered the merchandise of the foremost layer of street-level vendors, and banners hanging from the windows of the upper stories fluttered in a brisk breeze, creating a colorful canopy that whipped and twisted overhead.

It was larger and cleaner than the nanobug market, and had bigger, permanent enclosures, some several stories high. Except for the generally rowdy and rank atmosphere, it could have been a regular city.

Pircifir's ship had a very powerful drive, and she knew they had traveled far beyond the planets in Vhiliinyar's immediate vicinity, maybe even beyond the planets where she and her people had been trying to contain the plague. He had declined her help or Ariin's on the bridge, and she could not get a look at the charts, so she did not know exactly where they were. She only knew she had never been here before, in any time, although as they had approached from the air, she had thought there was something familiar about its color scheme.

The inhabitants were human, as far as she could tell, with a few other species sprinkled in among them. There were also companion animals and beasts of burden. She wondered if anyone had a litter of kittens. She'd need to start looking for a new cat now that Khiindi had turned into Grimalkin.

She didn't suppose he'd want to turn back, and even if he did, it wouldn't be the same.

Besides the vendors, there were entertainers of all sorts. Jugglers juggled everything from balls to small dogs. Mimes who surely had to be of nonhuman stock struck poses and seemed to morph into exaggerated, cartoon imitations of audience members. Dancers shuffled, twirled, leaped, and tapped. Although some of them wore the same kind of street clothes and shipsuits favored by the vendors, others wore bright, if somewhat tattered, costumes, spangled with tarnished embellishments. You had to get pretty close to see the tatters and tarnish though. From a distance they looked splendid. At least Khorii thought so. Ariin snickered and said she saw where Akasa had got her start. Grimalkin was most attracted to the dancers, some of whom wore very little clothing of any sort. Pircifir had obviously been here many times, and strode purposefully through the crowds, ignoring the strange and tantalizing displays, shows, and foods all around them.

Khorii didn't see any litters of kittens, but there were talking dogs, counting horses, and camels who could spit at a target and hit it dead center many feet away. The crowds gave that corral a wide berth.

Tall and striking as Pircifir and Grimalkin were, had she not been able to read their thought patterns, she'd have lost them in the crowd. Grimalkin occasionally did a protective check on her but was mostly enjoying himself. Pircifir seemed to have specific objectives.

Ariin tried to keep up with him as well. *"He's the one who will find the aliens they make houses from,"* she told Khorii. *"Not you or your overgrown kitty cat. You may be tagging along to sightsee, but I happen to have a mission."*

"Let me know when you accomplish it, so I can be sure

and take the credit then," Khorii told her tartly. *"I wouldn't want to disappoint you, after all."*

They were both surprised when they fetched up unexpectedly behind Pircifir as he stopped to talk to a man standing in front of gaudy signs displaying all manner of alien life-forms. "Hurry, hurry, hurry," the man's recording blared over his dialogue with Pircifir, "see the beautiful humanoid symbiont bonding with the serpent—she slithers, she shakes, she rolls in the belly of the snake." The picture behind him showed a female wearing very little. Whether Grimalkin's interest was aroused by that or by the fact that the female was depicted as being within the body of an enormously long and convoluted reptile, Khorii was unsure. The face of the snake had a faintly humanoid look to it, too, she thought.

"Of all the things to take an interest in," Ariin fumed. Then, *"Oh, I see now."*

"What?" Khorii asked. Although the market was exciting, she found the sensory overload was giving her a ferocious headache. *"Could you please touch your horn to my head?"* she asked. To her surprise, her sister did as she asked at once.

"Look there. Remind you of anything?"

"The incredible morphing tunnel, ladies and gentlemen. It is what it eats! It slinks on its belly or walks on its feet. It crawls, it rolls, it climbs and dives. It changes colors and shapes in the twinkle of an eye. Hurry, hurry, hurry."

"You see it, don't you, Pircifir? That's it, right?" Ariin asked, tugging at the sleeve of his shipsuit.

Pircifir smiled. "Three tickets, please."

He took the tickets, tore them, and turned to give them to the girls. The barker gaped. "How much for the unicorn twins?" he asked. "Can they do tricks?"

"You'd be surprised," Pircifir told him with a wink. "But they're not for sale. "

"Maybe you'll change your mind when you've seen the show," the man said, with a bow and an expansive wave to the wonders beyond the ticket booth.

Khorii heard Grimalkin growl low in his throat as he joined them and demanded a fourth ticket. He was trying to protect her, she realized, her and Ariin both, and seemed to think he had to be both Khiindi and Elviiz for her. It was sweet, but she didn't know if she'd trust him if he took a fancy to the lady symbiont in the snake's belly.

She and Ariin headed for the section of the tent marked with the poster of the incredible morphing tunnel, but Pircifir strolled toward the lady symbiont's section.

"But—" Ariin protested.

Grimalkin caught it and whispered to both girls, "Shhh, mustn't tip our hands by seeming too interested in any particular thing."

The huge snake was sleeping and had to be prodded awake by a bored man reading something colorful and flimsy. It writhed and coiled, its head and upper body rising several feet above the floor of its cage as it swayed back and forth. Its eyes were quite beautiful, slanted gold and not slitted, but with wide pupils, and regarded them sadly from under a fringed hood.

"Where's the lady?" Grimalkin asked the man. Another prod, the snake hissed more in pain than anger, and the coils spread to reveal what Khorii saw at once was not a lady at all but a growth of some sort that was vaguely shaped like the torso and head of a human. She felt the snake's pain and realized the growth was probably killing it.

She had done so much healing in the past *ghaanye* that it was almost automatic for her. Khorii stepped forward. She couldn't hiss. Her vocal cords were not capable of producing the sound. But she projected calming, shushing thoughts to the serpent, and it lay back down again, still uncoiled.

Grimalkin grabbed her by the hood of her shipsuit as if trying to pick up a kitten. "Khorii, don't! That's a dangerous creature!"

"It's okay," she told him. "She knows I'm trying to help her. She won't hurt me."

Grimalkin held on to her arm, forcing her to listen while he related an ancient folktale about a lady who had saved a serpent's life when it was freezing to death, on the condition that the dying reptile refrain from biting her. "So the lady put the snake inside her coat next to her heart and warmed it on her breast. It recovered and she was pleased until the moment she felt the fangs sink into her skin. 'But I saved your life and you promised not to bite!' she protested with her dying breath. 'Why did you kill me?' 'Because I'm a snake,' the serpent replied. 'so don't whine. You knew I was a snake when you picked me up.'"

"If she bites me, Ariin can heal me, or you can take me back before this happened, okay? But she's in a lot of pain," Khorii told him softly.

Grimalkin released her. Pircifir looked on with interest as she stepped forward again.

"Bring your hurt to me," she told the snake. *"Press that part of you to the bars and I will heal you."*

The bored-looking keeper roused himself, but Pircifir planted himself between the man and the serpent.

The snake shifted, her scales rippling as she coiled herself so that the outer coils filled the back of the cage while her head and the coil containing the lump pressed against the bars. She regarded Khorii with a tragic expression, which Khorii hoped did not mean that the snake regretted that as soon as it was healed it would, as in the story, be compelled by its serpentine nature to bite her. While Khorii was fairly certain that the measures she'd outlined to Grimalkin would save her life, she also thought being bitten by something that size would hurt a lot.

The coil pulsed slowly. It was dry and smooth except for the irregular lump, where the scales poked up along it. Some of them had rubbed off, revealing dark, ichor-filled sores.

Shushing the serpent again with her mind, Khorii motioned it to press farther forward. When it was close enough, she dipped her head to touch the lump with her horn. The snake hissed again, and Khorii assured it that she was not going to poke or prod the tumor with her sharp-looking horn, but that it would make the hurt go away.

She felt the snake's head swaying above her and was startled momentarily when a drop of something wet fell past her nose and sizzled on the street just beside her foot. Glancing up, she saw the fangs protruding slightly from the snake's mouth, venom dripping. A few feet away, she heard Grimalkin hiss in surprise, and she held out her hand to him, warning him not to come any closer.

Khorii knew the secretion of the venom had been involuntary, and the snake rippled with what could have been apology. She touched the tumor with her horn while the snake concentrated on trying to refrain from dripping venom.

She felt the tumor begin to uncoil its wadded cells inside the snake's body as it began to disintegrate, then she realized why the serpent looked so sad. This was not a real tumor, but the calcified bodies of the snake's young that she had ingested before she was captured. Instead of reabsorbing into her body normally, they had congealed in a lump, then grown hard and putrid inside her and sickened her.

Khorii jumped back as the snake's mouth yawned. Grimalkin grabbed her shoulders, Ariin her arm. But when the serpent opened its mouth wide, it was to let out a terrible belch of the worst imaginable stink as its body finished digesting the mass, and the coil became smooth again.

The snake wound its long body in a tight coil and regarded Khorii with those beautiful eyes again. Then it slowly dipped its head, as if bowing in appreciation of what the young Linyaari had done for it. And all during this time, the man who was supposed to be tending the snake watched the entire event with his mouth hanging open. Then, when the snake belched, he fainted dead away.

chapter 6

Grimalkin and Pircifir did not actually stick around for the snake's complete recovery. The keeper who had been in charge of stimulating the snake was still passed out, either from fright or the stench of the belch. The visitors thought it best not to revive him. The stench followed them into the next exhibit, the incredible morphing tunnel.

The interior of the tent was bare—no cage, no keeper, not even a flutter in the sides of the tent. The fabric was stretched incredibly smooth and tight, from the slightly raised floor to the conical ceiling.

"Where is it?" Pircifir asked.

"Hurry, hurry, hurry, step right up and see if the floor comes away on your boot," Ariin suggested.

He gave her a quizzical look as she set her boot deliberately on the material raising the floor of the tent up off the street. Her foot came away with a sucking sound and she held the sole up to show him that it was covered with a sticky mucus. "You're looking at the tunnel's first trick. It's become the tent's entire interior."

"How do you know that?" Pircifir asked her.

"It's a time thing, brother," Grimalkin told him.

From behind them came a low, self-satisfied chuckle,

and they turned to see the barker. "You didn't go inside," he chided them.

"It would eat us," Khorii said.

"Don't be silly, little girl. It's perfectly safe." He brushed past them and stepped inside. "Too close for you? How about a window right—here?" With a stick, he drew a domed shape on the side of the "tent," crisscrossing it with marks. The marks sucked in the material between them so that it stood in ridges. At first, the film left between the ridges was opaque, but gradually it became transparent, and Khorii saw a spitting camel walking past, led by his trainer.

"A higher ceiling? Watch!" He swished the stick in a circle above his head, and the cone lengthened, then, as the swishes became broader, widened again until the ceiling was approximately a meter higher. "Perhaps you'd be happier in a dome?" he asked, and ran around the room, his coattails flapping as he poked and swished at the wall until it spread into a dome shape.

"A castle?" Grimalkin asked.

"A small one, maybe," the man said. "This is just a small tunnel, after all. I'd have to feed it a lot more tents and cages to have enough to make something larger. But it has lots of bigger brothers and sisters where it comes from."

"Where would that be?" Grimalkin asked.

"A trade secret, my hairy friend. A trade secret."

"What if we wished to place a custom order?" Pircifir asked.

"I'm a showman, not a merchant," the man said. "I search the universe for these wonders, but they come from a great distance, and I've no intention of going back there."

Pircifir named quite a hefty sum, but the man said, "You have little insight into the soul of an artist like myself, sir. My assistant told me that your little friend here ruined the symbiont effect of my serpent, and now you wish me to disclose the secret source of my other act. I couldn't possibly consider that without a truly intriguing and appealing replacement—such as the unicorn girls there."

"We're not—" Khorii began, but Pircifir crooked his finger to Grimalkin and called him over.

"You can't sell us," Khorii protested.

Grimalkin reached back to pat her arm reassuringly, and she caught his warning glance and a flicker of eye movement in the direction of the barker. Tuning in, she wasn't surprised to find that the showman had more than simple bargaining on his mind.

"Once I have those twins caged, I can move them far away before their owners discover that I've told them to look in the wrong sector instead of the one where the tunnels were actually found. Maybe I can go back to their planet and get some more and do a really classy act, unicorn princesses in a castle tower kind of thing. Ought to be a big draw, along with these girls making stuff like the snake's tumor disappear."

"Did you also catch the real location of the tunnel planet as he thought about it?" Khorii asked Ariin.

"Yes, but I have no intention of telling those two until we're back safe aboard the ship. I don't want to be on display again."

"We might be able to come to an agreement," Pircifir said. "But you have to throw in your current specimen as well. These girls are quite extraordinary."

"No way," the man said. "I need that specimen. I'll take one of them for revealing the location where you can get your own, and the other one in payment for ruining my snake act. That's the best I can do."

"Very well," Pircifir said. "Your loss. Come along, girls."

The showman shrugged shoulders unusually broad and muscular for someone of his otherwise-slight build. He smiled philosophically and waved at them, trying to make them think this was the last they'd see of him.

"He's following us," Khorii told Grimalkin. She had decided she really didn't like Pircifir all that much. For a moment there, she thought he actually might have sold them. And while Grimalkin's history showed him to be anything but trustworthy, he had been, for the most part, a nice kitty who had been her friend, or at least seemed to be, for a long time.

For the first time in her life, she was among supposed allies, all of whom had given her reason to mistrust them. It didn't exactly frighten her, well, not too much, but it annoyed her that they couldn't be better behaved, and it also made her rather sad and disappointed. Not even Elviiz was smart and invulnerable anymore. Everything had changed far too much lately to suit her.

"Yes, and so is his trainer, who is actually his partner," Grimalkin told her. "While they are watching us, they're leaving the specimen unguarded."

"What does that matter? It's not ours. Ariin and I read the knowledge of where to find their original planet. Let's just go there instead."

"I want that specimen," Pircifir said.

"We noticed," Ariin snapped.

"Don't be difficult. I never meant to leave you behind, and you know very well he could never hold you. All you'd have to do is return to your humanoid guise and convince him he'd been hoaxed, and he wouldn't even want to keep you."

Khorii started to tell him that they couldn't do that, but Ariin stepped on her foot.

Grimalkin smoothly intervened. "How do we know that, brother? An unsavory character like that would find some way to recoup his investment. Best get the ladies safely stowed aboard the ship before we continue."

"Continue what?" Ariin asked suspiciously.

"Why, our mission, of course," he replied.

"This is our mission, you silly cat," Ariin snapped, but Grimalkin just grinned an amused grin at her.

"I realize that. But Pirci and I cannot complete our mission with you hampering us."

"It was my mission with Pircifir before you two came along," Ariin said.

"Please be more cooperative, or none of us will accomplish anything here," Pircifir told them.

Much against Ariin's will and Khorii's inclination, the girls returned to the ship, whereupon the two Friends left again.

"When are you coming back?" Ariin demanded.

Grimalkin waved his hand. "Sooner or later." Khorii was reminded of the wave of his Khiindi self's retreating tail as he sauntered off to do exactly as he pleased.

As soon as they disappeared, Ariin was back out the hatch.

"What are you doing?" Khorii asked.

"Following them, of course. This was my idea, and that cat of yours isn't going to leave me sitting on a spaceship while he steals it to reingratiate himself with his friends."

"We can't follow them. They're gone."

"Yes, but we know exactly where they're going, don't we?"

"I suppose. They'll be trying to steal that thing as soon as everyone is asleep."

"Of course they will. And they're bound to run into trouble. The man who owned that thing is as shrewd as they are. The Friends always think they're smarter than everyone else, and really, they can be so transparent because they never ever give anyone else—not even us—credit for having any brains at all."

"You can't go alone," Khorii said. "Those streets are not safe. Didn't you feel that stew of greed and anger and violence all around us?"

"No, but I have not led the sheltered life that some girls have. I don't expect everyone to like me and admire me and want to be my friend."

"That's a good thing," Khorii thought, but mostly to herself. "Nevertheless, if you're going, I'm going, too."

Ariin huffed, but then seemed to reconsider. "Come on then."

Khorii followed her, but almost at once wished she hadn't. The market was emptying by the time they walked back through the gates. People crossed in front of them, dark shapes in a dark city, and melted into the nearby buildings. The rugs and stalls full of unusual merchandise had magically disappeared. No spitting camels or even heavily laden beasts of burden wandered the streets. Banners were rolled up, tattered bunting flopped listlessly against the buildings. The more enticing smells of their earlier visit had faded, and the more noxious ones intensified. The temperature had also dropped sharply. The girls were well protected by their shipsuits, but Khorii's cheeks were cold. From the shuttered windows and closed doors, she felt that she and Ariin were being watched. It wouldn't be hard. Their hooves clopped against the pavement louder than any other sound. Lights blinked out in twos and threes, then in entire banks as they walked farther down the street toward the carnival tents.

"Decided on a career change after all, did you, ladies?" The barker's voice inquired from somewhere behind them.

"How did that happen? People shouldn't be able to sneak up on telepaths," Ariin thought indignantly. *"Why can't we read him now?"*

"We don't actually know who he is exactly, do we?"

Khorii asked. *"Perhaps he has some special abilities himself. Shielding, for instance."*

"We got worried about the snake and decided to check on her," Khorii said. "Is she all right?"

"How should I know? I turned her loose," the barker said. "A giant snake is not rare enough to be of any use to me."

"Where did you turn her loose?" Khorii asked. "How will she survive?"

"I don't know, and I don't care. But I can't support a beast that size if she's not working. You two, on the other hand . . ."

"Khorii, watch out, he's—" Ariin began. Normally they would have been able to know their opponent's intent, but again, he was frustratingly blank. Then a net was cast over both of them, and they were expertly rolled up in it like the prey of a huge spider. Rough hands shoved them off their feet and dragged them into a doorway.

"You don't want to do this, really," Ariin projected at their captors. *"This is a very bad idea."*

"I don't think this pair is sensitive enough to respond to your pushing, Ariin," Khorii told her.

"Now that we've got them, what are we going to do with them?" the man who had been the snake's keeper asked. "We'd better lie low and keep them out of sight in case their gentlemen friends come looking for them."

"They're long gone," Ariin prompted. *"They didn't own us. When they refused your offer, they didn't ask us if we wanted to work for you."*

"That's right," Khorii added, though her prompt wasn't as subtle as Ariin's. *"I've always wondered what it would be like to be in show business."*

"There, you see? My sister wants to work for you, too. You should take this net off of us before it damages us. It's too tight. Besides, you can't show us to people all bound up like this. There's nothing interesting or unusual about that."

"Take the net off, Sileg," the barker told the snake keeper.

"What if they get away?" Sileg asked.

"We have to let them loose sometime so we can work on their act. Besides, I have the feeling that they might enjoy our kind of life. The door's locked, the windows are barred and their friends are nowhere in sight. Maybe they got bored with this pair."

"Maybe you've been hitting the bottle again, Pebar. They all looked pretty chummy when they left here earlier."

"All I'm saying is that they certainly disappeared fast enough after leaving these two at their space vessel," Pebar said. "The fact that the girls tried to follow them indicates some sort of a falling-out, don't you think?"

"I'm telling you, Pebar, don't count your take from these two until that ship leaves here for good."

"Then send a boy to keep an eye on it and report back to us," Pebar told him. "And hurry back. We've work to do with these two."

chapter 7

I t's okay now, Pebar. The ship is gone," Sileg reported
when he returned.

"Did you make him think that?" Khorii asked Ariin.

"N-no. I didn't." Ariin sounded shocked.

*"How can the ship be gone? Did they really go off and
leave us?"* Khorii could not believe that Pircifir and Grimalkin would just desert them.

*"Most likely they didn't even realize that we weren't on
board. I have tried to tell you how little notice these people
take of anybody else. Can you see now how important you
were to your precious Khiindi?"*

"I hope that's it," Khorii said stubbornly. *"Because if it
is, they'll be back as soon as they do notice we're gone. I
know you hate Khiindi—I mean, Grimalkin—but I think being my cat all those years changed him. He isn't bad, and he
does care about me."*

"Good for you. He doesn't give a dead stinkweed for me."

I can see why, Khorii thought to herself, then felt bad
about her unkind, if honest, reaction. It wasn't Ariin's fault
she was like this, it was just her response to her own certainty that Grimalkin and Pircifir had abandoned them. But
Khorii knew that wasn't the case.

As they debated what had happened, Pebar and Sileg untangled the net and released them.

"You understand now, little dears, that you are alone except for us," Pebar told them as he pulled the webbing from their legs, torsos, and finally their heads. "We will feed, shelter, and protect you in exchange for a little honest work. Now then, what else can you do other than ruin my snake act?"

"We're healers," Khorii told him. She and Ariin had reached a silent agreement that their best course was to play along until they could find some way to free themselves. Either the ship would return for them, or they would find another way out. Ariin still had her crono and once their hands were free and they were unobserved, they could easily just return to the time before they left the ship. "We're sorry we cost you your act, but we simply can't help it. If something is injured, sick, or in pain, we cure it. It's our nature."

"Hmm, sounds useful," he said, turning on a lamp.

The girls rubbed circulation back into the places where the nets had cut into them. Khorii thought Ariin looked very funny with her face gridded and dented by net marks, but then realized she looked the same.

"It's going to take a little retooling on our part though. Expensive. We have to let people know we're in a new business and even though you girls will be paying your way soon enough, I'll be out of pocket in the meantime." The lamp's light glinted from his greedy eye and the crono on Ariin's wrist at the same time. "Here, that looks expensive," he said, snatching the crono and pulling it over her hand before the feeling had returned to it again. "That should help offset the expenses."

"Look at it closely. It's not precious metal. It's old and worn. It doesn't even keep good time. It's worthless." Ariin projected as hard as she could, but Pebar pocketed her crono

without looking at it again and began hauling heavy chests out of corners and down from high shelves.

Sileg helped him with other chests until there were six in all. Then the two of them hauled out bundles of fabric, billowing armloads of gauzy sheers from one trunk, stiff folded packets as unyielding and inflexible as heavy packplas, brilliant silks from another, and pots of paint and brushes in the last.

Pebar held up a sheer white robe to Khorii. "Put this on."

Obediently, she slid it on over her shipsuit.

"I meant take off what you're wearing and wear this instead," the man said, with exaggerated patience.

"It looks better over the other clothes. Purer. It will make a better act," Ariin nudged.

Since nudity and false modesty were not Linyaari traits, Khorii had already unfastened the wrists and neck of her shipsuit, and started to pull the filmy garment over her head.

"No, no. On second thought, leave the suit on and put the gown on over it. Yes, I like it. The gown lends the ethereal quality we're seeking, but the suit lends a certain purity that will go well with the tinge of sacred awe your talent should inspire in people."

"Yeah, Pebar, and it's not like there was anything to them. They're way too skinny to fill the gowns out right. I'm going to have to take the shoulders in and lower the belts on the gowns as it is," Sileg, apparently a critic of both tailoring and female form, declared.

"Fine, fine. Now then. Billing. The Healing Horned Princesses?"

"How about The Healing Horned Priestesses instead, Pebar? Gets the religious angle that way, too. People will feel like they're dropping offerings in a collection plate instead of paying admission."

"Ye-es. In fact, if they're as good with people as they are with snakes, we could change our entire approach. Turn the tunnel into a temple and sit the girls up on a throne, have the marks bow as they come in and make donations appropriate to the healing they need. And how deep their pockets are, of course. I like it. I like it a lot. We should change our image too, Sileg. To fit in with the ambience."

"Yeah, we could be like temple deacons or something."

"Exactly. The helpers of the divine ones who take care of all the mundane details, like money."

"We're not divine and we're not priestesses," Khorii thought exasperatedly. *"And those two are certainly not any sort of spiritual functionaries."*

"No, but our gift is true, so we're not fundamentally misleading anyone. Play along till I can steal my crono back, anyway."

"I guess we'll have a chance to help people while we're waiting," Khorii agreed. *"Right now it seems we haven't got any other choice."*

The next day, the alien tunnel's exterior had become a cobalt, gold, and carnelian tent, the colors achieved by feeding the appropriately dyed silks to the organism. Khorii and Ariin, clad in their white shipsuits with the skirts of the white wispy gowns spread around each of them like the petals of a lotus, sat on a pair of altarlike thrones and waited. And waited. And waited. So did Sileg, who stood behind them with a fan of rather mangy feathers.

"Don't you two know how to do anything but sit?" he complained. "Why don't you go out front and juggle or tumble or something."

"You'd have to change your new sign then to read 'The Tumbling, Juggling Healing Horned Priestesses,'" Khorii pointed out. "It would be more fun than sitting here, but I don't think it would project the dignified and reverent image you're trying to achieve."

"I suppose not," Sileg was forced to agree.

"Sileg!"

"What?" the man answered irritably.

"Get out here and go find us some gimps! Preferably some with loud mouths."

"Where am I going to find those?" Sileg asked.

"There are beggars on every street corner with terrible injuries. Go get some of them."

"Yeah, but most of the injuries are fake, Pebar. They don't want to be cured."

"Who cares what they want! There's another new act up the street that isn't depending on the marks to come to them. Flying Tigers. Can't figure out how the ifrit they do it. They're amazing and astounding, but they can't make anybody feel any better, so go drag some miserable sot in here for the girls to cure."

"How about you recruit the gimps, and I'll change the set a little so the tent is open and the girls are in plain view. This sacred thing is fine, but if the marks don't see the girls doing their trick, or the gimp getting healed, they're not going to be flocking over here with their money."

"That's where the big mouths come in," Pebar said. "But you do have a point. Fine. You work on the display, pull back the draperies some, and I'll go recruit some gimps and sickos."

"You two seem to have a very good working relationship," Khorii remarked to Sileg. "Your employer listens to you and heeds your advice."

"He's not my employer," Sileg said. "He's my brother. We learned our craft at our mother's knee, and sometimes at her foot. We're fourth-generation showmen."

"Has your family always used aliens in your acts?" Khorii asked. "Like the tunnel and the snake and—well, us?"

"No, we're the first. But you can't just go with all domestic talent these days. Too much competition. So, during the off-season we go talent scouting."

"That must be exciting, and dangerous, with creatures like the snake and the tunnel."

"Expensive, too," Ariin said. "Space travel isn't cheap."

"We pay our way providing entertainment for the crews," he said.

"But with large fierce creatures like the snake and the tunnel, how do you persuade your transports to haul them for you?"

"The snake is pretty standard wildlife cargo," he said. "It was only the growth that made her special." He gave Khorii a resentful look.

"I'm sorry," she said. "I was trying to help. I didn't realize I was ruining things for you."

"Ruined it for her, too. She may have had a bellyache before, but she'll starve now or get captured by some restaurant and served up as round steaks."

"How horrible," Khorii said, shocked at the consequences of what she had thought was a helpful act of kindness at the time.

"But speaking of food," Ariin cut in, "we're getting really hungry. Is there a patch of grass nearby where we could graze while your brother fetches the—what did you call them—gimps?"

"Nothing like that around here that I know of. When you prove your worth, maybe Pebar will buy you some snake steak."

"We're herbivores," Khorii told him. "Vegetarians."

"Then maybe he'll let you each buy a piece of fruit from one of the vendors."

A few very long boring moments later Pebar returned, towing a beggar behind him. The beggar appeared to have no legs and sat on a cart to which Pebar had attached a rope.

Hauling the poor man before the girls in much the same way Khiindi had often presented Khorii with a rodent, Pebar stood back with his arms crossed over his chest, and said, "Do your thing, o' healing, horned priestesses."

Khorii and Ariin looked at each other and at the man. *"Uncle Joh said some horns once made his fingers and RK's ear and tail grow back when they'd been cut off, but I don't know if we can do legs."*

"You've had more experience at it than me," Ariin replied. *"The Friends never need healing, and neither do the Others. I didn't even know we could do that until I came forward to meet Mother and Father."*

Khorii got down off the throne and knelt beside the wretched man. Even before she knelt she had smelled him, but fortunately her horn purified the air around him immediately, making prolonged proximity to his scabrous person much easier to bear. Besides the missing legs, he had thick crusts around his eyes, nose, and mouth, oozing sores on other exposed surfaces, raspy breathing and bleeding, and cracked calluses on his palms and knuckles. "How long ago did you lose your legs?" Khorii asked.

"Born without 'em," he said, with a pugnacious jut of his chin. "Leave me alone. I'm missing prime time and Blind Orange Anderson has been eyeing my corner."

"How can he do that if he's blind?" Ariin asked.

"Don't worry," Pebar said. "He's next. Heal this one, and I'll go get the other one."

"I'll have to see your stumps, sir. I'm not sure I can do anything for you if you were born without legs but . . ."

"Just mind your own business," he replied, jerking back from her. Khorii sat back on her heels, puzzled.

Sileg grabbed the man and twisted his arm up behind him. "Go ahead and horn him, girlie. Now shut your mouth, Stumpy. You're getting a freebie as it is."

Khorii shook her head, perplexed by the man's behavior, but Ariin, with a bored yawn, got down from her altar, brushed past her sister, and laid her hands on the man's shoulder and her horn against his forehead. "Calm down and let's have a look," she said. "I don't know what you are so upset about. I'm the one who has to touch you."

"Nobody asked you to," he said. "Let me out of here!"

Gritting her teeth, Ariin yanked on the bottom of his robe. She was, like most Linyaari, quite strong in proportion to her size, and the man found himself flipped over backward. He fell off the cart, onto his rear, his perfectly good legs trapped halfway out of the depression in the cart where he knelt while begging.

"You had legs all along!" Khorii said.

"No, no, you cured me," he said, pulling them back under him and covering himself with the robe to escape possible stares from the passersby. "Now leave me the 'frit alone and let me get back to my business."

"We can cure illnesses and injuries, but we don't clothe them with a horn touch," Khorii said.

"Pebar should have known. Stumpy's a phony."

Stumpy pulled his legs off the cart and stood, a bit unsteadily. Looking down at his hands, he said, "Aw, damn. Will you look at this?" The bruises and calluses were healed and the bleeding cleaned up. He wiped his face on the hem of his shirt, and his skin came away crust- and scab-free. "I'm going to have to grow them calluses back again," he complained. "It's going to hurt."

"We can—" Khorii started to offer, but he glared at her.

"You two have done quite enough. Ruined the whole day for me." He gave an indignant sniff, then sniffed again, experimentally. "Well, I'll be! You did cure me after all." Blowing his nose on his sleeve, he said in a clear voice. "Had a terrible cold, pneumonia probably, and it's all gone now. That's worth something."

"Hallelujah, it's a miracle," Sileg said in a flat voice. "Go forth and take word to the multitudes, brother."

"What's in it for me?" Stumpy asked.

"You already got a free healing," Sileg told him.

"That don't pay for shill work and lost time at my place of employment," the man haggled.

"Half a copper for each referral then," Sileg said. "But don't try to scam a scammer. We'll check with the marks."

"Done," Stumpy said, and knelt back into his cart. In an obsequious whine he said to Khorii, "Give a poor callusless fellow a tow back to his corner, pretty missy?"

"I'll kick your worthless arse around the rings of Octavia Prime if you don't crawl on out of here right now," Pebar said, hauling in another man, this one tall and thin with rust-colored skin and sparse white hair. He wore dark glasses and clung to a white cane.

He was no more blind than the other man was legless but had better manners. When Khorii cured the arthritis that made it hard for him to sit on his street corner for very long, he gratefully promised to move to another corner, minus the glasses, and shill for the girls until the act caught on.

This produced enough business to bring in a woman with female complaints, a man with indigestion, and a sick infant. The parents of the sick infant were well-off and donated enough that Pebar agreed that the girls could each have not only a piece of fruit, but all of the wilted flowers the florist cart had to offer.

Once they had eaten, the girls cured several more cases before the market closed, by which time Pebar had made plans. "We'll drag the snake's cage inside the tent," he told Sileg. "They'll be safe enough in there. Kind of poetic justice in a way that they replace the snake, isn't it?"

Sileg rolled his eyes.

Khorii thought that he was beginning to like them and feel sympathy for them that he wouldn't reveal in front of his harder-hearted brother. Still, it did not keep him from closing the front of the "tent" and snapping the lock on the cage. Apparently it would take some more time to work on him.

"Maybe tomorrow night you could nudge him into forgetting to lock the lock," Khorii suggested.

"Perhaps I will. My evil persuasive nudges that you so despise have done us so much good so far," Ariin replied sarcastically. *"Let's get some rest. I'm sure my horn is clear as glass after all that healing we were forced to do."*

chapter 8

Khorii was tired enough to sleep despite captivity, the cage, and the fact that she was slumbering inside an alien life-form. However, her dreams changed sometime during the night. They became full of doorsteps and trash in the streets, and dark, ugly passages full of slimy, rotting refuse where, for some reason, she was looking for food.

Then, joy of joys, she found it—large, juicy, filling and of no use to anyone except its fellow scum dwellers. Giving it no time to turn on her, she struck. It shrieked once before she bit it, then swallowed it and began digesting. But she did not wish to digest down here, nor to sleep the long sleep she needed while she did it. Although she had been released, cast out, she returned to the only nest she knew in this place.

Khorii's mane ruffled with a breeze and she heard a rustling, sliding sound. What an odd dream. She'd never dreamed of killing a live creature before. She wondered why she felt no disgust or repugnance.

The rustling was closer and louder now. When Khorii sat up, she saw nothing at first, but as her eyes adjusted to the light, she spotted a long, low mound where none had been. Then the front end of the mound rose and fanned out into a scalloped hood the size of a land lorry's wheel. Large golden eyes glinted in the dark, and Khorii briefly smelled the acrid scent of venom that she had smelled once before. Then she sensed movement and something soft and wet touched her hand. She recoiled with a start, but realized that it had only been the snake's tongue extended in greeting rather than attack. While that registered, the hood closed, the snake's head returned to the floor, and it wound its length around the cage.

Khorii had no idea how Ariin would react if she woke to find the snake wrapped around them, or how Pebar and Sileg would react. She entertained a brief fantasy in which the snake attacked the two men when they came in the morning and forced them to release the girls, but she realized the flaws in that dream even as she conceived it. The snake's thought processes did not extend to opening locks or relationships between two-legged people. She—the snake—was simply looking for a safe place to rest and digest her meal before hunting again.

Whatever reaction her sister or the others might have when they found the snake in the morning, Khorii found the creature's presence oddly comforting. She was sure the snake remembered her, at least, and far from fearing the creature, she felt, however unrealistically, protected by its presence.

When she awoke, however, it was to the lock snapping open and Sileg's voice saying, "Brought you girls some grain to break your fast."

"Clever of you," Ariin said ingratiatingly. "You may notice that our horns haven't the color they did before your brother began hauling in the gimps yesterday. We can only do our healing if we're well rested and nourished ourselves."

"So I figured. You perked right up after you ate that first bouquet of posies last night. I told Pebar that as business picks up, we need you in top form. By today word will have got 'round, and you'll be drawing a larger crowd."

"Oh, joy unending," Ariin said.

The snake was long gone, and Khorii wondered briefly if she had only dreamed the encounter. Then she saw the round hole in the side of the tent enclosure and how the sides bowed out at the bottom in the approximate diameter of the snake's girth.

As Sileg predicted, there were more people, a steady stream of them at first, then a large crowd gathered outside the entrance to the tent. Many carried crying children, and that became tiresome as the day wore on. Khorii wished their horns could abolish the noise permeating the air the same way they could cleanse it of bad smells. A lot of the children were just tired or overexcited, and a very gentle horn touch was all that was required to calm them. A few were frightened by the horns or the girls' appearance and required extra time. For the most part, though, the injuries were slight and the healing not too draining. The donations were not draining the pockets of the marks either, however, and this did not please Pebar and Sileg.

They worked steadily into the late afternoon. The child Khorii had been about to calm with a horn touch suddenly bellowed and leaped down from her mother's knee, running to the front of the tent. Khorii followed. A huge crowd clumped from just outside the tent all the way up the market street, where it parted to let another group of people pass through the center.

A deep, echoing roar, which had nothing to do with the roar of the crowd, rolled down the street. Khorii knew at once it came from some great beast, though she had never heard its like before. "What is it?" she called to the people outside the tent.

"One of the flying tigers crashed into a building. He fell from the air and is injured."

"We have to go help the poor thing," Khorii said, twisting to tell Pebar and Sileg.

"They can carry the cat here," Pebar said. "That's what I told them when they came to get you before, while you were shutting the kids up. So you just go back and think healthy thoughts, and pretty soon everyone will know what you can do and where to find you."

The bellowing roars and the excitement of the crowd increased by the second. Then suddenly there was a great downdraft that shook the entire tent itself. Four gold-and-black-striped paws appeared in the doorway. Then a long, clubbed, striped tail and black-furred wings attached to a sturdy but lithe feline body the size of a flitter followed, backing into the room. The massive head, fur bristling along the top and down the neck, appeared last, the mouth open in a white-fanged roar that terrified all the onlookers into a fast retreat.

"That would be the other flying tiger," Khorii's informant squeaked excitedly from a safer distance.

This cat stalked through the crowd, parting them easily so that the delegation bearing the injured body of the other flying feline could advance with greater speed.

"Smart cat," Sileg remarked. "You'd expect it to maybe guard its buddy and attack all comers. This one seems to have had some crowd-control training."

Twelve large men bore the injured animal on some sort of stage or platform, which they set down at the tent's entrance. Khorii knelt beside the cat. *"There's something familiar about him,"* she told Ariin.

"Isn't there just?" Ariin replied. *"Hmmm, I wonder, could it be because we know that shapeshifters who specialize in feline forms could be lurking nearby, spaceship or no?"*

"Help me then. Shapeshifter or not, his wing really is broken," Khorii told her.

"Meow?" The Grimalkin flying tiger's thought sounded heartrendingly like little Khiindi.

"Hush, kitty, I'm here." She laid her horn against the most obvious fracture. *"Does that feel better?"*

The great body rumbled beneath her in a rusty purr, but she still felt pain emanating from it. His right hind leg, she thought, but to her surprise he lifted his uppermost forepaw and placed it on her knee. When she saw the gleam of metal beneath the fur, she understood. The crono.

Khorii healed the damaged leg. Then, shielding the paw with her body so that neither Ariin nor their captors could see, Khorii stretched the crono's band wide enough to pull it off over the paw, and slipped it onto her wrist, shoving it far up inside her sleeve so that Sileg and Pebar wouldn't relieve her of it as they had Ariin's. *These pesky robes are actually useful for a change,* she thought.

Feeling a gust of hot breath across the back of her neck and shoulders, she twisted her head to see the other tiger— Pircifir, no doubt, monitoring her movements. She looked around, but didn't see Pebar and Sileg until she spotted them far from the tent, watching warily from the front of the crowd. The tigers made them nervous, it seemed. *Good.*

Ariin wouldn't touch Grimalkin, but she stood beside Pircifir as if consoling the great cat in his worry over his companion. Pebar roared, "Do something!" to his brother almost as loudly as the tigers had roared. Sileg departed and returned with a chair, with which he cautiously approached the tent, jabbing the chair legs in Pircifir's direction. Pircifir, with a slight flutter of his wings, made a flying leap and knocked Sileg and the chair back into Pebar and the crowd, then stood over their prostrate forms, growling ferociously.

"Leave the beasts to us, Deacons," Ariin called cheerily. "I don't believe they like men. We will stand guard over the sick one tonight as he rests and heal the fear in the other tiger's mind so that tomorrow, they may return to their tasks, as gentle as housecats."

Most of the crowd dispersed, but there were no more patients for the girls that day. When the market had closed, Pebar returned with a gun, which he aimed at the tigers, who were sitting together grooming each other. Behind Pebar, Sileg came with a net. But while the two men were practiced at capturing and taming wild animals or those without awareness, they were no match for the shapeshifters. The tigers split up, took to the air, and harried the two men all the way down the street. Khorii and Ariin laughed until the tigers returned.

Ariin drew the "tent flaps" closed with gestures similar to the ones she had seen Sileg use the night before. Meanwhile, Khorii searched through the costume trunks stored behind the altar. Once they had a degree of privacy, the tigers returned to humanoid form, and Khorii presented them with her gleanings from the trunk. A multicolored garment with full sleeves, a great red ruff, and matching trousers pleased Grimalkin greatly, though he chose not to wear the oversized shoes and large, floppy hat that went with it. The spangled tights and top hat were the only items that fit Pircifir, but he was amused by them, especially the shiny fringes, which he played with in true cat fashion for a few moments before returning to the matter at hand.

"I see no reason to delay our departure any longer," Pircifir said.

"Then you came back with the ship?" Khorii asked. "When we heard it was missing, we thought you had deserted us."

"It is not our custom to leave crew members behind, especially when we have already declined to sell them to unscrupulous persons," Pircifir answered with a grin.

"However, we did want to ensure that those two rascals would think we had left the planet, which is why we took off," Grimalkin said. "Then we needed suitable disguises to enable us to locate you without being 'seen,' so to speak. I came up with the flying tiger persona, and here we all are."

"Then the ship is out there?"

"By the time we get to the spot where it was, it will be," Pircifir said. "But first we must find a way to transport the specimen. I don't suppose you two have gained any insights into its nature and manipulation while you've been living and working within it?"

"Not really," Khorii said. "But if we can wait a while, and be quiet, someone else might be able to help us."

"We're not waiting for that stupid snake!" Ariin said. "It's dangerous, it's too big to take with us, and it would only delay us when at any moment Pebar and Sileg could return with real weapons and imprison or kill all of us."

"I don't think so," Grimalkin said in a growl worthy of his tiger self or Khiindi on a bad day.

"Just until after everything has gone quiet," Khorii said. "She slithers up from the sewers. That's the only place she can find something to eat."

"Oh, lovely," Pircifir said.

"Our horns can deal with the smell," Khorii said, pleading with him. "She is not an ordinary snake, and she has lived with the alien form long enough to consider it a friend, I think. She came in last night as we slept and wound herself around the cage." When they wavered, Khorii voiced one other intuition she had about the snake. "I believe they may have been captured together. Perhaps she is from the same place and can help us with others like this one."

"Why would she do that?" Pircifir asked.

"Because we may be taking her home," Khorii said. "And she communicates with me a little. I can't quite explain it."

"Fine. Are you going to feed her, too?" Ariin asked. "I don't think she lives on the same things we do."

"We could catch the two who captured you and feed them to her," Grimalkin suggested.

Khorii smiled in spite of herself, then frowned just as quickly. "That is not humorous. She prefers large verminous rodents from the sewers, I believe."

Grimalkin grinned. "I'm beginning to like this snake."

"She fed last night. I don't think she has to eat often, and she sleeps a lot. She may be quite nearby. She's not afraid of Ariin and me, but men's voices might frighten her."

Grimalkin nodded and put a finger, still sporting a long, curved nail, to his lips. Pircifir nodded once also, indicating his understanding, and the two settled down to wait.

Khorii was the first to see her serpentine friend and she sent a clear image of herself and her friends leading the snake and the tent to their ship and taking off into space. "*Is this,*" she inquired, "*something you would agree to?*"

She had no plans for what to do if the snake did not agree, and was chagrined when the creature rushed at her, toward the closed tent flap, tripping her in its coils, sweeping Ariin along in the same fluid movement.

"No go, eh?" Grimalkin asked.

Khorii took hold of Ariin and pulled her out of the tent. Before they were all the way out, Grimalkin and Pircifir tumbled after them.

"I thought you said this snake was a friendly, reasonable beast!" Pircifir said indignantly. He had no more than gained his feet, however, when the great iron cage and the costume trunks, even the ornamental urn concealing the stout metal box in which donations were deposited, came flying out of the tent.

"She seems to be evicting everyone and everything," Grimalkin said, then jumped back as the snake's head appeared in the flap opening, rapidly followed by the rest of her.

Khorii motioned the others back away from the tent. "She

wants us out of the way is all," she said. The snake whipped out of the tent and began coiling herself around it. It obligingly compressed behind her body, growing taller as she wound herself into a smaller and smaller coil around it. Then she lifted her head and adjusted her coil so that she pulled the top-heavy form down until it was a flat, compact disk.

"I'll be 'fritted," said Grimalkin, who had apparently picked up some of the local parlance. "The serpent was packing it up for us."

chapter 9

The snake allowed Khorii to carry the alien disk. It was a bit more than she could manage, so she balanced it on the snake's back, right behind the head, and held it steady while the four of them walked, the snake undulating beside Khorii. Outside the market, Pircifir and Grimalkin each stuck out a hand for the girls to hold. Pircifir's other hand was raised, the sleeve pulled back to show his crono.

"We can't go yet," Ariin said suddenly, snatching her hand back, and stopping abruptly.

"Why not?" Pircifir asked. "One would hardly suppose you'd developed a fondness for this place."

"Pebar took my crono. It's mine, and I want it back," she explained.

"Actually, it's mine," Grimalkin said.

Pircifir, still believing the girls were Friends in a strange guise, asked, "Why would she have your crono?"

"She stole it."

"When? You had it—"

"I had it before I was injured. I'd stolen it back from an earlier self, but long after that, and after this, she stole it from Akasa, who had stolen it from me."

"You've been spending too much time dirtside, brother," Pircifir said. "It's not healthy.

"I'm not leaving here until I get it back," Ariin said.

"She has a point, I suppose," Pircifir said. "Our devices should not fall into untrained hands. Other people cannot properly appreciate their usefulness and might end up somewhere they've no wish to be."

Grimalkin did not betray the Linyaari to his brother as "other people."

"I'll turn back into a flyger and pounce it out of him," he offered.

"No," Ariin said. "I don't trust you. You won't give it back."

"She knows you well, brother," Pircifir said, with a resigned sigh. "We'll all go. Join hands again."

They did, and in a blink the darkness disappeared and the sun returned. Along with it was the ship. That was a very good thing, Khorii decided, since a throng of people spilled from the market square, carrying all sorts of implements that could be used as weapons. At the throng's front were Pebar and Sileg, bearing a tranquilizer gun and net.

Pircifir apparently made a mental adjustment to the crono, because in the next moment they were all strapping themselves down as the takeoff sequence began.

The snake coiled loosely at their feet, her tail anchoring the disk.

"You tricked me!" Ariin accused Pircifir.

"Nothing of the sort, my dear. We will return again to retrieve the misappropriated crono once we have completed our mission. Unless you have decided you do not want to be part of the crew on this historic event? If so, just say the word, and you can go back to life in the carnival until such time as we deem it convenient to return for you."

"It's not like the time matters," Ariin sulked. "With the cronos, you can go back and forth and never lose a moment."

"Up to a point that is certainly true," Pircifir agreed. "But I find loops tiresome. I am the captain, and you are here on my sufferance, and I say that this now is the time we will leave to seek the home of the alien shapeshifter. We do have a lot of time, but other resources are more limited. Fuel for instance, and oxygen."

"But—" Ariin began. She saw a fallacy in that statement somewhere, but before she could protest, the ship sliced through the planet's atmosphere, and they were once more in space.

Had it been up to Ariin, despite her wish to take credit for solving the future alien menace, they would not have found the planet. She refused to divulge the coordinates she had picked up from Pebar and Sileg. However, Khorii had the same information, and Pircifir and Grimalkin were such seasoned travelers they had no trouble locating the homeworld of the "alien tunnel."

The closer they got, the more intrusive the snake became. She took to coiling behind their chairs and raising her head to loom over them, dripping venom from her fangs, making small scars on the deck as she scanned the viewscreen. If ever an animal could be said to be anxious for something to happen, this one was anxious to reach her home.

"Surely she wouldn't recognize our course," Grimalkin said. "I doubt her kind excel at astronavigation."

"Perhaps it's an intuitive mechanism," Khorii said. "But I feel sure she knows. After all, you knew things as a cat that people didn't think you could know—"

"That was different. I was a superior sentient being in cat form, and nobody knew that."

"We don't know that she isn't one, too," Khorii said. "I

wish I'd thought to bring a LAANYE along before we left our time."

Whether or not the snake was a superior sentient being, she seemed to realize she was among friends. The rest of the crew were frightened of her at first, and annoyed by the holes in the deck her venomous dripping caused—it was actually a drool of sorts, and Khorii thought it might be a nervous response. Later, they grew used to her and nicknamed her Nagaine, the name of a serpentine shifter who once dwelled among the Friends. Grimalkin wondered if the original Nagaine might even be a founder of the snake's race. He himself had initiated the population of feline breeds on several worlds.

As they drew nearer to the coordinates Khorii and Ariin had gleaned from Pebar and Sileg, the serpent began shaking her tail and would not leave the bridge. Finally, she remained in coiled position, with her head raised as the ship entered the target planet's orbit, flattening only as its gravity caught hold of the ship and pressed the crew deep into whichever soft surface they had strapped themselves.

When they had landed, it took one glance out the viewport for Pircifir to say, "Nagaine leaves the ship first. We will learn how sentient she is when she joins them."

He nodded to the viewport, which showed a rocky but writhing terrain filled with other large serpents in various stages of locomotion, some flat out and undulating, some semicoiled, some coiled, others coiled with heads raised, all postures with which Nagaine had made them familiar.

"You can go now," Khorii told her. *"Please tell your people we mean them no harm and hope they feel the same. We would like to keep the tent thing."* She touched the disk. With seeming reluctance, Nagaine withdrew the length of tail she had coiled around it.

"Are there more like it here as well as more of you?"

Ariin asked her. *"We'll want many of them. Remember, we cured you and brought you home, so you owe us—"*

"Nothing," Khorii interrupted Ariin's thought. *"But if any of your people need our healing skills, we would be happy to treat them."*

"And if they want to show their gratitude by bringing us more of these, we'd call it even," Ariin said, with a frown at Khorii.

They weren't sure if Nagaine understood or not, but she writhed eagerly through the hatch and twined herself down the gantry, then dropped to the ground and was instantly caught up in a large tangle of snakes.

Khorii felt Ariin shudder beside her.

"If we're going to go down there among those, I want enough of these things to make houses for everyone in Kubiilikaan."

"We don't barter our skills, Ariin. We heal because it's needed, not to make people give us what we want."

"As if we could make that"—she shuddered again at the writhing knots of snakes below—*"do anything! I don't think the tunnel came from the same place. I think we just got the coordinates of the snake planet, not the tunnel planet, and we should go now. Besides, I don't think the tunnel was ever a plague. The only thing I ever saw it eat was those silk flags. It's probably just a similar organism, not the same thing."*

"I know. It looks the same, but it doesn't behave the way the ones the plague made did, does it?" Khorii agreed.

"We think we should just go, Pircifir," Ariin said. "This is where the snakes live but not the tunnels."

"I disagree," Pircifir said, and directed her to look again at the viewport. The balls of snakes had been so repugnant to her that Ariin had looked away as soon as possible.

Most of the snakes were now retreating in waves but others crawled forward, pushing large balls with their noses, herding them toward the ship. Then the pushers, all but one lone serpent who was as clearly Nagaine as the others clearly were not, retreated beyond the rocky hills.

"There's our cargo," Pircifir said, with a satisfied smile.

"How do you know that's what we want and not snake eggs full of baby snakes that will hatch as soon as we get into orbit?" asked a crew member who, like Ariin, was still shuddering from the spectacle presented by the sea of snakes.

"Well, for one thing, would you send your babies off to be born on a foreign ship?" Khorii demanded. "Neither would Nagaine and her species."

"You don't know that."

"I do," Khorii said.

"She does," Grimalkin agreed. "Besides, when we take them, we will have the tunnels and can train them to be houses. Look—one is pulling out of disk shape already and forming a cone. We'd better go collect them before they turn into tunnels again and slither off after the snakes."

Pircifir bravely led his crew to the ground, where he and Grimalkin opened one of the disks to show the crew there were no snakes inside. Then the gifts were loaded.

One member of the crew, the one Ariin remembered from the ball, came forward with a cleaning rag. "I'll just give these a good mopping," he said. "I guess all these alien snakes are a bit sloppy about the mouth, like Nagaine."

As he rubbed, the disks moved with the motion of his rag. Fascinated by their antics, he swiped one way, then another, testing them. He stayed with the disks in an oxygenated cargo hold. He was still experimenting when they returned to the bridge.

Returning to Vhiliinyar with their cargo, the crew had the life-forms unload themselves, all but the original one, which Pircifir kept to experiment with on the ship. "I can't wait until they see these in the city," Pircifir said. "I believe the tunnel shape is probably the one they assume most naturally because the serpents use them as shelters. A handy relationship, but apparently not a symbiotic one, or the serpents would not have relinquished them so readily. The crew has found that with a little training, each creature can be turned into a vast variety of shapes."

"In the future, they will provide the perfect variable facade dwellings for our shapeshifting species," Grimalkin assured him smugly.

"I don't know how you ever remember all that," Pircifir said. "It's all I can do to keep track of the present and the past, never mind the future."

"I'm extremely gifted," Grimalkin admitted.

"Now can we go home to our own time?" Khorii asked Ariin. *"We're not going to learn anything further here. I mean, now."*

"You're forgetting my crono," Ariin said. *"I want it back."*

"It's not yours anyway, it's Grimalkin's."

"He's got another one—or you do. I want mine back. He and Pircifir promised we could return once the mission was accomplished. They agreed that it wasn't safe to leave the crono with Pebar and Sileg."

Khorii sighed. *"I just want to go home and see how our parents are and if Elviiz is any better."*

"If we revert to a time shortly after we left, they won't be any different at all. You may as well stop whining so we can finish what we've started."

"Nevertheless, I want to go home now. Maybe you don't care what's happening to everyone, but I do."

"You can't leave without me."

"Yes, I can. I have Grimalkin's other crono, remember. You'll have to convince Pircifir to use his to do what you want."

"You have to help me convince Pircifir at least. He likes you better than me. Everyone does."

"That is not my fault," she pointed out. *"Use your push."*

"He's become a bit used to it," Ariin complained. *"Please?"*

"Oh, very well." The two of them sought out Pircifir, who was supervising the fueling of his vessel. To Ariin's surprise, he seemed almost as eager as she was to return to the blue-green paisley planet they had recently visited.

Khorii left Ariin to discuss the departure with Pircifir while she sought out Grimalkin.

"So I see no reason why I shouldn't go home now. I'm figuring you don't want to come and be stuck as a small cat again. But I thought you might want to come with me long enough to reclaim your crono so you could come back here. I mean, now."

Grimalkin's back was to her when he said, "But, Khorii, you can't go without me! And I can't stay here when you go. We're a team. You need me. Khorii and Khiindi, Khiindi and Khorii, that's how it's been ever since you were born."

"But it wasn't your choice," she said. "I respect that you were forced, and I'm old enough now to look after myself."

He turned around with a "hmm?" that was half a purr. On his face was the same cagey expression he wore when he had, as Khiindi, just devoured some hapless living creature. "Not quite yet, Khorii. Perhaps Khorii could manage without Khiindi or Khiindi could manage without Khorii for a short time, but Ariin and Pircifir will be needing both of us, and we will need to be there. The patient cat catches the fattest birds."

That was not the sort of argument to win her over, but obviously, now that Khiindi had Grimalkin's sleeves back, he had something up them. And Ariin was right about one thing, at least. They could use the cronos to return to her family before they left, so it didn't actually matter that they had been away so long. Their family would never know. But she knew, and she missed them. Still, she didn't even need to worry about what was happening while she was gone. With the help of the crono, all she had to do was picture things as they had been, and she could be in the midst of them once more and watch events unfold with everyone else.

It was very handy. Nevertheless, she began to understand Pircifir's dislike of loops.

Ruined!" Pebar growled, when he and Sileg returned to the spot where their trunks, a few props, and the iron cage marked all that was left of their livelihood. "It's gone, all gone. No snake, no tunnel, no horned priestesses, nothing. We've been robbed."

The crowd, suddenly and inexplicably deprived of its prey, had quickly dispersed. The market bustled around them now, and it wouldn't be long before some other act tried to usurp their little piece of street.

Sileg opened the trunks. "So we have. Someone got back here before us and made off with the costumes. We could sell the trunks and the cage, I suppose. Start over. Book passage on another scout ship. Nothing here for us. Or is there? Lookit here, the lip of the urn is broken, but nobody saw the cash box."

He picked up the urn and smashed it against the cage. The metal cash box jingled to the ground.

"That's something," Pebar said, opening the box and extracting a fairly good take for the two days the horned girls had been with them.

Sileg scratched his head, then his beard, dislodging several fleas. While the girls remained, his infestations had vanished, but now that they were gone, his unwelcome tenants were back with a vengeance. "We should have been nicer to them, Pebar. We could have had a class act and plenty to share. They weren't bad kids, but they were just kids. They wanted to go home, and you can't blame them for that."

"Simple 'kids' don't have flying tigers that turn into humans as guardians," Pebar told him. "I wonder where they're from anyway." Putting the cash into one of his pockets, he touched a piece of cool metal and pulled out the strange watch he'd taken off one of the girls.

"There's got to be more where those came from. Ones who'd like to join us, maybe, or at least ones who don't know any winged tabbies," Pebar mused.

Sileg touched the watch. "Honestly? I never heard of girls with a horn in the middle of their foreheads and healing powers before. Now, in olden times, there used to be unicorns, but they went extinct a long time ago."

While he spoke, Sileg stroked the face of the watch thoughtfully, remembering the pictures he'd seen of unicorns in the woods around castles and that sort of thing, way back in times before space travel, before Terra had to be reterraformed the first time even. What that must have been like! "They not only had healing powers, they could clean water and neutralize poison, and they say a little of that horn dissolved in water could restore a fellow's manhood."

Before he said the last word, the air around Pebar and him blurred strangely. It also suddenly smelled so different he found it hard to breathe. The familiar piss, spice-sweat, and smoke scent of the market had been replaced with something so thin in its clarity that he had trouble pulling it into his lungs.

The street was gone, and he stood ankle high in a fast-moving stream, though Pebar stood on a rock in its midst. Instead of traffic and people passing all around them, there were funny-looking brown poles covered in fluttering, fragmented green canopies so full of holes they'd never keep the rain out.

Trees. That was what they'd been called back in the olden days when such things were needed. A bunch of trees was a forest. They were soaking their—well, his—feet in a forest stream.

Most remarkable of all were the creatures that had been startled by their instant appearance and were now running away from them. White as the skin and hair of the priestess girls, these creatures had four legs instead of two. But each of them also had a single spiral horn in the middle of the forehead, much longer than the horns of the girls, and very sharp and fierce-looking.

"Unicorns!" he whispered to Pebar.

"What?" his brother asked, his eyes wide as he tried to take in all of the differences confronting him.

"Poachers!" someone else cried, and a horn sounded. "Poachers have come to take the last of the king's unicorns. Cut them down, men!"

never send a Friend or a cat to do a Linyaari's job,"
Khorii grumbled, as she and Ariin waited on the ship
while Grimalkin, in Khiindi form, and Pircifir, his features
and clothing modified to resemble those of the local residents, searched the market for Pebar and Sileg. "Khiindi's
probably been chased up the side of a building by a dog or
another cat, and Pircifir has spent the last hour trying to rescue him."

"You're just jealous," Ariin replied. "And you're careless.
I just bought your homeworld and profitably sold it to the
Consortium. You are now a player without a planet on which
to stand. I win." They'd been passing the time by playing an
ancient game Pircifir had stored on the ship's computer.

Disgusted, Khorii looked out the viewport and saw the
pair returning down the Market Road. They had parcels, but
did they have the crono?

"They're not there," Pircifir said as soon as the two were
back on board again. "The cage is still sitting there, housing
a very suspicious-looking, undernourished dragon, and the
trunks are being used as seating by the dragon's keeper, but
the lad says neither he nor anyone else have seen Pebar and
Sileg since they tried to heal the flying tigers."

"That would be us," Grimalkin added, lest the girls had forgotten.

"Of course. But where have they gone? Did they book passage on another scout ship? Sileg said they did that sometimes to find new acts."

Pircifir shook his head. "I inquired at the shipping office, but no one has seen them there either. We also asked if they had been peddling the crono recently, only we simply asked about jewelry. No one noticed them approaching anyone. In fact, they seem to have just—vanished."

"So now what?" Ariin demanded of Grimalkin. "We just pack up and leave, and I take your word for it you didn't get the crono back and decide to keep it for yourself?"

"It is mine in the first place," Grimalkin pointed out. "But I was in cat form the whole way. I wouldn't have had any place to hide it."

"And I don't suppose you wish to accuse your skipper of lying, do you?" Pircifir asked, with a dangerous undergrowl.

"Er—what's in the parcels then?" Ariin asked.

"Some pretty robes we saw in the market that we thought you might like," Grimalkin said. "We knew you'd be disappointed about the crono, and these have lots of shiny things on them that sparkle in the light. Very attractive."

The robes were pretty and had hoods that might be handy for disguising horns, Khorii thought. But they were chosen with a small cat's eye for fashion—one was bright aqua and one was sapphire blue and both featured mirrored and beaded ball fringes dangling from the hems and sleeves and trimming the hoods.

"They're really—er—shiny, Grimalkin, Pircifir," Khorii said, inwardly groaning. "Thanks."

"We thought they might make you easier to find if you got lost," Grimalkin said.

"So you could find us among crowds of other single-horned people we've seen lately?" Ariin asked sourly.

"For Uncle Hafiz's parties maybe, too," Grimalkin said. "For when you go back."

"I'm not going back without my crono," Ariin said stubbornly. "And don't say it's not mine but yours, because you have one—or rather, Khorii has it. That's yours."

She pointed to Khorii's wrist, where the crono peeked out from between a pair of beaded baubles bobbling over the back of her hand.

Khorii said, "The odd thing is, both of you are right. This is Grimalkin's, but so was the other one. They are, in fact, the same crono from different times. I suppose the separation on different people must be why they didn't merge back into a single item. But I wonder—do you suppose this one might know where its counterpart is?"

Pircifir shrugged.

Grimalkin said, "That was my next suggestion."

Grabbing hold of her sister, Ariin said, "Don't you dare take it anywhere without me along."

Pircifir said, "You needn't worry about that. The ship and all of us will go whenever she programs the crono to go. Just don't visualize any tight places, Khorii."

"I am counting on the crono to do the visualizing for me," she said. Instead of a place, she imagined Pebar with the crono on his wrist and Sileg at his side.

Whereupon the ship swiftly proceeded to stay exactly where it was, but after quite a lot of blurry activity visible in the viewscreen, everything else had changed.

"Trees!" Khorii said happily, looking out at the bark-and-leaf-covered spires and umbrellas surrounding them. "And a little glade with a stream! We can graze. I was getting ever so tired of old grain and nutrient bars."

"I could eat one of the trees!" Ariin said. "But where are we, and where are Pebar and Sileg?"

"And what's that and who are those?" asked Pircifir, pointing up beyond the trees in the direction where the market had been. The huge city market, with its flapping banners and bunting, had been replaced by a large, smoke-blackened, and forbidding-looking stone structure. Four towers topped with large teeth guarded each corner and a central building with a peaked roof, from which flew a purple-and-gold banner.

"I can't make out the insignia on the crest," Grimalkin said, "but I am pretty certain it doesn't say, 'sale on melons through Saturday only.' That's a castle is what that is, and there are no doubt troublesome politicians living there who will neither understand nor tolerate our presence here."

A half dozen men in metallic shipsuits mounted on horses also wearing some sort of protective apparel galloped into the forest. From within the trees in a direct line from the riders there rose a cloud of dust, indicating more riders ahead of the ones who were visible. Pircifir switched on the external auditory sensors, and the sound of clattering and thudding, such as one might hear at a Linyaari race or a particularly lively party, flooded the bridge.

Khorii caught all of that in a flash, but then she also saw something else, downstream from the riders in the opposite direction. The noise flushed four Ancestors from where they grazed among the bushes beside the stream. Their heads rose, horns shining in the sunlight, and they leaped and fled for the trees.

"Poachers!" someone cried, and that was when she saw Pebar and Sileg, who had been hidden by the ship's fin when it appeared over the top of them. They apparently hadn't noticed it, or had mistaken its bulk and shade for something more indigenous, for they ran without a backward look.

"Cloak!" Grimalkin ordered, and Pircifir stabbed a button.

The horsemen passed before the viewport, splashed into the stream, and crossed it, chasing Pebar and Sileg.

Khorii gave her former kitty a wondering look. "You knew we were going to be here, didn't you? You remembered. This is where and when the Ancestors were rescued, and we did it."

"We're going to, yes," Grimalkin agreed.

"That's why you bought these in the market, isn't it?"

"Pircifir did. I was out of pockets at the time," he said modestly.

"As disguises, they're much too flashy," Khorii said, and began picking at them, tearing loose the thread binding the glittering ball fringe to her robe.

"But that's the best part!" Pircifir protested.

She pulled the fringe off a sleeve and handed it to him. "Fine," she said. "Then you wear it."

"We have to attract their attention, Khorii," Grimalkin told her.

"This will only frighten them. It glints like the armor the hunters are wearing. Besides, as legend has it, the Ancestors were telepathic, even on Terra, at least with us they were."

"Us being Pircifir and me," he said. "Your kind wasn't made until later. Couldn't have been."

"But that's where we came from—later," Ariin pointed out.

"And the legend never said we weren't there," Khorii said, ripping the fringe from her other sleeve. To her annoyance, she noted that Ariin wasn't following her example. "Just that you Friends were. Anyway, if we're to retrieve Ariin's crono and save our forebears, we'll have to leave the ship."

"That doesn't sound like a good idea," Grimalkin said. "Did you see those long stick things they were carrying? And the long blades at their sides? They looked rather savage and distinctly hostile to me."

"Then change into a pussycat and hide in the bushes," Ariin snapped.

"We'll need the element of surprise," Pircifir told his brother thoughtfully.

"Take the creature," Grimalkin suggested.

"It's bulky."

"Yes, but it can provide cover. If it can look like a house, it should be able to look like a tree, and we can hide inside it."

A trumpet blared from within the forest, and Khorii said, "They've found something. We need to be very quick."

"You girls carry the creature, and we'll run ahead in wild-cat form," Pircifir told them.

"Just don't forget it's my crono," Ariin said. "And don't forget to wait for us before you take off this time."

The Friends did not dignify her admonition with an answer but changed into large tawny cats with very sharp claws and very long fangs, and leaped out the hatch, their sandy tails switching as they bolted into the underbrush.

Khorii looked at the disk. "Maybe they should have turned into giant, galloping tortoises so they could carry this on their backs. We can hardly move quickly and carry it, too."

"If we're in the right spot, we don't have to be quick," Ariin said. "And maybe it will compress further."

Between the two of them, they squeezed the disk together until it was half its former size, then Khorii tucked it under her arm before they, too, left the ship.

The shouts and cries of men were muffled by the foliage, but Khorii was sure she could hear Pebar and Sileg. "No!" one of them screamed.

Khorii started to run for the voice but Ariin tugged at her arm. *"We stop here. Let's make a tree while nobody is around."*

"But they're being hurt!" Khorii cried.

"I'm weeping within," Ariin said nastily. *"As long as the*

hunters don't take my crono, I don't care what happens to those two. Make the tree."

Khorii was about to tell her to do it herself when she heard more screams and some familiar roars. *"Only because Grimalkin and Pircifir are helping them,"* she said. *"You can't just go abandoning people to their fate like that when they're endangered, Ariin. It's* ka-Linyaari, *is what it is."*

"Is it? I wouldn't know. If you'll recall, unlike those of you privileged enough to afford principles, I wasn't brought up in Linyaari culture."

"Your problem is that you feel so sorry for yourself, you have no sympathy left for anyone else."

"I have begun to realize that far from its being a problem, it can be quite an advantage not to worry about the entire universe before helping myself. It has always been clear to me that if I didn't, no one else would."

"There you go again. Maybe that was true at one time, but now you've got me and our folks and Elviiz and all of our people, and Pircifir and Grimalkin . . ."

"Oh yes, your sweet kitty who did such a great job of looking after me when I was smaller and more helpless than an infant."

Disgusted, Khorii turned her thoughts from her sister and to the project at hand. With hands flying, they urged the disk to grow tall, spread at the top, and grow some more.

"It's the wrong color," Khorii said. *"I don't think a mud-colored tree is going to fool anybody."*

"Pull it down, and we'll make it a hill instead. We can hide inside a hill. Hurry!"

"I don't like the sound of the roars," Khorii said. The roars were now not just angry but frightened. *"Grimalkin and Pircifir are in trouble now. I can feel it."*

"Make the hill," Ariin ordered tersely. *"There. It's big enough to step inside. Hollow it out. Bigger. Bigger."*

Ariin plunged into the body of the now amorphous mound and began spreading her hands and feet, spinning in circles to take up as much room as possible.

Khorii was about to join her when she heard the trumpet again, and hoofbeats coming out of the forest. Ducking behind the new hill, she saw the huntsmen approach, dragging nets behind them. One carried two men bound up together. *"Hah! Serves them right,"* Ariin said, when Khorii conveyed the sight to her. *"See how they like being netted."* Inside the other net, tawny fur wriggled and writhed while its fierce roars reverberated up and down the stream.

Suddenly the talk stopped and the lead horses thudded to a stop. "Halt," one of the hunters said. "Where are we? That hill wasn't there when we came past!"

Ariin had been using Khorii's eyes to watch. She gave the hunters a mental nudge. *"The hill has always been here. It's as old as—as old as the hills."*

"What are you talking about?" another of the riders demanded. "Hit your head back there or what? That hill's always been there, hasn't it, men?"

"Sure that's—uh—that's—I'll think of the name in a moment."

"The Hill is all I can think of," another man said. "Maybe we ought to name it."

"Fine. King's Hill. That's safe enough."

"Bit confusing since there's quite a number of those scattered about the kingdom."

"All the better. If it already has a name, that's probably what it is. King's Hill, I mean."

"Unless it's the queen's."

"True."

While the men were debating, Pircifir and Grimalkin had stopped growling and were applying their razorlike fangs and claws to the net. It was made of some organic rope stuff, and the two cat forms used their advanced brains to destroy the net's fibrous ropes and widen the holes.

Pebar and Sileg were not doing nearly so well. Their net was stained red. Someone was bleeding.

"We could use a diversion," Khorii suggested.

"Good idea," Ariin said. *"You run out in front of their knives and pointy sticks, and while they're killing you, I will dash out, grab a knife from one of them who isn't using it on you, and cut loose the two men who held us prisoner."*

"Can't you create a better one? I'm becoming a bit worried about you, sister. Your special talent failed you several times where Pebar and Sileg were concerned, and now you can't seem to use it to help us again. I think you may be losing your touch."

"I could make the hill change shapes," Ariin replied. *"That might get their attention, but it would spoil the hill's usefulness as cover."*

"Too bad we don't have a way to uncloak the ship and cloak it again really fast. That would get their attention."

Khorii could feel Ariin trying to think of diversions, and she, in turn, tried to imagine how she could use the crono to help release the captives.

She was still pondering when the first soldier clucked to his horse to continue, and the others began filing past.

Suddenly the road ahead vibrated with hoofbeats, and the trumpet sounded again. "Hark! After them!" The lead rider cried, and with much clanking and clattering, the others bolted after him.

"Lose the nets. They'll only slow you down," Ariin pushed the hindmost riders. As if they had received an order from their leader, the two men turned and almost slashed their horses' tails in their haste to release their extra burdens.

As the men rode out of sight, Khorii and Ariin left the hill's shelter to help the former captives extricate themselves from their nets. Pebar and Sileg were both wounded—Pebar's hand was nearly severed at the wrist, and Sileg bore a deep wound in his side. Ariin healed Pebar first, reattaching his hand, then Sileg. Grimalkin and Pircifir had also sustained stab wounds and slices, but they, too, were soon mended. Khorii stroked Grimalkin's fur as she would have done to calm Khiindi.

The big cats wasted no time running after the horses.

"Where are they going?" Pebar asked.

"Back into trouble, I'd say," Sileg answered.

"They're saving the last of the Ancestors," Khorii said. "I know it happens, but I don't know how."

"What are you two doing in this time?" Ariin asked the men.

"No idea, girlie. No idea at all," Sileg said. "One minute we was admiring that watch he took off you, and the next thing you know we're here and there were unicorns. My best guess is this is a dream and actually, we were talking about unicorns and then had bad pasties at the stall, so of course we're dreaming about them, and you, for that matter."

"I'm dreaming the same thing," Pebar said. "So I must have eaten the pasty, and you're not here at all. You're in my dream."

"As handy an explanation as any," Khorii said. "Just keep dreaming among yourselves while Ariin and I sort this out."

chapter 11

We have to save them," Khorii told her sister.

"That's what you always say. We're always saving something. Why don't you think of yourself first for a change?"

"But you know it's true this time. This is how it happened. This is how the Ancestors came to Vhiliinyar. We brought them there."

"I'd like to believe that. I'd like to help them. But this is an accident. You can't possibly know that this is how it was supposed to happen."

"Not that I think 'supposed to' matters where our history and the cronos are concerned, but it makes sense. When Grimalkin and I were searching the time device for you, we saw you and Pircifir leave on the mission to find the tunnels, but you didn't come back. And yet we knew that you did, and Pircifir brought the aliens back to make the changing houses. That was why we decided to come with you. It was always kind of vague, the story I was told growing up about the Friends hearing the Ancestors' 'cries of despair from space as they passed near the planet.'"

Ariin snorted. "Is that what they told you? I doubt the

Friends would recognize cries of despair if they even heard them in the first place."

"Grimalkin would—or at least Khiindi would have. But more than likely he'd think it was prey ready to fall into his paws. And he certainly wouldn't recognize it from space. Probably we wouldn't either. But it makes sense that we're involved, don't you see? We share the psychic bond with the Ancestors and the healing, all of that. They just helped us, and I'm sure that they're counting on us to help them."

"Let's call them, then, and they can hide here until the king's men are gone," Ariin agreed, then broadcast, *"Unicorns, Others, come here. We will hide you and take you to safety."* She listened for a response. *"Nothing. They must be out of range now."*

"There's a song," Khorii said. *"I think it was made up by Linyaari long after the Friends brought the Ancestors to Vhiliinyar, but it is called 'Gathering the Grandparents.'"*

She sang:

"Grandmother, Grandfather, come hither, come here
Find love and protection from death, pain, and fear
Come hither, come hither, come swiftly, come fast
We come from the place where your lineage lasts
Grandfather, Grandmother, come here to this song
On our world your lives will be happy and long
Where there are no hunters to trouble your days
But vast hills and valleys of green fields to graze
We are your grandchildren, from time yet to come
We heard your screams as you ran from the hunt.
Though you are our past, we have come your aid
We are your future, so be not afraid."

"It's just a stupid little song, Khorii. They can't hear you from here," Ariin said.

"Maybe they could if you joined in, and we broadcast."

"They didn't hear me before. They're too far away."

"You weren't singing. Songs penetrate the consciousness more easily than mere words. It's a scientific fact."

Ariin snorted.

"Try at least. For them."

Reluctantly, Ariin began singing, and, to both girls' surprise, her voice was in natural harmony with Khorii's.

They sang it through three times. Pebar and Sileg looked puzzled, since the words were in Linyaari, of course. Pebar complained, "You're going to draw the soldiers back with all that neighing and snorting."

"Hush," Khorii said. "Did you hear that?"

In the distance, another mind was saying to his diminished herd, *"Hush, did you hear that?"*

The girls sang the song another three times and felt the herd swerve in flight and double back toward them.

"We'll need to show ourselves," Khorii said. "Pebar and Sileg, stay here and be quiet, or we'll leave you behind for the king's men."

"They'd probably be a lot friendlier if we turned you and your friends over to them," Pebar speculated. "We need a better bargain than that."

"We'll give this hill creature back to you when we're done with it so you can start your act again," Khorii promised desperately.

"That leaves us half as well-off as we were before we met you, and you ruined our lives," Pebar said. "How about the tunnel and one of the unicorns?"

"We'll do better than that," Ariin promised so quickly and definitely that Khorii knew she was up to something. "Much better. But you have to be quiet and stay out of sight. If you spook the unicorns, they'll run away and be slaughtered, and I will do my best to see that you are, too."

"Shut up, Pebar," Sileg said. "That's good enough for me."

He folded a piece of the inside of the hill around them, making a separate room, and Khorii read him, briefly but enough to know that he would keep his word and see that Pebar did as well.

Grimalkin and Pircifir followed the king's men as they trailed the unicorns into the forest, but the creatures swiftly eluded their human pursuers. The two Friends hid in the brush while the armed men's horses snorted and stamped impatiently as their riders tried to decide which direction to take. Finally, they headed back to the road.

"We should change now, too," Grimalkin told his brother. "Our new friends won't like wild cats any more than they like human hunters."

"Change into Others?"

"I've done it before," Grimalkin assured him.

They completed the change and began tracking the herd, but there was no need. Before they had passed back across the loop of the stream the unicorns had jumped in their flight, the herd turned back and charged straight at them. Grimalkin and Pircifir wheeled in their tracks and sprinted off, leading the herd.

"Follow us!" Grimalkin called to them.

"Begone!" the stallion trumpeted. "You trespass in our forest!"

"We came to save you," Grimalkin announced, because he now knew that was the truth, however accidental the circumstances.

The stallion ignored him and reared on his back legs, slicing the air with his front hooves in a challenge.

"Stop that, Hraffl," one of the mares told him. When he ignored her, she butted his flank with her head, unbalancing him. "It's not like there are enough of us left that we can afford to kill anyone over border disputes."

"They smell funny," the youngest mare said.

But the third mare galloped past them, then skidded to a stop, listening, "Hark! You males have raised such a commotion the king's men heard. They are returning. Flee!"

They wheeled again to leap back into the forest but the hindmost mare stopped suddenly, her right forefoot quivering in midair, her ears twisting to hear. "Listen. Do you hear that?"

The others halted. Grimalkin listened. Khorii and Ariin were singing.

"What are they up to?" Pircifir demanded. "This is no time for music!"

But the stallion and his mares turned yet again and trotted out of the glade and down the road, toward the ship and the hill.

"They've come!" a mare said, with a quiet sigh. "As it was foretold. We are saved."

"That's right," Grimalkin said, following, "That's what we were trying to explain to you before your leader attacked us. We are your Friends. We're here to help."

They didn't seem to hear him, but continued following the girls' summoning song.

"Don't give them all the credit!" Grimalkin protested. "It's our ship and cronos, after all."

"Mine, you mean," Pircifir corrected him. "But that matters little. They'll never make it. Look!"

The dust cloud, clattering hooves, and clanking armor were almost upon them once more. The trumpet blared as the hunters spurred their mounts forward.

The unicorns hesitated.

"Cover their flank!" Pircifir commanded.

"They're armed, and we're not!" Grimalkin protested, but the men attacked them again.

Pircifir reared, and would have charged, but the king's

men were well prepared this time. Before he could strike, three arrows pierced his white chest, he snorted bloody foam, fell on his side, and lay unmoving. Before Grimalkin could think how to get his brother back to the girls, one of the King's men leaped from his horse, raised his sword, and severed Pircifir's head from his body.

Grimalkin saw only the first stroke because he ran away in a hail of arrows, following the unicorns blindly, not thinking of strategy or trickiness or anything else but dodging the deadly darts.

The girls had stopped singing. The ship was cloaked, and there was only the hill. How to enter it? Did it matter? Would they see him? Khorii stepped into his path. Grimalkin swerved to avoid her and stared into the cavelike entrance of the hill. His sides heaved, and his mouth frothed. Two arrows had found their way into his hide—one in his left hindquarter and one in his right side. But all around him the unicorns crowded. He changed to man form, grimacing at the hurt the arrows caused, and Ariin threw him a shipsuit. Before he donned it he pulled the arrows from his flesh. On either side, a unicorn horn touched him lightly, and the pain from the arrows was no more.

"Where's Pircifir?" Khorii asked. "We need to go now."

"He's gone," Grimalkin said, and was amazed to find his face was wet with more than sweat. "They killed him. Beheaded him. Even we cannot survive that."

The horsemen thudded up to Khorii and halted, looking puzzled. She tried to look as innocent as possible, keeping her head still so that the hood of her garment covered her horn.

The leader bore a great bloody sack slung across his saddle. "What have we here?" he asked his men, regarding Khorii. "Little maid, we hunt a herd of unicorns. Have they passed this way?"

Trying not to look at the sack, she pointed down the road and said in the most archaic language she could remember from Uncle Joh's vids, "They went thataway."

The men clattered away, for the moment taking no more interest in her. She ran back down the road to where Pircifir had fallen. If the men thought to be rewarded for bringing back a unicorn's head, they might be disappointed. Upon death, presumably after the men took his head, Pircifir had returned to his humanoid shape. There was nothing she could do for him, she knew, but she tenderly removed his crono from his lifeless wrist. She galloped back toward the hill.

The ship reappeared, which meant that someone had deactivated the cloaking device Pircifir had carried in his uniform. The unicorn herd, trembling and wild-eyed, walked out of the hill, followed by Grimalkin in a shipsuit, then Pebar, Sileg, and Ariin.

As the others entered the ship's open hatch, Khorii compressed the hill as much as she could, handed it up, and climbed in after them. As she did, the king's men returned, looking up in awe at the ship. A unicorn glared down from the hatch at the men, daring them to hurt Khorii, but they made no move to do so.

"Look! The maiden was a fairy, and she is carrying the beasts into her magic castle."

With a touch of the crono, the men, the forest, and the castle vanished. Khorii imagined that they had probably decided her magic castle was a vehicle after all, but she didn't care.

They returned to Sileg's and Pebar's time and silently, the two men departed. Before they left, Khorii returned the original alien dwelling to them so they would be able to make a living. The crono was firmly back on Ariin's wrist, the crono of Grimalkin's Khorii had kept back on his own. Khorii carried Pircifir's crono, and was not sure what to do with it.

Grimalkin was surely the late captain's next of kin, but he had no need of the instrument now.

The journey through space was longer and harder than it had been on the way there. Grimalkin said very little and seemed preoccupied. Khorii thought he might be grieving.

"You can return to an earlier time and bring him forward, can't you?" she asked. "You did that with my grandparents and my uncle, I'm told."

To her surprise, Grimalkin shook his head. "They were not of our race, and their demise or survival made no difference on many time paths."

"So Pircifir's dying was more important than when our relatives died?" Ariin challenged him.

"I'm not sure. But he never returned from this journey. Originally, you didn't either," he told Ariin. "But I think, if Pircifir came back, the Others, your ancestors, would not have been saved. I must consult all sorts of archives and ancient time lines to sort it out, but I think that's the way it goes."

The sneer faded from Ariin's face even as she said, "Oh, come on. That can't be right. You're immortal, aren't you?"

"Apparently not," he said, and spoke no more of the matter for the rest of the trip.

Back on Vhiliinyar, a flurry of training and building occupied Kubiilikaan and its inhabitants. The unicorns were the second great wonder to emerge from the ship in a very short time. Khorii and Ariin stayed on board the ship this time. "I think seeing the unicorns just now will confuse them enough," Khorii said. "They can worry about our kind later on."

To her surprise, this time Ariin agreed with her.

Grimalkin off-loaded the unicorns by himself and arranged for their care and feeding. Then he returned to the ship. "It is time to continue our true mission," he said.

now I want to go home, to our own time. I want to see how Elviiz is and tell our parents what we've discovered," Khorii said. "And Ariin, I think you've gathered enough credit, helping to discover the source of the Friends' shapeshifting houses and rescuing the Ancestors of our race."

Grimalkin inclined his leonine head, shrank back into his Khiindi body, and hid under Khorii's chair.

All Ariin said was, "We'd better take this ship. We might need it."

Before she could change her mind, Khorii concentrated on the quarantine compound where and when they'd left their parents, Elviiz, Maak, and Uncle Joh.

The countryside blurred past the viewport, moving through centuries of time. The unicorns they rescued had meanwhile bred, been born, bred among themselves, and eventually died, and at some point the Linyaari race had somehow been created.

The blurring cleared. Outside it was morning again, and Khorii saw a meadow, with Ancestors ranging around it. In the center was the *Condor*, Uncle Joh's patched-together ship. Beside it was the pavilion where her parents lived now.

Some distance away sat two other pavilions, their flaps fluttering in the breeze.

She reached down and picked up Khiindi, who mewed mournfully. It was easier than she had expected it would be to forget that her lifelong companion could at times transform himself into a man, a flying tiger, or a unicorn. She petted the stripes between his ears and patted his side consolingly. He hadn't said much about missing his brother when he was in man form, but now that he was a small cat again, his grief showed in his eyes and his plaintive cry. The crono hung around his furry neck.

"You two took your time!" Elviiz said, sitting up when they stepped into his pavilion. Maak had assembled tools and surgical instruments, chips and diodes, and was methodically laying these on a pallet lying beside Elviiz's.

"We found a spaceship!" Ariin told him cheerfully.

"Where?" Elviiz asked.

"On the shore when we went to see the LoiLoiKuans."

"How is it that no one found it before?" Maak asked.

"I don't know," Ariin said. Khorii stayed out of it. This was Ariin's story. Let her talk her way out of it. "It's very old. I think it might have been buried, and the terraforming dredged it up somehow."

"Highly improbable," Maak said.

Ariin shrugged, and said, "Maybe . . ."

Khorii sighed. *"Just tell him we'll explain later, when the operation is complete, and we can explain to the others as well. We'll have to tell them. We need to figure out the significance of what we found out about the dwellings and how the information might help us with the plague creatures. Unless you've figured it out already?"*

"I'm working on it," Ariin said.

"It is good you have returned," Maak said. "It is time to neutralize my son's nerve centers so he will not feel pain. I will need you to heal the incisions I make once I have inserted the necessary modifications."

"Father," Elviiz said, "will I still be able to thought-talk once my nonorganic functions are restored?"

"That is one of the few things I do not know, son," Maak replied.

Just then they heard the sound of a flitter. A moment later, seven tall Linyaari, five in white tunics, two in multicolored clothing, entered the pavilion.

Maak looked up at them from where he knelt beside his instruments. "I am required to warn you that you are in an area bordering a quarantined enclave. I have been declared disease-free but—"

The entrance of the seven had masked the sound of a second flitter. Now they were joined by Neeva, Melireenya, and Khaari.

"It's all right, Maak," Neeva said. "These five are esteemed physicians who are deans of the new medical college on narhii-Vhiliinyar. They are Riiri, Kaafri, Naarli, Raarilya, and Hruf. These two are techno-artisan Guild Masters Faari and Hriinye, the most skilled electronics and bionics engineers among our people. They offer you their skill to assist with the repair of Elviiz. Since Melireenya, Khaari, and I performed the initial healing of the organic modifications necessary to preserve Elviiz's life, we felt our insights into his condition would be helpful as well."

Neeva introduced Khorii and Ariin to the new team.

A flicker of curiosity showed in Riiri's eyes as she addressed them. She had no doubt heard of Ariin's return from the past and Khorii's work on the plague. In fact, she might have been among the rescue teams Khorii had assisted in the past, but she did not remark on the fact. Instead she said, "Invasive forms of healing are best performed by others whenever possible."

Neeva placed a hand on each girl's shoulder. "She is correct. This healing will involve far more than the application of horns. We are here to assist Maak because our intervention in Elviiz's case has made has his reconstruction far more complicated than even his father realizes."

Ariin looked puzzled, but turned to go with a shrug. Khorii started to protest.

Elviiz reached up and touched her arm. "It is true, little sister. Some disassembly of my organic parts may be required to make room for the inorganic enhancements with which Father originally endowed me. If you were an android like me, you would no doubt find the procedure instructive. However, since you are an organic being with certain emotional sensibilities of which I have recently become aware, you would probably find it more upsetting than helpful. Therefore, since there appears to be adequate technical and medical support to Father's endeavors, I would appreciate it if you would wait outside until I have been adequately modified. I trust the results will be worth the wait."

Looking into the dim gray of his weak, organic eyes, Khorii perceived an unexpected emotion. She realized her brother was embarrassed for her to see him with his skin off.

She knelt and touched her horn to his forehead. "I'll wait outside, Elviiz, if that is your wish."

"It is," he said. "Your presence may also have a beneficial effect on the emotional state of our mutual parents."

She nodded and stepped out of the pavilion. Ariin was already grazing outside the quarantine circle, deep in conversation with their parents between mouthfuls of succulent grass. Mother and Father nibbled thoughtfully while Uncle Joh paced the meadow around them like the tiger RK thought himself to be.

The situation would have seemed calm and in hand except

for the mournful meowing of Khiindi, who prowled beneath Pircifir's ship as if looking for his lost brother.

"Can't you shut him up?" Uncle Joh demanded. "What the coz is wrong with the critter anyway?"

"He's sad, Uncle Joh," Khorii told him, having to shout a bit to be heard across the quarantine circle and over Khiindi's cries. "He's suffered a loss."

The *Condor*'s captain stopped pacing and, with more patience than most people would have thought he possessed, said, "Then pick him up and pet him or heal him or something, can't you? I don't see how anyone can concentrate on major surgery with that yowling going on. Tell the cat we're sorry for his loss, but we don't want to lose Elviiz, too."

Khiindi's cries stopped in midhowl. Perhaps he remembered that it was Elviiz who had stopped Marl Fidd when the young thug had swung Khiindi by his tail and thrown him into a pool. Elviiz had always treated Khiindi as if he were a feline younger brother, in the same way that Khorii was a Linyaari younger sister.

Her sometimes-cat ran to Khorii, who scooped him up and petted him, consoling herself with the softness of his coat.

Everyone waited all day long. They knew the surgery must be intensely difficult, because for many hours there was no direct thought contact from any of the people working on Elviiz.

"On the other hand," Mother told the girls when Khorii wondered again what could possibly be taking so long, "nothing very bad has happened, or we would know it already."

At one point Uncle Joh looked up at his ship and excused himself. When he came back, he said, "Just Hafiz and Karina checking in to see how the boy's doing. I'm surprised Hafiz didn't have a device installed in the tent so we could have an Elviiz-cam broadcasting from here to narhii-Vhiliinyar to MOO."

Mother rolled her eyes in amusement. "Don't say that too loudly, or Uncle Hafiz will hear you on his *Condor*-cam and make it happen."

Finally, at sunset, Maak came to the pavilion flap. Khorii rushed over, followed by Ariin. "How is he?" she asked.

"As well as can be expected, I am told," he said. "You can see for yourself. He wishes to see you."

She entered the tent cautiously. Maak's voice had never become as expressive as Elviiz's but even so, there was some disappointment in it, a lack of conviction about the success of the restoration.

Elviiz was listening to what sounded like instructions from the two techno-artisans. Neeva, Melireenya, and Khaari passed Khorii as they left the pavilion. Neeva's expression was apologetic, and she touched Khorii's arm consolingly.

Khorii couldn't see why. Elviiz looked perfectly healthy. He was even sitting cross-legged on his pallet as he touched various parts of himself in response to the techno-artisan's instructions.

The techno-artisan handed him something. Elviiz lifted a pair of goggles, then seated them over his nose and ears. "Our people are working even now on a fully functional adjustable lens that will be able to superimpose all of the functions of your bionic eyes on your organic ones. But until then, these should work. There is also a full sound-modulation function built in and enhanced olfactory sensors, all controllable from your implant."

"Thank you," Elviiz said politely, and put the goggles in place.

"Elviiz," Khorii said, as the techno-artisan rose to go. "How do you feel?"

"Enhanced!" he said. "Not as good as before in many ways, but they were able to augment my skeletomuscular system and nerve synapses, restoring most of my strength. Chip implants have restored my memory banks, although frankly accessing them is a bit more of a problem than it used to be because my brain is almost entirely organic. But that is a good thing, I think. Say something to me."

"Uh—hi, Elviiz?"

"No, I mean silently, in thought-talk."

"Elviiz, you have no idea how concerned we have been about you. Ariin and I have much to tell you."

"What?" he asked, but a huge smile lit his organic lips, which opened over his molecularly bonded ceramic-and-steel teeth.

It was Ariin's idea," Khorii said later, as the family stood as near to each other as they dared, having a celebratory graze. Even Elviiz tore up grass and chewed it, but his enhancements were too strong. He tended to rip away the roots as well as the grass and end up with big clots of dirt dangling from each mouthful.

Ariin explained in great detail how her observant nature and discerning eye, not to mention her instinct for behavior patterns and her sense of danger, had led her to notice the similarities between the mutable dwellings of the Friends and the newest form of alien menace.

"That's my girl," Aari said proudly, although until recently he hadn't known that she was, of course.

"Very clever of you, dear," Mother said. *So did you find out why that was?"*

Ariin had to admit that they hadn't really, but mentioned casually that while they were detecting, they had helped rescue the unicorns who would eventually become their Ancestors. She didn't say a word about Pircifir. After giving Elviiz a welcoming ankle-twine, Khiindi made himself scarce. He did not want to be around, apparently, when the girls told their parents that their daughter's pet cat was their old trickster nemesis, Grimalkin. However, Ariin didn't mention Grimalkin either. If their parents noted any holes in her story left by the absence of the shapeshifting brothers, they said nothing.

When Uncle Joh returned from the *Condor*'s galley to join them, he was carrying a plate of long white noodles and round fragrant balls in some sort of red sauce. He sat on the ground beside him. "So what did I miss?" he asked. "And say it out loud, people. It's not like I have ears in the back of my head—or—well, you know what I mean."

Ariin started telling her story again, but Uncle Joh had trouble with her Linyaari accent when she spoke Standard. Khorii started to interpret for her but caught a warning thought from Ariin. She was afraid Khorii's version would include the parts she had purposely omitted. So their father gave their friend a quick sketch of Ariin's story.

"So the damned thing ate my treasure, did it?" was Uncle Joh's first response. "That's a shame. Good thing you girls found its homeworld. I know you Linyaari don't believe in killing stuff, but could we just track it down and hurt it a little? That was a really good treasure."

"We don't know for sure it was the same thing, Uncle Joh," Khorii said quickly. "The dwelling creature is not hostile or harmful in any way, and the serpents were cooperative and intelligent beings. Certainly they did not seem to have a connection with the plague—just the resemblance Ariin noted."

"They do have something to do with it," Ariin insisted. "You know they do, too, Khorii."

"Well, you girls did say you traveled back in time to find

it—it would have been a long time ago on their planet, too. It kinda makes you wonder what they've been up to lately, doesn't it?"

"We're going back there," Ariin told him. "We have our own ship now, but we wanted to return and tell you first."

"And to invite Elviiz to come with us if he feels well enough," Khorii said quickly. She had caught a fleeting thought from Elviiz that now that she had a sister, she seemed to think she didn't need him any longer.

"If I won't be too much trouble," he said, with an unandroid-like tone of resentment.

"On the contrary," Khorii said. "I've really missed you. Khiindi, too."

"You have?" He sounded more surprised than she would have believed. He had always seemed so arrogant to her before, but she wondered if it wasn't just that he enjoyed and was proud of being needed. Of course, now that he was more organic, he probably experienced emotions like pride and pleasure more than he had in the past, but still, her own jealousy of his abilities had always shaded her feelings about him.

"Yes," Ariin said, with uncharacteristic warmth. "It is so good to have you to turn to for information and guidance when things go wrong and to be able to count on your strength."

That was enough to stop him in midgraze. He stood there thoughtfully chewing a clump of dandelions into his mouth while dirt showered off their roots. *"Thank you both,"* he told them mentally, since his mouth was full. *"It is of course my primary function to inform, guide and protect my sister— sisters. And Khiindi, of course."*

"Of course," Khorii agreed.

"And good luck with that!" Ariin said, referring to Khiindi.

chapter 13

J ust so he knew they really wanted him, they asked Elviiz to fly the *Pircifir* to MOO. "It will be excellent practice with my new modifications," Elviiz agreed enthusiastically. "On the whole, it seems that my injuries have provided me with the opportunity for a significant upgrade, even though it functions somewhat differently from my former artificial systems."

The *Balakiire* caravanned with them. As *visedhaanyi ferilii,* or ambassador to alien races, Neeva said she felt it was within the scope of her duties to accompany them to the alien world and enter into diplomatic relations with the inhabitants, serpentine or tunneling. Khorii also secretly believed that Neeva was coming along to keep an eye on them at her mother's insistence, but said nothing.

The *Mana* had remained on MOO, where their friends, Captain Asha Bates, Jaya, Sesseli, and Hap Hellstrom, who had returned to the *Mana* after helping a borrowed Federation tanker deliver the LoiLoiKuans to Vhiliinyar, met them along with Uncle Hafiz and Karina. Hafiz was very enthusiastic when he heard about the mutable dwellings. "Think of what such places would be worth!" he said, rubbing his hands together.

"But Uncle Hafiz," Khorii told him, "the reason we went to find out about them is that we fear they are what's eating everything else in the universe now."

Hafiz nodded sagely, "This indicates to me that far from being an alien menace, they are an intelligent and perceptive species well aware of the need to eliminate competition in the marketplace."

Melireenya could not suppress a long, expressive snort of derision. Hafiz had been very generous to the Linyaari, but sometimes his viewpoint was far more alien to them than that of the mutable dwellings.

Captain Bates also guffawed. "Mr. Harakamian, it's hard to figure you and the Linyaari allied together—sort of like the Warlord Attila at a Quaker meeting."

Hafiz huffed through his long, curled, and meticulously waxed mustache. He wasn't sure whether to be flattered or insulted. "Attila was a delightful person, once one got to know him. I sold him many, many caches of armaments in the past. I am unfamiliar with the people that he was meeting in your analogy, Captain, but I assure you my relationship with the Linyaari people is one of perfect harmony and understanding and eventually, I hope, mutual benefit."

Captain Bates sobered. "I didn't mean to offend you, sir. Khorii has told me so much about how wonderful you have been to her people, and of course your assistance in providing support for them as they battle the plague is praised throughout the universe." The captain was redeeming herself now. "I have a strange sense of humor sometimes. Must be my upbringing."

"Think nothing of it, dear lady," Hafiz said graciously. "Now then, before the next phase of your mission, we must enjoy one last feast together, yes?"

Khorii was pleased to fortify herself before they set out again. Flitting about in different times and spaces, she sometimes forgot when she had last grazed, and Uncle Hafiz always provided such delicious and beautiful floral center-pieces for his Linyaari guests.

When Khorii asked if anyone had heard from Jalonzo about how things were going in Corazon, the city that had been her family's headquarters in the Solojo system, where the plague seemed to have begun, her friends looked at her oddly. "He's not home yet, Khorii. The tanker only left two days ago," Jaya said. Of course. Unlike Hap, Jalonzo was returning home after tanker duty.

Khorii felt disoriented, experiencing temporal vertigo. She, Ariin, and Khiindi had traveled light-years back and forth and many years, centuries even, in time and yet in her own time line only two days had passed since she left her friends on MOO.

How did the Friends manage to keep this all straight? Especially the ones like Grimalkin and Pircifir, who traveled through time and space so frequently? Maybe that was part of why Grimalkin had been so careless of the feelings of others. He passed through people's lives, arriving before their births and after their deaths, so they were rather like moving shadows for him. Khiindi jumped onto her lap and yowled at her. Except for Pircifir. Losing his brother can't have been unexpected, since Grimalkin had already outlived his sibling when he first stole Ariin. But the loss was fresh now, and Khiindi was not letting her forget it.

When the meal was done, Ariin said, "We should be off now. It's been nice to see all of you again, but I think that my family is all the help I'll need to solve this puzzle. Naturally, you'll be the first to know when we've figured out how it happened and deliver the solution."

"We're going, too!" Jaya said.

"Why? Your ship is large and clunky. and you can't travel through ti—" she stopped. She had been about to say that they couldn't travel through time, but she didn't want to share the secret of the cronos, Khorii realized. Khorii thought that a bit over-cautious. She trusted these people.

Neeva didn't care what she was going to say. "I think it would be wise to travel as a fleet to this planet. If the mutating creatures are indeed connected with the plague by-products, then it makes sense to have a ship in orbit in case the creatures devour the ship on the ground."

Even Ariin couldn't argue with that. Once both the *Mana* and the *Balakiire* had downloaded the serpent world's coordinates from Pircifir's ship, and all three were reprovisioned for the journey, they set off.

Khorii had missed her friends and spent a lot of time on the com unit filling them in on how they had located the creatures. Captain Bates was especially interested in their time travels and their encounter with Sileg and Pebar. "Coco and I belong to the Selegiznas," she said. "There's also a Pebarzigna tribe, and they're supposed to be related."

Ariin, who had been eavesdropping while Elviiz piloted the ship, looked over Khorii's shoulder into the com screen, and snorted, "It wouldn't matter to Pebar and Sileg if you were their own daughter. They'd still sell you if they were offered enough."

Captain Bates grinned. "And that observation, my dear, gives you stunning insight into my almost native culture."

"But you're not like that, Captain," Sesseli said, leaning affectionately against her. The little girl patted their former teacher's hand. Sesseli was almost seven now, Moonmay's age, but she seemed younger than the freckled and red-headed Moonmay. Sesseli's wide blue eyes and blond curls (presently braided and beaded by Captain Bates into the distinctive coif she had created for the *Mana*'s crew in the approved manner of the shipgoing tribes) and her rounded, soft features made her look even younger. "You're nice," she assured Asha Bates.

The captain hugged the child. "You're pretty nice yourself, kiddo. And the thing is, even if the tribes live by their wits, to put it politely, there are as many good people among them as in any other group. They just hide it well with outsiders."

"Sileg wasn't bad," Khorii said. "I think he'd have been willing to let us go if it hadn't been for Pebar."

"They both got Pircifir killed," Ariin said, as if Pircifir had been her relative rather than Grimalkin's.

Khorii started to correct her and say that it was saving the unicorns that got Pircifir killed, but Ariin knew that already.

Khiindi mewed piteously, and Sesseli looked as if she'd like to pick him up and kiss him between the ears as she so often had when they'd traveled together.

Khorii patted Khiindi consolingly but refrained from any of the more extravagant gestures the little girl would have offered. Although it was hard to believe her little cat was also Grimalkin, even when she'd seen him turn, it was also hard to forget how much trouble he'd caused for her family. But Khiindi didn't seem to think what he did in another form counted. He rubbed his head against Khorii's jaw and pawed at her while mewing in a heartbroken fashion. Relenting, Khorii hugged him and petted his head. As Khiindi, he seemed to have the emotional needs of a small cat as well as its form, and she and he had been babies together. The first time he suffered a loss, no matter the circumstances or who he actually was in another guise, was not the time to rebuff him.

The journey seemed longer with the three ships caravanning, and Ariin was disgusted to realize that the other two, much newer vessels, were faster than the *Pircifir*. Even the clunky old *Mana* had to reduce its power to keep from outstripping the ship.

"Elviiz, can't we go any faster?" she asked.

"We are utilizing the same flight plan you used in the past," Elviiz said. "If my father and I had had the opportunity to upgrade this vessel, possibly we could achieve greater acceleration, but I cannot do it in midflight. I could not ever have done it in midflight," he added. "It is not that I am still impaired from my traumatic experience. It is not that I am reluctant to go near them again. Fear is not part of my programming. I—"

"I get the point," Ariin said.

At length, they reached the serpent planet's outer atmosphere.

"We will land, and the rest of you can orbit and wait for us," Ariin told the personnel on the other two ships. Before anyone could protest, she said, "After all, the serpent race knows us."

"That was many generations ago," Neeva pointed out. "There is no guarantee that their descendants will recognize you. In fact, the race may well have died out. Certainly I have never encountered their descendants in my travels."

"The thing is," Ariin said, "we may need to time travel, and this is the only ship capable of it as far as we know."

"It's the cronos that permit the time travel, as you very well know," Khorii protested indignantly. "We could give one of them to Neeva or Captain Bates, and they could time travel as easily as we can."

"We couldn't do it without landing. Besides, I'm not giving mine up, so you'd have to do it."

Khorii considered that. The problem with surrendering all of the time-travel capability was that she felt some residual loyalty to Grimalkin. Admittedly, he was not himself all that loyal, but he made a good kitty, and she thought he would eventually redeem himself. If only he could return to his original form, he could convince the people who forced him always to be a small cat to unfreeze his form. She didn't want him to be her cat just because he had to be.

So she said nothing further as they descended to the planet's surface. She realized it should have changed somewhat since their last visit, but the landscape had altered in the particularly barren and horrific way that all of her people recognized as the result of a Khleevi invasion.

At first she thought the serpents had survived, because she saw long squiggles on the landscape as they descended, but the closer the ship came to landing, the more she saw that the squiggles were monstrous long mounds covering the planet's surface. No trees, water, or other living things remained. She grieved for the beautiful serpents that had been here. It seemed to her such a short time ago.

Ariin said, "Well, it looks like we found the alien monsters in their new incarnation anyway."

"No," Khorii said. "That's Khleevi scat." Ariin wouldn't know about it, of course. She had been raised in the time before the first Khleevi invasion and had been into space only one round-trip in contemporary times. Khorii had seen the devastated worlds during her travel to Kezdet. Stories of what Vhiliinyar had looked like before the terraforming were rapidly becoming legend in her culture, with her parents (and Ariin's, she reminded herself, and Elviiz's) playing a major role.

"Khleevi?" Ariin asked. "But they're all dead, aren't they?"

"Yes, but so are most of the worlds they invaded. Ariin, I don't think we should land."

"Why not? We landed before?"

"Because your theory seems to be correct. I believe the mutable dwellings and the plague and this planet are closely related. If we land here, we may expose ourselves and the ship to the original plague at its strongest. All of our horns combined wouldn't be powerful enough to cleanse us. If we didn't die, we'd probably end up in quarantine, and before you say that would be good, it might be a totally different quarantine than the one our parents and Uncle Joh are in."

"We have to land. If we don't, it's a wasted trip. You're just saying this to prevent me from finding the cause and the cure for the disease. I can see how the mutable dwellings are connected with the last phase of the plague's development, but not the earlier part."

"I can't see that either, but I'll bet it has something to do with the Khleevi. I promise you that you do not want to time travel on this planet without knowing exactly when to go to avoid the Khleevi. If they had anything to do with the plague, and it did involve the beings on this planet, we won't find out any more here without going back to that time."

Ariin said, "We can put the cat out with the extra crono, and he can time travel back to meet your bug-eyed monsters."

Khiindi hid behind Khorii and hissed at Ariin.

Elviiz said, "We are joining our companion vessels in orbit."

Khorii felt ashamed. She had been so busy arguing with Ariin she'd forgotten that Elviiz was actually in charge and would, of course, take the most prudent course.

"Thanks, Elviiz," she said. "Guess we'd better let everyone know we came a long way to learn very little."

"That is not precisely true," her brother said. "As we skimmed the surface, I was able to take readings that may be useful."

"How did you do that?" Ariin demanded.

But Elviiz simply smiled enigmatically and, Khorii thought, in the same smug way he used to smile in his former incarnation.

Once the three ships were well away from the Khleevi-ravaged world, Elviiz said into the com unit, "I suppose you would all like to know what I have inferred from the evidence I gleaned on the world we just visited."

"Pray enlighten us," Khaari said.

"Don't tease, Elviiz," Jaya chided him. "What was that all about?"

"From geological and thermal time signatures, I can definitively say that this world was the last visited by a particular swarm of Khleevi, who did so at the same time their fellow monsters were being exterminated by their own young after attacking narhii-Vhiliinyar."

"There was more than one swarm?" Ariin said. "I never heard anyone talk about more than one swarm. I thought our parents had eradicated them."

A chill shot through Khorii like a laser bolt. "Then that means there are still Khleevi alive, conquering innocent planets like this one and eating them up?"

"That cannot be," Neeva said. "We would have known."

"We didn't know they existed to begin with until they invaded our sector," Khaari reminded her. "The universe is immense, after all. These may have gone somewhere else."

Elviiz held up a hand so that all could see he had more to say on the matter. "I do not believe they survived as Khleevi."

"You think the serpents killed them?" Khorii asked.

"The serpents or some other life-form on the planet at that time," Elviiz replied. "My sensors detect extremely large deposits of a mineral now known to our scientists as khleevium because it was not known before the Khleevi came. It is found in their carapaces. Interestingly enough, as much scat as there appears to be on the planet's surface, it is not enough to indicate a Khleevi occupation of great length and intensity. Allow me to show you something." He tapped a small circular socket on the instrument array, and a picture of the planet's surface as they had just seen it appeared on the screen. The image rotated, showing that, despite Elviiz's implication that the occupation had been comparatively short, nothing much was left on the surface except for the mounds of Khleevi scat. Elviiz highlighted one of these and zoomed in.

"Do you see how this has been interrupted? A chunk has actually been removed. Here, here, and here"—he highlighted and zoomed in on a scattering of other scat—"we see the same thing. Something came along after the Khleevi were no longer there to prevent it and devoured their scat."

"Ewwwww, gross," Jaya said. "Elviiz, I didn't really need to know that."

"Yes, Jaya, I believe you did. I believe it is very important to the creation of this plague, if my sister Ariin's assumptions are correct, and the beings of this world are connected to what seem to be by-products of the plague."

"Do you think the Khleevi and these serpent creatures completely destroyed each other then, Elviiz?" Captain Bates asked.

"Yes, I do. Of course, it is also likely that although the serpents ultimately destroyed the Khleevi, the Khleevi had damaged the planet so profoundly that there was no longer sustenance available for the serpents, completing their own eradication. But this is mere conjecture on my part. I do not have sufficient data to confirm my hypothesis."

"Do we need to go back there, then?" Khorii asked. "Could you tell more if we did?"

"Not in the present time, no," he said.

"It's too bad there's not a time device on this planet like the one on Vhiliinyar," Ariin said. "Then we could track everything that happened on the chart without having to go there."

Khorii shook her head. "The Khleevi invasion on Vhiliinyar destroyed the waterways and conduits for the time machine. It kept it from working properly there, and it probably would here, too."

But Neeva said, "Not necessarily, Khorii. The remote part of the timing device was damaged, which was why people kept disappearing from the scouting parties. But the device itself was intact, and it was possible, with a few minor repairs, to trace time backward, if not forward. Nevertheless, such a device does not exist here, and physical travel is too risky without some way to determine when the Khleevi actually invaded."

Elviiz said, "I believe I can do that, *visedhaanyi ferlii* Neeva, and I would gladly take the risks upon myself to broaden our database, but my father says he is too temporally grounded to time travel. I suspect the same is true of me, unless you think the recent modifications in my structure may have altered that?"

"I can't say, Elviiz," Neeva replied. "They may have, but none of us are going to try. Not only would we endanger ourselves by risking interacting with the Khleevi again, but we risk their gaining access to the present time. They almost did during Khornya and Aari's last encounter with them, when the master device was damaged."

"My father has spoken of it. He was at the controls when the Khleevi came through," Elviiz said. "He valiantly fought with them to defend my Linyaari parents and our world."

"Yes, he did," Neeva agreed. "He was very brave."

"But not very familiar with the device," Ariin said. "Had he been, or had our parents been more skilled with it, such a thing might not have happened. It was always perfectly safe during the time I lived near it in Kubiilikaan. It simply requires a skilled technician."

Her gaze narrowed as it settled on Khiindi, who blinked up at her innocently.

Khorii caught her look. "Stop it, Ariin. There's no device like that here for him to operate, even if Khiindi was Grimalkin and not a little cat again. We'll just have to find another way."

"Okay," Jaya said. "I have another question that has nothing to do with time machines. Elviiz, if the Khleevi and the snakes killed each other, and they do have something to do with the plague, how did the plague spread to other planets?"

"Yeah," Hap said. "And if someone found the disease here and took it to the Solojo system, where it's supposed to have started, how did they get there without dying?"

"Does your data tell you anything about that, Elviiz?" Neeva asked.

"Maybe," he said. Khorii had never heard him use the term of uncertainty before. It indicated to her that he had indeed become more organic, and perhaps more fallible. "I will reexamine the images with a sensor I am now designing that will determine where there have been landings within the period between the Khleevi's invasion and now."

Elviiz, although somewhat differently configured, appeared to be fully recovered from his injuries. After a brief interval, he said, "Yes. One vessel did land here. You can clearly see its imprint in this section—" He zoomed in on another highlighted portion of the planet, where a slight round indentation roughly the size of the landing surface of a Linyaari ship could be seen if one squinted. A lot. "You may notice that the track of the ship resembles one of our own egg-shaped vessels. In fact, according to my calculations, it is exactly the same landing pattern as the VL58PK series, as it is now known."

"You think one of us landed here and created and spread the plague?" Neeva asked.

"I did not say that. I merely indicated that the person or

persons who did so landed in a vessel that makes a print identical to that of one of our own models."

"Perhaps one of the rescue teams, or a scouting mission, landed here briefly," Khaari suggested. "I will check our fleet's collective memory."

Her search took longer than it had taken Elviiz to design his program to detect the ship. Finally, she looked up, shrugged, and said, "It wasn't one of ours, Elviiz. They're all accounted for. Except for our recent excursions as rescue teams, we haven't taken many journeys. For one thing, not many of our ships survived the dual invasions of the Khleevi. We took what we could with us to narhii-Vhiliinyar, but during the second attack, the ones still docked on our new world were destroyed. Including all of the VL58PK series."

"Nevertheless," he replied, "the print matches."

"There weren't many made to begin with," Melireenya remarked. "A dozen were ordered, though only eleven were ever registered with our fleet. That is odd. I wonder why. There's another possibility, too. Khaari, check and see if our emissaries—the ones the Khleevi murdered—were flying VL58PKs at the time."

"Do you think the Khleevi captured the ship and used it to land here?" Khorii asked.

"It seems doubtful. Khleevi are larger than we are, and the controls would be difficult for them to operate. I would suspect they'd have simply eaten the ship, as they did everything else in their path."

Elviiz said, "As the more recent menace has done? The plague devours organic matter, at least at a certain stage of development, and the after-product devours the inorganic matter."

"But why here?" Ariin asked.

"The Khleevi destroyed worlds indiscriminately, Ariin.

They did not have reasons or an overall plan as we know them," Khorii said.

"I don't mean why did the Khleevi attack this world. I mean why did something on the world apparently survive the attack or at least mutate the Khleevi into the form of the plague and its aftermath? And how was a ship that apparently belonged to our fleet involved? This is beginning to remind me of something, too."

"What do you mean?" Khorii asked.

"Think about it," Ariin said. "Which race had a connection with this planet and used beings from it to make their lives more comfortable? Which race is so self-involved they might have come here, seen something they didn't like, changed it to be—I don't know, more portable, easier to control, prettier—and taken it away again without any concern at all about the consequences? Whom do I know well and whom have you met recently who might do something like that?"

"Surely not!" Khorii said. "But why?"

"It was probably all a clumsy, stupid mistake," Ariin replied. "For all their arrogance and supposed abilities, they're a bit slipshod at times."

chapter 14

At least Ariin can't blame me for the plague, Grimalkin thought as he meticulously licked his coat into gleaming, top-cat shape. He had been with Aari, Acorna, Lariinye, or Khorii during the times in question, and had been confined to small cat form since the end of the second Khleevi invasion. He eyed Ariin warily. Of course, a skilled time traveler like he might have looped back to bring the plague and its aftermath down on humanity, but why would he? He only meant the best for his Linyaari descendants and their human friends and all of his descendants on all of the other worlds he'd visited as well. Anyway, he was sure he wasn't responsible. He'd have remembered something like that. He remembered things that hadn't even happened yet.

As for his fellow "Friends," he was much less certain of their innocence in this matter. Some of them were explorers, as Pircifir had been, some were not mere explorers but diplomats, problem solvers, and the founders of great races, as he himself was. But some were tinkerers.

Odus and Akasa came to mind. They, like the rest of his race, had been gone from Vhiliinyar long before the Khleevi invasion. Personally, he'd been away off and on long before that. He remembered well the day he stopped back to pick up a few things at his old dwelling only to find that the city was no longer there. He'd had to find it underground, and use the time device to pick up his clean laundry! That was the trip during which he discovered poor Aari restrained on a laboratory examination table, the victim of the tinkerers who were trying to use him to invent his own race.

Then he and Aari had gone traveling in time and space, and he had simply never bothered to find out where the rest of his own race went while he was off adventuring, founding the Makahomian noble dynasty and inspiring their religion, rescuing Acorna's parents, and helping defeat the Khleevi. He'd just been too busy to track down the rest of them.

According to Linyaari legend, his people had traveled to other worlds to help other people. But the legend probably confused his own intrepid deeds with those of his fellow shifters, most of whom were not as kindly, well-meaning, and empathetic as he was. So if one of them had done this, had mutated what remained of the dwelling and serpent races into the plague and its aftermath, who had done it and where had they gone? There was only one way to find out. Khorii and Elviiz were absolutely correct, of course. It was much too dangerous. He wished there was some way he could send Khorii at least to one of the other ships while he did what was needed, but he didn't see how he could manage it while trapped in small cat form.

He could, however, manipulate the cronos Khorii carried. Ariin kept the one she had stolen on her wrist and up her sleeve, but Khorii still had Pircifir's in her pocket. Khiindi had a very light paw as a cat burglar, although Khorii had never been aware of that particular talent. He'd had to shelter the child from a few of his more unsavory accomplishments, but she knew who he was now, and, besides, she had to grow up sometime.

As she engaged in earnest discussion with Neeva and

Jaya while Ariin coached Elviiz on the finer points of plotting their course, Khiindi snaked a paw into Khorii's shipsuit pocket. It closed with a tab in the middle but he easily slipped his paw into the wristband and pulled it out the side without her noticing.

To find the right time, he focused on the ship that would have landed here, and the place it landed. He narrowed his search to that single vessel and tried not to include any other features of the planet. Pircifir's ship, the only other ship from Vhiliinyar that they knew for sure had landed here, lacked the distinctive egg shape and fanciful decorated hull featured on the Linyaari ships. A VL58PK was egg-shaped, and the hulls tended to be particularly gaudy for some reason. His mind blurred that image a bit, concentrating on such a ship landing here at some point in the past.

A point without Khleevi, he fervently hoped.

It would be really helpful as well if it were a point farther back than when he had been frozen in small cat form, but there was no way to guarantee that.

"Jaya? Neeva? Where are you?" Khorii asked. Then she asked Elviiz, "Where did they go?"

Ariin exclaimed, "We're time traveling. That blasted cat!" She lashed out with a kick that should have sent Khiindi flying across the room but only succeeded in grazing Grimalkin's shin as he reached for Pircifir's spare robe, still hanging from a hook near the hatch.

"Tsk, tsk, Ariin, I'm surprised at you. After all, isn't this what you wanted in the first place?" Grimalkin asked as he shrugged into the robe

"So I *can* time travel?" Elviiz asked. "Father will be so pleased!"

Grimalkin studied the viewport. The egg-shaped ship was just landing. No Khleevi were evident.

He hailed the ship, "Linyaari vessel, identify yourself immediately. You are in grave danger and if you proceed, will bring even worse danger to the entire universe."

"Grimalkin, you wily cat." Odus's smug face appeared on the com screen. "You're only saying that so you can keep the secret of our dwellings to yourself. On our new world there is room for much grander homes, so I've come to acquire more of the creatures to serve us."

Before Grimalkin could utter another word, Ariin snatched the crono, which he still held only on the tips of his fingers in the same way his paw had held it in cat form. The viewport blurred, cleared, and Neeva's voice demanded, "Where are you?" followed immediately by, "Oh, there."

But her voice was muffled by the folds of Pircifir's robe covering Grimalkin/Khiindi's ears as it settled on top of him.

Ariin scooped him up roughly and tossed him off the bridge into the corridor, then closed the hatch.

Khiindi turned to scratch at it, and had opened his mouth to utter his most heartrending, plaintive, offended meow when the hatch irised open again and Khorii scooped him up, cuddling him, kissing him between the ears and petting him. "Even though you only do it part-time, you are the cleverest cat in the universe, Khiindi. My sister didn't even give you time to explain that you knew we could go back in time while in orbit without risking the plague, and we both heard Odus, so now we know he was here. He must have had something to do with it. He's such a nasty man."

"Stop that," Ariin said. "Honestly, you and that—that being—are making me ill. You know what he is—how can you coo to him as if he were a sweet little animal instead of a wicked, manipulating, cunning, selfish, scheming shape-shifter?"

Khorii looked levelly at her sister, "You need to be more *linyaari,* twin girl. You hold a grudge far longer than is customary or healthy. Khiindi as a cat has never done you any harm, and the harm Grimalkin did you is long over."

"That's easy for you to say, you with the loving family and the normal childhood frolicking through the fields and grazing at will, not being questioned about your every movement or thought."

"I can see why you would be annoyed about that. However, that's no excuse for mistreating Khiindi when he's just trying to help. Even as Grimalkin, he has only done his best to keep us safe and has never raised a finger or a paw to you in any form. He's sorry for what he did. He's trying to make it up to you, but you just keep being nasty to him. If you can't forgive someone who is only trying to help undo the harm he was compelled to do to you and all of us—we were deprived of you after all, and now that we have you, you're too angry to be much fun—then we will never solve the problem and find a cure for our family and everybody else."

After glowering at Khiindi so hard his little cat body trembled in Khorii's arms, Ariin's face shifted moods, her eyes lowered for a moment, and when she looked back up there were tears in them. Khiindi knew she had been reading her sister as well as listening to her. The truth—that they were all in this together and the plague was more than an obstacle to keep Ariin from her family—was finally sinking in.

"I'm sorry, Khiindi, Grimalkin. But you shouldn't have stolen the crono."

"Two of the cronos are his," Khorii pointed out. "And the other one was his brother's."

Khiindi mewed. He really did miss Pircifir, but there was no harm in vocalizing it to emphasize to Ariin that she was not the only one with feelings.

"We are the ones borrowing the devices from him, not the other way around," Khorii said judiciously. Khiindi purred with satisfaction. She was such a fair girl. Sometime when he was back in two-legged form again, he must remember to compliment her on that.

"So Odus is the one behind the plague?" Ariin asked. "It figures."

"Actually, we don't know that. We just know that he was here after the Khleevi and before we learned about the plague. Shall we continue talking to Neeva and our friends and decide what our next move should be?"

Ariin nodded. Elviiz looked at her expectantly, and she said, "Yes, that will no doubt be helpful." Khiindi, absolved and vindicated, decided it was time to lick himself back into shape again.

"What happened to you?" Jaya asked.

Knowing that his sisters were still a bit upset, Elviiz answered for them, "It is nothing, really, Jaya. My sister's feline companion Khiindi is actually a time-traveling shape-shifter from one of the two races that created the Linyaari. He took it upon himself to take us back in time while still in orbit here to determine if the ship I had detected belonged to the person he suspected. This person is of his own race, and apparently has been known to exercise poor judgment in the past. It was indeed this person, but before Khiindi could remonstrate with him, Ariin became alarmed and returned us to this time."

"That certainly explains it," Captain Bates said.

"Yeah," Hap said from behind her. "I was going to guess that next."

Sesseli smiled proudly. "Khiindi is such a smart kitty." Khiindi gave a little purr. Sesseli was his favorite human. Khorii, of course, was his favorite Linyaari, but humans did not come any better than the little girl who had once used her telekinetic gift to save him and who had always understood him better than anyone else, even Khorii. She had always simply accepted that he was the most splendid and admirable creature she had ever encountered. He could accept any amount of childish mauling from someone like that.

"So who is this character your cat suspects?" Captain Bates asked.

"Odus the Odious," Ariin answered. Now that she had decided to be nicer to Khorii and Khiindi, the full weight of her scorn and disgust went into pronouncing the name of the being who had been, she realized now, not her mentor, as he'd liked to claim, but her tormentor. "He was there. We saw him and heard him on the com unit. "

"Can you go back to that time and stop him from doing it?"

"I don't know. But I don't see how we could without landing or making direct contact that might also infect us or our ship."

"If you think he didn't do it intentionally, you could use the com to warn him of the consequences of his actions," Neeva suggested.

"Odus? Excuse me if I scoff, Mother-sister, but he doesn't listen to anyone ever."

To Khiindi's amazement, Ariin turned to him, and asked, "Am I right, Khiindi, or do you think we ought to go back?" She held out the cronos. "We will go if you want to, and I won't interfere this time."

Khiindi stared at the device, considering. It hadn't occurred to him before, but the child, however misguided about his own noble intentions, was correct in her assessment of Odus, never a favorite of his among his brethren. Perhaps she had some potential after all. He turned his back on the cronos, raised his foot, and proceeded to cleanse the area under his tail.

chapter 15

I don't imagine it's worthwhile to try to find this Odus now," Neeva said. "He probably died of the plague, don't you think?"

"Perhaps not, if he was the one who deliberately engineered it," Ariin replied.

"Ariin, I agree he was totally odious," Khorii said, "But I don't think he was actually evil. Why would he do such a thing?'

"I don't know. He probably didn't know he had until it was too late to undo. But I very much doubt he suffered by it. His sort never do."

Since Odus's sort was the only sort Ariin had known until recently, Khorii decided that although her sister's viewpoint might be a bit warped in some instances, she was probably generally correct.

"In that case, we should find him and see if he can help undo this latest scourge," Neeva suggested.

"Okay, but where do we look?" Jaya asked.

"His race left Vhiliinyar long ago," Neeva said. "Well, most of them anyway. I am unsure how to explain the continuing presence of Khiindi's alter ego."

"Khiindi is part of our family," Khorii said. Khiindi

looked up from his bath and blinked twice before returning his attention to his tail. "Grimalkin is the name of his alter ego, and he befriended my father. It got—well, complicated, and as Ariin will tell you, sometimes what he did didn't work out very well, but—"

"But he was your family, just like he's your kitty now," Sesseli said, having apparently no problem with the change in her feline friend's status.

"About like the tribes were my family," Captain Bates said, with a wry twist to her mouth. "Although my mother was the only blood relative I had, sometimes I thought my adopted ones screwed up my life so much I'd have been better off as an orphan."

"But no matter how good they are, sometimes you feel that way anyhow," Jaya said. "Sometimes I wanted to believe my parents—and my aunts and uncles and cousins, who were other crew members on the *Mana*—"

"I didn't realize that, Jaya!" Khorii said. She felt bad that she had failed to understand, or even sense, that part of Jaya's predicament as the sole survivor of the *Mana*'s crew.

Jaya nodded. "Yes, there were a lot of them. They all had opinions about everything I did, everything I said or wore. Sometimes I used to just feel smothered and as if there was nobody left for me to be because they were so overpowering. And they did things that upset my plans and hurt my feelings and embarrassed me. I never had any privacy."

"But you really miss them all now and wish like anything they were all back again," Sesseli said, with a sigh.

"Not all of them, no," Jaya said. "But my mom and dad I miss all the time. And—well . . ."

Hap silently patted her shoulder. Sesseli buried her face in the fur of the kitten she was carrying.

Moonmay said, "It's true kinfolk can be a trial and a tribulation at times, but I miss mine just the same, and I'd miss them more if I knew I'd never again have an opportunity to be peeved with their antics."

"Fine," Ariin said. "I already apologized. Now what we need is a way to find Odus and make him stop the plague. If he's able."

Elviiz nodded sagely. "My fleeting impression of this individual, based on both data collected and my newly acquired intuitive powers, is that he is perhaps overly optimistic about the extent of his intellect and does not think his hypotheses through to all of their possible logical conclusions before acting on them."

"That sounds exactly like him. So what do we do about it?" Ariin asked.

"We have two points of reference with which to work," Elviiz replied. "One is that Odus visited this planet and apparently left it again. The other point is the *Estrella Blanca,* originating in the Rio Boca region of the Solojo system."

"But the plague may have come from a passenger more likely to have been traveling from Dinero Grande," Khorii said. "The people on the *Blanca* were all very well-off, so unless the carrier was a crew member, it could have originated on the passengers' homeworld."

"Dinero Grande sounds like this Odus bird's style," Hap said.

Captain Bates nodded, "He does sound like he considers himself a high roller."

"He could have been on Dinero Grande, I suppose," Khorii said. "We might have missed him."

Ariin snorted. "He wouldn't let anyone miss him. I doubt he's there anymore, if he ever was, but if he was, you can bet there will be some trace of his magnificent presence other than the plague."

"Would all of the Friends have moved together to the same place, do you think?" Khorii asked her sister. She wished

Khiindi could be Grimalkin again at least long enough to help them figure out where the others of his race had gone. "The only one I've ever heard much about is Grimalkin, and we know where he is and that he and Pircifir were more inclined to go their own way than the others."

"It may not be necessary to find the rest of them as long as we find Odus," Elviiz said. "I will change course immediately for the Solojo system, and suggest that the *Mana* and the *Balakiire* do the same."

"I have a better idea," Ariin said.

Elviiz looked up inquiringly and with some incredulity.

"You aren't familiar enough with the time device to have thought of it, brother," Ariin told him. "None of us have searched it for the whereabouts of Odus and his people because we didn't realize there would be a problem. But it should tell us when they left Vhiliinyar for the last time, and I'm sure if we look hard enough, there would be some data concerning their destination if they had one when they left."

Elviiz beamed. "That is an excellent idea, sister. We will have to travel backward to a time before the Khleevi, but if we avoid them and eliminate other time periods in which we know the Friends still inhabited our world, we should be able to find what we seek very quickly."

"In no time, you might say," Captain Bates said.

"Can we come, too, this time?" Sesseli asked. "Please?"

"Sorry, Sess," Khorii told her, "But it's best if we split up now. The *Mana* should go ahead with the original plan and look for Odus or clues about him on Dinero Grande while we search the timer."

The little girl looked sullen for a moment, but Captain Bates said, "That works for me. Besides, we can check up on Jalonzo and the others in Corazon. If there's still a city there after the crawly things eat their way through it."

"The *Balakiire* will assist the *Mana*," Neeva told her.

"Other Linyaari will be available on Vhiliinyar if my sister's daughter's children require help. You may be in need of our skills to make some of the quarantined areas safe for exploration, and many of our rescue teams have returned home already."

When the *Pircifir* returned to Vhiliinyar once more, Ariin pulled back her cuff to reveal the crono. Then, before consulting it, she looked at Khorii, Elviiz, and, finally, reluctantly, at Khiindi.

Digging into her pocket, she extracted the crono she had taken from Grimalkin and held it out. "I still don't trust you," she told him. Khiindi blinked his large gold-green eyes at her twice, then cautiously stretched out a forepaw and snagged the device with his claws, pulling it back to rest between his front legs and his belly.

"That is a very good idea, sister," Elviiz complimented her.

Khorii added, "Brilliant! For all his faults, Grimalkin has done more time travel than either of us, especially in the time before his people left Vhiliinyar. Having him choose when we visit will—er—save time."

"He was apparently near when the VL58PK was manufactured. Otherwise, how would he have acquired that particular model?"

"Oh, Elviiz, you're new to time traveling, or you wouldn't ask," Khorii said, with a sigh. "It gets very complicated. But you're right in saying that it is a lead—and perhaps the first one we should follow. Khiindi?"

She picked up the robe Grimalkin had worn and held it up while, outside the ship, time blurred by.

The ship remained docked in Vhiliinyar's new docking bay. The port had been constructed not where the original one was, Khorii knew, but close to the site of the original techno-artisans' complex. The current complex was being built up around the port. This made sense, since most of the goods modified by the artisans arrived in the port and also, particularly for the shipsmiths, would need to leave from there.

When time stopped blurring, the viewport was level with the top of one of the huge pavilions in which the work of the techno-artisans took place.

A large, oval-shaped ship poked at the top of the pavilion. The first coat of gilt and painted shielding had been applied to the hull, the details sketched out on top of it for later embellishment.

Although soft light still infused the pavilion, the moons of Vhiliinyar had risen, and the night held none of the noises Khorii associated with shipbuilding and repair from her earliest acquaintance with it.

The pavilions, as she knew, could be erected and dismantled depending on the amount of work the artisans had to do. Every precaution was taken to preserve the good meadowland beneath the floors of the temporary structures. Techno-artisans liked to graze as much as the next Linyaari. This was not the scantily furnished and crowded port/technical complex she had known from babyhood, however. This complex was beautifully laid out in a spiral from a large central guildhall and work area where the special coating compounds for Linyaari ships were mixed and the clan records were kept. The ships were each dedicated to individual clans and their members who were starfarers and were named for prominent starfaring ancestors. This was the old Vhiliinyar, before the Khleevi invasion, and at that time, according to her lessons, many Linyaari had never been in space, preferring the peace of their home meadows. They maintained the homeworld and its culture and customs, and cared for the Ancestors while the more adventurous of their race explored space, set up trade agreements with other worlds, and befriended other species. Until the arrival of the Khleevi, she was told, the Linyaari had never had a true enemy, so far as they knew, in the entire universe.

Though it was a bit difficult to see beyond the pavilion and ship that blocked most of the viewscreen, she counted eleven more pavilion hangars arranged in the spiral tightening around the guildhall.

"Let's have a look," Grimalkin suggested. He was two-legged once more, clad in Pircifir's robe. He took the time to strap the crono securely to his wrist this time.

"I'm glad we came at night," Khorii told Ariin. *"I know when we've time traveled before we've gone back to times before we were born, but this seems so familiar, I feel like we might run into Father when he was a boy. Mother won't even be born for another two* ghaanyi . . ."

They left the ship to explore the other pavilions.

Every single one of them held one of the VL58PK models, each in the process of receiving its shielding coat of elaborately codified decorative swags, swirls, and embellishments.

"I thought the story was that one of these was never delivered," Khorii said.

"I'll bet Odus probably used time travel to confuse the techno-artisans somehow or other," Ariin suggested. *"It would be his kind of joke."*

Grimalkin spoke in a low tone. "It's as I thought. The ship we saw was here. I visualized it in this place, and here it is."

But as they stared at the ship in question, with its purple orbs and golden swags on a pink background, Grimalkin's nose went up as if he were still in cat form.

Elviiz said, "My olfactory sensors detect the odor of fuel. I also feel slight vibrations coming from the ship. Our quarry is already aboard the vessel and preparing for takeoff."

With a controlled whoosh, the fabric-clad structure of the pavilion's pinnacle retracted, leaving the ship's nose open to the moonlit sky.

"Quickly, back to our own ship if we are to catch him," Grimalkin said. They ran back to their ship and reboarded, but at no time as they ran the relatively short distance did they see or feel the other ship leave its moorings. By the time they were back on the bridge of the *Pircifir*, however, the twelfth pavilion stood open and empty, though no other vessel ascended into Vhiliinyar's night sky.

"It vanished," Elviiz said. "Most unscientific."

"He timed it!" Grimalkin said. "Of course, and we must do the same."

He stared at the crono again, and the landscape outside the viewport changed once more. They caught a glimpse of the ship Odus had taken on the ground just before it lifted toward the moons.

The techno-artisans' compound was gone, as was the spaceport. In the distance were the mountains and the gleaming sea, but no sign of the city of Kubiilikaan or its own spaceport.

"Please return to your seats and strap yourselves in for liftoff," Elviiz said in an oddly pleasant and mechanical voice. "We will be leaving in a precipitous manner in pursuit of the vessel now exiting Vhiliinyar's atmosphere."

"Perhaps we will be invited to join him," Grimalkin suggested. He touched the com button. "Greetings, friend. Leaving so soon? I was hoping you might give me a ride in your elegant new transport."

Odus's gleeful and rather shiny face peered back at them from the com screen. In front of him, Akasa was seated, checking her lips in her reflection from the viewport. "Grimalkin! Haven't seen you in a while, old cat. What is that antique tube rocket you're flying? Are those your children?"

"He doesn't remember me?" Ariin asked.

"If Grimalkin isn't frozen in cat form, then he hasn't taken you to his Council yet as far as Odus knows."

"I'm beginning to agree with Pircifir about not liking time loops. This one seems to have tangled itself."

"Remember that the Friends knew all about our race before they had Grimalkin abduct you. So maybe Odus came way forward in time to hijack the ship and in his time line, you don't exist yet."

Grimalkin answered smoothly, "Never mind them. I've been looking for the rest of our people, Odus. When I tried to go home after an extended journey, Kubiilikaan had vanished. I found it, using the crono, but it was deserted. Where did everyone go?"

"Oh, you know, here and there," Odus said vaguely. "Decided to leave Vhiliinyar to the Linyaari and the unicorns, actually. I was hoping we might create a more stimulating race among us, but the Linyaari aren't especially interesting. They graze, they build things, they philosophize and sing, but I ask you, old cat, where's the drama in that? Except for being bipeds, they seem to have acquired none of our traits. Most disappointing."

"He put me through all that testing to try to create our race, and now he thinks we're boring?" Ariin said indignantly. *"If he was in range of my hooves, I'd show him boring!"*

"Hostile thoughts are probably counterproductive right now," Khorii cautioned. *"Can't you push him to invite us along?"*

Ariin pushed.

"If you think that bucket of bolts can keep up, I'll show you," Odus said. "I have a brief errand on the way back, however. We left our dwellings behind. They were dying anyway and in poor repair, despite the technicians' best coaxing and care."

"Perhaps you could just give me the coordinates in case we lag behind, our vessel being less modern and splendid than your own," Grimalkin suggested, with a modesty Khorii felt anyone who knew him would find transparent.

"Not that simple, old cat. This journey will involve a bit of a jump forward on the old crono—best synchronize."

Grimalkin nodded affably and pretended to do so, but Khorii knew he was doing nothing of the kind. They knew very well when Odus would make that fateful jump to the Khleevi-ravaged planet.

"I'd still like the coordinates for our people's new home," Grimalkin told him. "Just in case we get separated. You never know what in the universe might happen."

"True enough," Odus agreed, and provided the information. Khorii noticed Elviiz listening carefully, and she was sure he was processing the coordinates.

"Try to stay close," Akasa said. "We won't be turning back to look for you."

"Nor should you," Grimalkin said agreeably. "Our ship is no match for that splendid craft you're flying."

When they broke off communication, Elviiz told Ariin and Khorii, "Before we go off-world again, I would like to speak with my father and with our mutual parents as well. We cannot determine the time of our next meeting with any accuracy, so while we are within such close proximity, spatially speaking, I wish to take advantage of the opportunity."

"Me too," Khorii said.

"Yes!" Ariin agreed, "Even though it is very frustrating to be able to speak to them only by com or from a distance."

Grimalkin said, "I have someone I wish to see here as well. And I would prefer not to do it in Khiindi form, which I would have to do if I went forward to your parents' time with you."

"We're not going to be all that long," Ariin cautioned.

"Nor will I!" he said cheerfully, and vanished from the ship. Oddly, his robe stayed behind.

"That Khiindi!" Khorii joked. "He forgets his coat if you don't remind him!" She picked up the garment and replaced it on its hook.

But Ariin was looking eagerly at her crono. This time when she used it something unusual happened. As usual, the scenery from the viewport blurred into streaks of color. However, this time the ship shuddered and shook as well.

"What's the matter?" Ariin demanded. "The crono says we should be when I set it for, but where's the field?"

Elviiz said, "I fear we may have to walk. The ship has arrived at the correct time but its construction has been unable to withstand the strain. From the log, it seems that the jumps we have made since Pircifir's death were much longer journeys in the temporal sense than the ones he customarily made. The Friends may be exceptionally long-lived, but apparently their inorganic devices have mortal limitations."

"Wonderful!" Ariin said. "So now we have a good idea how the plague began, who was responsible, and where he went, but you're telling me we have no way to get there?"

chapter 16

We'll speak to Uncle Hafiz about it," Khorii said to calm her sister. "I'm sure that for such an important journey he will have a vessel he can lend us."

"Hail him now!" Ariin said.

But when Elviiz tried the com unit, he shook his head. "I am sorry, Ariin, but this vessel seems to be as deceased as its former pilot. I could resurrect the com unit given time, but first, I really do wish to see our parents."

Although Khorii agreed with her brother, she found his repeated insistence on the matter a little odd. Perhaps it was due to the increased proportion of organic matter in his makeup. He was telepathic now, after all, even though he seldom used thought-talk, perhaps because he had not yet become accustomed to doing so.

The three of them left the ship. It was resting—and rusting, Khorii noted sadly as they departed, between the planet's main port and the burgeoning techno-artisan complex.

They stopped to graze on the outskirts of the complex. Nothing anywhere was as good as the grass and wildflowers of home, Khorii decided. As she rose from her grazing posture, a shadow passed overhead.

"A flitter," Ariin said. "Perhaps we can catch a ride."

She waved at the vehicle, which circled back and settled on the meadow. The hatch rose and the familiar face of Maati, their father's younger sister, peered inquiringly out at them.

"I thought you three were off on a secret mission somewhere. Back so soon?"

"Yes, Linyaari Father-sister Maati," Elviiz said. "A portion of our mission dictated our return to Vhiliinyar, and we wished to see our family before embarking on the remainder of our journey."

"Besides which," Khorii added, "our ship seems to have kind of fallen apart. Could you give us a lift?"

"Certainly. I was actually on my way there with supplies and to say hello. We just returned from our own mission. Was your ship attacked by the new menace? Many have been. It has become difficult to maintain vessels in working condition."

"I believe ours simply succumbed to age and overuse," Khorii said. But she wondered if passing so close to the planet where they believed the plague had originated might have contributed to their ship's malfunction. If it had Elviiz should have been aware of it.

They crowded aboard the flitter, Khorii sitting on her brother's lap with the security strap across both of them, Ariin holding a large bag of imported cat food, no doubt bound for the belly of RK, the *Condor*'s feline first mate.

Maati landed just outside the pavilions that had been erected for the twins and Elviiz. The *Condor* remained in the middle of the quarantine field, and when they arrived, Uncle Joh was chewing his mustache as Maak beat him at Multilingual Scrabble® while the twins' parents looked on, amused. "Numerical equations don't count as words!" Uncle Joh growled.

"You are incorrect, Captain," Maak replied. "Mathematics is a language and therefore its expressions are allowable under the rules of Multilingual Scrabble®."

"Never mind him, Maak," Mother said. "He tried to claim that the Linyaari words we constructed during our turns didn't count either because he was unfamiliar with them. Oh, look! The children have returned!"

Maati, Elviiz, and Ariin advanced to the quarantine barrier—an area of trampled grass—while Khorii followed. Approaching the others while watching her parents, Maak, and Uncle Joh abandon their board to trot toward the barrier, Khorii was aware of something out of place. Not exactly wrong, just different. Then she decided it was not something out of place but something missing. None of the people beyond the quarantine barrier had blue dots dancing around them any longer.

She gave a delighted gasp, bounded past Elviiz and Ariin, and leaped the barrier to run to her parents. "You're cured!" she said.

"Khorii—?" Elviiz began to protest.

Belatedly, Khorii turned back, took her twin's hand, and pulled her toward their mother and father, then threw herself into her mother's arms. "Oh, Avvi! I thought I would never feel your gentle touch or Father's strong arms again!"

Father had scooped Ariin up and was twirling around and around in the grass. RK danced around them, meowing excitedly at the happy reunion.

"Don't I get a hug, too?" Uncle Joh asked Elviiz, who, having firmly shaken hands with Maak so that neither of them damaged the other with their great strength, gingerly patted Captain Becker on the back.

For a fleeting moment, Khorii maintained a light finger touch with her mother while replacing Elviiz to give Uncle Joh a one-armed embrace. Then Mother broke contact to join Father in hugging Ariin. Khorii piled on. Elviiz patted each of them tenderly on the shoulders and backs, so as not to break them.

Then everyone, including Elviiz and Maak, who had worn his special bionic horn adaptation during his stay on Vhiliinyar, touched horns. Only Uncle Joh and RK were left out of that. Then Uncle Joh wrapped his arms around as many of his friends as he could while RK twined around their ankles before becoming annoyed by their lack of gratitude for his attention and climbing the leg of Khorii's shipsuit. RK was a massive Makahomian Temple Cat, so she could not ignore him. Although his claws did not penetrate the cloth, he almost pulled her to the ground.

When the interlude was over, Uncle Joh clapped his hands and rubbed them together, saying, "Okay, we've all been sprung. Now what? Wanna go up to the com unit and tell Hafiz to kill the fatted cauliflower in your honor? I'm thinkin' party time!"

Mother said, "Maybe. Certainly we should stop by and be briefed on the latest events, but I am anxious to get back to work."

"Yes," Father said. "The family that stops plagues together—" He looked at Uncle Joh. "It is a Terran aphorism. Can you finish it appropriately for our situation?"

"Sorry, buddy. 'Drops eggs together' is the closest I can come. Somehow I don't think that conveys quite the sentiment you're trying to express."

Those remarks and a lot of other giddy nonsense marked the occasion, but once all of them were again aboard the *Condor*, Khorii sobered enough to check the ship for blue dots. She was relieved to find none. Perhaps, since the plague had not been able to kill anyone here, it had also been unable to continue its course and mutate into the matter-eating monsters. Certainly everyone present who had been infected was alive, healthy, and unavailable to provide ghostly collections of molecules to consume the inorganic matter that would eventually provide them with mass similar to that of the shapeshifting dwellings.

Ariin roamed as far from the others as she could while staying in sight, inspecting the ship's interior. "What kind of ship is this?" she asked. "I haven't seen one like this before."

"Of course not," Uncle Joh told her. "The *Condor* is a unique synthesis of the best bits of the best technologies of many worlds and cultures. Right now she's in tiptop shape because I have passed lo these many Standard months tweaking her. She'd be even better if I could have had access to my salvage stash."

"About that, Uncle Joh," Khorii said. "I'm sorry our news about the *Blanca* and your other salvage there was so upsetting to you."

"I can't be upset today, sweetie," he said, brushing it off. "My buddies Aari and Acorna have been reunited with their kids, and we are all free again. Nothing can mar that. I'm ready to celebrate!"

"The latest phase of the plague ate the *Blanca*, and probably by now has eaten the rest of your salvage," Ariin told him. "We have not checked lately, but it may have destroyed much of the inorganic matter in its path, including the derelict ships it attacked in its plague form."

At first they thought the low growl was coming from RK, but it was actually coming from the *Condor*'s captain. "First it almost kills me and my friends, then it locks us up and away from all the action, now it's eating my salvage? It must be destroyed!"

"We are in agreement," Ariin said. "And that is a good thing. You have a ship. Ours is no longer functional."

"Is it salvageable?" Uncle Joh asked with an acquisitive twitch of his left eyebrow.

"I believe so," Elviiz said. "Parts of it at least. Perhaps among us, you, Captain, my father and I may be able to save some of the electronic data in storage, which I think will provide much valuable information pertaining to our current mission and to the history of the Linyaari people."

Uncle Joh then showed one of the rare flashes of sensitivity that often took Khorii by surprise. Taking Ariin's hand, he asked, "That okay with you, Little Girl? I know you claimed that ship. Okay if we salvage her in exchange for transport for all of us to go kick this miserable medical monster in its star-farting behind?"

Without hesitation, Ariin nodded gravely. "I only hope it won't take too long."

"Don't you worry about that, honeybun. The Droid Boys and the cat and me have got a system."

They lifted off and flew the *Condor* back to the spaceport, close to where Khiindi/Grimalkin had left them.

While Uncle Joh, Elviiz, Maak, and Father worked at dismantling and hauling away the most useful bits of the *Pircifir*, Khorii grew increasingly nervous. No one noticed because Ariin was busy regaling Mother with somewhat edited tales of their adventures. While she kept in the cronos and *Pircifir*, this time Khorii noticed gratefully that she omitted mention of Grimalkin. Mother and Father had their own issues with Khorii's erstwhile kitty, and she was glad that Ariin didn't add any more fuel to that fire just now.

chapter 17

Grimalkin faced an unexpected dilemma. Actually, he should have expected it. If he returned to the *Pircifir* and the young people in their chosen time destination, he would be in small cat form again. That he knew. But when he consulted the time device to try to determine when his people abandoned Vhiliinyar and where they might have gone, he also accessed the time the twins and Elviiz had visited. He hoped there was some way of connecting with them during an earlier era that predated his cat curse.

That was when he saw the avatars for Aari and Khornya, as well as their children, Maak, Becker, and Khiindi's perpetually grumpy alleged sire, Roadkill, coagulate within the *Condor*'s avatar and leave the quarantine area, arriving a short hop later at the spaceport. Where the *Pircifir*'s avatar should have been was only a marker, and it decreased further after Aari, Becker, Maak, and Elviiz made repeated trips from the marker to the *Condor*.

Obviously while pursuing his own interests and investigations, Grimalkin had missed something important. Skipping forward on the time map a few hours, he saw all the avatars back aboard the *Condor*, and very little left of the *Pircifir*.

Then, amazingly, the *Condor* departed, with his own avatar not aboard.

Quite correct. He had no intention of returning to be trapped in small cat guise aboard the *Condor* with a cured Aari and Khornya. The youngsters had undoubtedly confided to their parents all about Khiindi the small cat's part in Grimalkin's rather convoluted role in their lives, history, and current predicaments. He couldn't think they'd be pleased to see him.

Poor him. Always misunderstood. What to do? He yawned, stretched, and turned from the time device, walking out of the building. He passed the few people on the street, reached the seashore, and continued toward the spaceport and, beyond that, the lovely meadow where the unicorns grazed.

A nap. That would settle his mind, and a dream might suggest a course of action, or at least be pleasant enough to delay any action at all while he prolonged the nap to enjoy it.

Until the last moment before departure, Khorii watched for Khiindi's return. Even though she knew he was also a powerful and troublesome being many times larger, older, and stronger than she was, in her heart he was still the Khiindi cat who had grown up with her and whom she loved. Even seeing the transformation to the hulking and devious Grimalkin had not erased the tenderness she felt when she thought of the fluffy little face with its pink nose, bright eyes, tufted ears, and thickets of whiskers. Why couldn't Khiindi have just been her cat? Why did it all have to be so complicated?

"Yaazi?" Mother's thought gently intruded. *"I didn't intend to eavesdrop but—Khiindi is Grimalkin?"*

"He's who?" Father's thought voice joined Mother's.

"I didn't tell!" Ariin protested. *"I didn't!"*

"Of course not, dear," Mother said. *"Your sister was so anxious about her pet—that treacherous trickster who makes*

*me wish we Linyaari were not such a peaceful people—that
she was broadcasting."*

"Ignition," Uncle Joh's voice said. "Hope you're strapped
in folks, cause we are going bye-bye now." The family was
seated together in an area that was one of the new improved
features Becker had grafted into the *Condor* during his
quarantine. Aft of the bridge and one level down by robolift, where previously only the Linyaaris' 'ponics garden
had been, there was now a semispacious lounge with the
garden as its focal point. A viewport larger than the one on
the bridge spanned the entire port side of the hull. The star-
board side contained a huge com screen. The seats were far
more luxurious than those on the bridge, and reclined fully
for sleep if crew members wished to doze outside their own
cabins. This was an excellent addition, since the bridge had
been designed for one, or at the most two people, and no
amount of modification had provided Becker with a better
floor plan that would allow him to pilot his ship and have his
friends around him at the same time. The lounge offered all
of the amenities of the bridge to crew members not actually
required to run the ship. It lacked only the long-distance and
broad-spanning sensory array that were the *Condor*'s remote
eyes and ears. Otherwise, everyone could converse and share
observations far more comfortably than ever before.

As the ship lifted skyward, Khorii turned from the port to
turn a guilty face to her parents. "I was trying to think how
to tell you about Khiindi," she said aloud. "I actually thought
Ariin would first, but she has been kind enough to leave it to
me, since he's my cat, even though she considered Grimalkin her enemy, as you do."

"He's not our enemy, Khorii, not exactly," Father said.
"He is one of those beings of whom Joh says if he is your
friend, then you have no need of enemies. By this he means
that with mostly benign or at least not deliberately harmful

intentions, Grimalkin can cause the people around him a lot of trouble."

"I think being Khiindi has been good for him, Father," Khorii said. "He has been very helpful to us lately, and has tried to make up for the trouble he caused."

Ariin snorted. "Don't get too carried away, sister."

"He has been the one who helped us pursue Ariin's idea that the Friends' dwellings were related to the latter stages of the plague. Even when she wasn't very nice—that is to say, even when he knew she was hostile to him, he persevered in trying to help us, and when we were in trouble, he and Pircifir saved us and risked their lives for us and the Ancestors. Pircifir was actually killed doing it, and Grimalkin is still very sad about that. And no, it wasn't his fault either."

"It was he who acquired the coordinates of the new home of the Friends," Elviiz said over the intercom. He was on the bridge with the captain and Maak, supplying the data from his own memory. "It will be instructive to see what, if any, impact the plague and its aftermath have had on that world and those beings."

"Instructive indeed," Mother agreed.

They stopped at the Moon of Opportunity so that Uncle Hafiz could personally welcome Mother, Father, and their friends back into the mainstream population, and stuff them with fragrant bouquets of delicious flowers and succulent mosses and ferns. Against Captain Becker's custom and wishes, Hafiz also insisted that they file a flight plan. Uncle Joh's exact sentiments, grumbled into his brushy mustache, were along the lines of "not needing a fraggin' leash."

What was really bothering the captain, Khorii thought, was that he did not like to navigate as other people did. His adoptive father, Theophilus Becker, had taught little Jonah the ins and outs of wormholes, "pleated space," and other anomalies of physics. Using these features, so frightening to most spacefarers, was second nature to Becker, and allowed him to take all sorts of shortcuts unavailable to those too wary or unaware of them. Confiding his real flight plan would be highly inconvenient, would slow him down, and might give away some of his secrets.

"Space is more perilous than ever before, my intrepid friend," Hafiz told Becker. "Communication since the advent of the plague is sporadic and unreliable. The Federation's collapse has removed all continuity and assurance of order and security. One truly no longer has any idea whom to bribe. In short, a lamentable state altogether. You and your crew are more precious to me than all of my wealth and treasure. Only by knowing your precise whereabouts can I send assistance should you require it."

Auntie Karina beamed and passed the marigolds. But as Khorii nibbled a blossom, she looked up to see Karina fling herself back against the low divan on which she and Hafiz were seated. The lady's ample flesh heaved her bosom up and down like a bellows, sending her lavender draperies fluttering like bright sails. Karina's eyes showed only whites.

Hafiz looked down at her with polite inquiry but no concern. He was used to such displays. "Yes, my beloved, you are having a vision?"

"A vision!" Karina's voice echoed. "I see danger, extreme danger. Bloodstained and poorly groomed people stand between you and your goal. And yet, there is danger to them as well. Oh, if only it were clearer." She raised her head, coughed, picked up the end of one of her draperies, and tried to fan herself with it. "It's a good thing my farsighted pharaoh insisted on a flight plan. I feel that more will be revealed to me at a later time. I'll have to get back to you on this."

Hafiz regarded his wife with a fond expression, then snapped his fingers so that an employee came running to lower the flaps of the pavilion beneath which they sheltered.

It never made sense to Khorii that they actually needed to shelter on MOO since the enormous compound was enclosed in its own bubble, and its weather and ecology were both artificial and manipulatable. But Hafiz evidently thought it necessary, and no one was willing to contradict him. He leaned across the table, his crimson-sashed belly tipping it so that the food slid toward him. "I have one small commission I would like you to undertake for me while on your journey," he said. "I own some property on Dinero Grande."

"That figures," Becker said, nodding. The name of the planet meant Big Money after all. Uncle Hafiz and House Harakamian owned some of the biggest money and other measurable wealth in the galaxy.

"It represents a considerable investment. I am concerned about its security, given the nature of the plague's unfortunate aftermath."

"Uncle Hafiz," Mother said gently, "we have some ideas now concerning how to stop that. We need to focus on that. We can protect . . ."

Hafiz held up one hand and pressed the other to his heart. "Dear child, you wound me! Can you with your Linyaari gift not discern the purity of my intention?"

Mother actually blushed. "I apologize, Uncle. Please continue."

"I sent my adopted son and heir, Rafik, to investigate the state of this property. I have had no communication, direct or indirect, since he left LaBoue on the new House flagship. I fear for his safety and that of his crew. My concern is primarily for them, though, of course, if your investigation reassured me as to the integrity of my property, that news also would be most welcome."

Khorii's family spent much of the journey telling stories and sharing thoughts in so much detail that Ariin began to feel almost as if she had been there, too. Though at first she treated Uncle Joh as a necessary but intrusive interloper, by the time she had spent a watch on the bridge with him and listened to his own versions of her family's adventures, she had adopted him, too. It helped, Khorii thought, that Uncle Joh occasionally made reference to how disappointed her parents had been not to have other children after Khorii's birth. Elviiz was a wonderful addition to their family, but they realized that he had another parent in Maak and was only theirs on loan, so to speak.

Two days out from MOO, the *Mana* answered the hail the *Condor* had been transmitting.

"We're waiting for you," Captain Bates told them. "We just left Rushima, where we dropped off Moonmay."

"Is there anything left of the planet?" Khorii asked.

"Many of the creatures were carried into space eating the pirates' shuttle. Even specters who resemble people who hated each other in life seem to band together in this form. The real ghosts have helped herd the newcomers to the dumps and quarries, where they can do the least danger. Moonmay's granddad says he can see where the creatures might be helpful if you needed to dig a well or a mine as long as you could get them to excrete the ore you need and go away afterward."

"I would be gratified if they would go away now," Elviiz said.

"Poor boy, of course you would," Captain Bates said. "Don't worry, Elviiz, we organics will protect you."

Sesseli said, "Moonmay and I thought up a name for the ornery critters." Moonmay's colorful expressions had already imprinted Sesseli's vocabulary. "They are inogres."

"Inogres?"

"Like the shapeshifting ogres in the old-time fairy books for kids, you know, the kind Puss in Boots killed? Ogres ate folks and animals. So something that eats houses and space-ships and inorganic stuff is an inogre. Get it?"

"It sounds like an excellent name to me, though I am un-familiar with the story."

"Oh, you'd like it, Khorii. See, there was this miller, which Moonmay explained to me is someone who lives in a mill and has a big wheel that he uses to grind other folks' grain. All he had was a cat and a boy and when he died, he didn't have any money because he was really kind and let people wait until they had enough credits to pay him for grinding their grain, only they never did. So the son thought he'd have to eat the cat to get by, then probably starve. But then something amazing happened. Even though the mill cat had never shown any sign of being a talking cat before, all of a sudden, as Moonmay said, he became downright chatty. Probably because he didn't want to get eaten."

"A cat who suddenly turned into a talking one, imagine that," Ariin said.

"Yes, well, like Moonmay said, most cats would prove their worthiness to their people by going out and catching mice and birds, thinking the people could eat the same things the cat ate. But Puss, which was the cat's name even though he seems to have been a boy cat, was smarter than that. He told the boy to get him some fancy boots and a fancy hat and some fancy gloves and a nice leather bag to put his kill in, and he'd make his fortune."

"That was not very clever of the cat," Elviiz said. "If the boy was so poor that he was going to have to eat his cat, how could he afford garments of that quality? Though small, boots that would fit a cat's hind legs would have to be custom-made, and that would be incredibly expensive, as would a hat small enough to fit his head and cut to accommodate his ears. This cat was taking a great risk making such demands."

"I'm sure he didn't demand it, Elviiz," Sesseli said. "He

probably asked really nice and purred and rubbed up against the boy, who actually liked cats and didn't want to eat Puss anyway. Moonmay says that probably among the people that owed the miller money there was a leather worker and a milliner, and the boy collected his daddy's debt from them to do what the cat told him. Because, like she said, if your cat started talking to you about ideas he had to make a future for you both, wouldn't you listen to him?"

"Not if you were smart," Ariin muttered.

Uncle Joh came into the lounge then. He had been sleeping while Maak and Elviiz took the bridge. "I always figured the kid stole the stuff he gave the cat, but Elviiz is right—boots that would fit a cat would have to be custom-made. Maybe the kid was good with leather himself and salvaged some to make them for the cat."

"You know this story, Joh?" Father asked.

"Oh, sure. I'll bet Acorna knows it, too, don't you, princess?"

Mother nodded, and said, "Yes, but until I visited Makahomia, it did not impress me. RK is an extraordinary cat, but even he had never shown any signs of wishing to speak or wear human apparel. However, had I read the story after our adventures with the temple cats, I would have assumed that Puss was a telepath. Now I am not certain that possibility is the only viable one."

Wearing an adorably cute frown, Sesseli said, "Do you all want to hear my story or not?"

"Sure, honey," Uncle Joh told her kindly. "Go on."

"Once the cat had his boots and other things, he hunted, but instead of catching mice and rats and songbirds, he caught stuff people liked—rabbits and quail and the like," Moonmay said. "Then, when he had a bag full of goodies, he went to the king and told him it was from his master, and pretended the miller's boy was a marquis, which was someone high up in the government back then." She made a puzzled face. "You'd think if the king was the head of the government and the boy was supposed to be the marquis, the king would know he'd never heard of him before, wouldn't he?" She shook her head. "Anyhow, when he'd given the king enough presents so that there was some name recognition associated with the boy as the phony marquis, and the king knew who Puss was, though he doesn't seem to have minded that he was a talking cat or thought it was a special thing in any way, the cat arranged for the boy to fake a drowning that got the king to supply him with fancy clothing and introduced him to his daughter."

"I do not see how this relates to ogres or inogres either," Elviiz said.

"Keep your shirt on," Sesseli said, channeling Moonmay once more. "The boy and the princess fell in love, and that was nice, but the king wanted to see where the boy lived before he'd marry off his daughter to the strange marquis, which shows he was smarter than most politicians, Moonmay said. Puss wasn't bothered about it at all. See, the ogre had eaten the king of a neighboring country and took over the kingdom himself. So Puss went through the ogre's land and told all the peasants to tell anyone who asked that it was his master the marquis who ran their farms, and not the ogre."

"You'd think the king would have known he had an ogre living next door," Jaya said.

"I think he did, but he was too afraid to look," Sesseli said. "Anyway, when the king drove by, all the peasants obeyed the cat, who had told them he was passing along the ogre's orders. Then the cat had his master take off his ragged clothes and jump into a pond and pretend to drown. When the king drove by in his carriage, the cat told the king his master had had his clothes and carriage stolen by thieves and was drowning, so the princess ran and jumped in the pond and saved him, then they both changed into some of the clothes the king and the princess had packed for the trip."

"That was before everyone used shipsuits when they traveled," Uncle Joh explained helpfully.

"Right," Sesseli said. "Then, while the princess was falling in love with the cat's master, Puss ran to the castle and killed the ogre."

"How did he do that?" Father asked. "If he was a little cat and it was a big shapeshifting people-eating ogre, wasn't that a bit difficult?"

"Oh, he lied a lot," Sesseli said. "But it was for the Greater Good."

"Any lies in this story you think might be helpful, strategically speaking, to our particular situation?" Uncle Joh asked, fluffing his mustache.

"Maybe. I'm not sure. He told the ogre that he was there to warn him that his master the marquis was coming to kill the ogre, and the ogre said how could he do that because, well, the ogre was an ogre. Puss said so was his master, and he'd just turn into a lion and eat him. So the ogre turned into a lion and—can you see where this is going already?"

"He told him enough lies to turn him into a mouse, then he ate him?" Uncle Joh said. Khorii thought it was kind of mean of him to spoil Sesseli's story, but the truth was that Uncle Joh really liked to be the main storyteller and somewhat jealously guarded his role.

"You cheated," Khorii said. "You're human, and you already knew the story."

"Sure," he said. "Why do you think I keep RK around? Security Chief in charge of ogre-slaying."

"I believe I comprehend your rather roundabout analogy, Sesseli," Elviiz said. "What we need to do with the aptly designated inogres is much the same as Puss did with the ogres. We need to persuade them to turn into something we can kill."

chapter 18

Once they entered what had been, until recently, Federation space, all three vessels in the small convoy began transmitting messages to the ship that had been carrying Rafik Nadezda the last time Hafiz had heard from him. They received no replies until they entered the Solojo system, when their probe was met with a distress signal, a digitized loop rather than an actual message, live or recorded.

The *Condor*'s scanner array, more sensitive even than the *Balakiire*'s, was the first to pick up the signal.

"It's coming from Frida," Khorii said from the copilot's seat. When the plague was in its early infectious stages, she had traveled to the moon's colony to heal the surviving victims with a baptism in the community reservoir. She found that if she purified water containing submerged victims, she could heal them all at the same time.

Uncle Joh opened the com, whistling for attention from the crews of the *Mana* and the *Balakiire*. "Listen up, people. We need to stop off on Frida Moon Colony. Rafik's ship is signaling from there."

But when they tried to contact Frida for permission to land, they received no response.

"That can't be good," Uncle Joh said. "Maybe we should

rethink all of us trying to land. One or two in a shuttle—"

"We should be the ones to go, Captain Becker," Neeva said. "You and most of your crew are convalescents, and possibly weakened by your previous infection. We are well rested, our horns are opaque, and are better equipped to assist any possible sick or injured people in case there has been a disaster."

It took a while for the shuttle to reach the surface, time in which the rest of the crews could only wait and watch, helpless with worry.

When the scouts landed, they found that there had indeed been a disaster, but there were no sick or injured people. There were no people at all. The *Balakiire* transmitted its view of the surface, and for the most part it showed nothing but an empty landscape, devoid of life.

"Where's the bubble?" Khorii asked, stunned. The bubble, or rather bubbles, had covered a large city of settlers, all of whom had been in perfect health when she left.

"What was it made of?" Uncle Joh asked her.

"Oh."

"I take your point, Captain," Maak said. "The inogres most likely devoured the bubble, exposing the settlers to the inhospitable atmosphere of the moon."

Their remarks were transmitted to the other two ships.

"Perhaps," Neeva said, as their sensors showed a few ruined bits of structure where the bubbles used to be. "But we are not seeing any human remains here."

"Have you located the ship yet?" Mother asked anxiously. Rafik Nadezda was one of the asteroid miners whose ship had intercepted her escape pod when she was an infant. The three men had raised her and were the human side of her family.

"Not—oh yes, that must be it," The images transmitted by the *Balakiire* stabilized, and the next thing Khorii saw was Neeva and Melireenya with their helmet hoods and gravity boots in place. They strode toward the ruins, moving white pillars against the ruined moonscape, and stopped at a stunted structure protruding from the ground. The tallest piece rose no higher than their knees.

They picked their way through it until Neeva bent down, then held something aloft.

"What is it?" Ariin asked from the lounge.

"A whiner," Uncle Joh said. "I could tell from the signal. It's a portable distress beacon not connected with the ship's main computer but programmed with its codes. It can be activated independently if the ship's other systems are disabled."

"Yes," Neeva said. "We've encountered several of these both on the ground and in space during other rescue missions."

"The signal is definitely from Rafik's ship?" Mother asked.

"'Fraid so, princess."

"There is no evidence of any human remains, recent or otherwise, and with the decreased oxygen available on this moon's unprotected surface, any remains would not have decayed quickly," Melireenya said.

"Perhaps they realized what was happening and evacuated, Joh," Father suggested. "Rafik might have attempted to assist in the evacuation and lost his ship in the process. This does not mean he was also lost."

"Yeah," Uncle Joh said. "But then, why hasn't he contacted Hafiz? And for that matter, I don't see any of those inogre thingies, do you?"

After relaying their findings to Uncle Hafiz via LaBoue, they continued to Paloduro, whose chief city, Corazon, had been a base for the rescue teams and housed a university that was the headquarters for research and rescue throughout the Solojo system.

There had been a spaceport there, but no longer. It and much of the city had collapsed. More of it was evident than had been the case on Frida, but it looked as if an earthquake had shaken everything down to its foundations. Instead of streets, undulating rolls of the sludgy inogre rippled and waved through the city. Puddling out from its center, the alien organism oozed tentacles into the ruined buildings on either side of the streets. When the tentacles withdrew into the main part of the beast, the ruins shuddered and collapsed to the ground.

"Where are the people?" Sesseli asked. Her voice quivered. "Abuelita and Jalonzo?"

"I don't know, but we're not landing here," Uncle Joh said.

Mother suddenly leaned forward and seemed to be concentrating very hard on something with a certainty that indicated she was using her special gift that told her not only the mineral content of asteroids and other objects, but had developed to the point where she could also intuit the contents of spaces beyond those she could actually see. Or maybe she was just reading the minds of some of their Corazonian friends, Khorii wasn't sure. She herself wasn't picking up any thoughts from them.

"They've fled the town," she said at last. "There are farmlands and fields surrounding the city. Since the inogres don't harm organic beings, the survivors are safe enough there, but because the plague blasted the plant life when it killed so many people, there's very little for them to eat."

"We still have supplies," Jaya said. "We can drop them some until they can be rescued."

"That may be a long time if all of the other plague planets are similarly afflicted," Neeva said.

The *Condor* had flown out of the city, past its industrial hem, and was overflying a field. The inogre had eaten the highways leading out there but appeared to have retreated back to its main body once the nourishment was consumed. Scallops of the sludgy creature protruded from the city's streets but didn't extend into the countryside.

"Maybe Rafik will be among the refugees in the field," Father said consolingly to Mother. "They probably evacuated Frida before the inogres took over the city."

"Doubtful," Maak said. "Elviiz was attacked in Corazon many weeks ago, so the city has been under attack since then."

"I'm afraid he's right, Mother," Khorii said. "We didn't hear anything about Frida being under attack before we came. Jaya, did you learn anything about the attack when you returned Jalonzo to Corazon?"

"We didn't. He went back with the ship and a crew supplied by Lord Hafiz. Look! There they are."

From their appearance, the crowd of people occupying acres of blasted fields could have been campers or attendees at some sort of festival. They wore everything from pajamas to very dressy clothing. Blankets and gourds littered the ground not covered by people, and a number of blackened areas marked spots where cookfires had smoldered. Most of the people were children, of course, since they were the age group least affected by the plague, but there were many elderly people among them, too. Because the Linyaari had healed the survivors, the eldest were in better health than they had been for many years. On the city side, a litter of pots and pans, small household devices, and other inorganic matter that might be attractive to the inogres formed a wide perimeter around the encampment.

Every face was turned skyward at the trio of ships approaching. The ships were directly over three of the occupied fields when Khorii saw the eyes of several people widen, their mouths make o's as if they were screaming, and their fingers point before they scattered in all directions.

"Uh-oh," Uncle Joh said. "We have stalkers. Hold on." He banked into a turn that aimed the bow toward Corazon again. What was left of the city was obscured by a towering tentacle of inogre, rising like a giant cobra about to strike.

"Remind you of anyone?" Ariin asked.

Khorii nodded. *"The serpent. Do you suppose there's another connection there?"*

"Probably."

Uncle Joh circled again, this time bypassing the fields to approach from the other side.

Captain Bates announced, "We're out of here, folks. We're less maneuverable than the *Condor* or the *Balakiire*. We'll return to orbit, load up a shuttle, approach from the unoccupied side of the encampment, and land long enough to bring supplies."

"Can't we evacuate some of them?" Jaya asked. "Jalonzo and Abuelita at least?"

"I doubt they'd come," Captain Bates told her. "And we don't have room for everyone. Besides, we're bound to run into a similar situation other places, and other than the room we have left on the ships, where do we evacuate them to? For the short term at least, if we can get supplies to them, they've probably found the best solution."

Khaari on the *Balakiire* said, "The tentacles have receded again. We're going to set down long enough for Neeva and Melireenya to attempt to regenerate the fields and see to anyone who may have been injured during the evacuation."

"Good idea," Mother said. "We can help with that."

When all of the Linyaari had been dropped off at the encampment, the ships returned to orbit to send shuttles to the *Mana* to resupply the refugees.

The first thing the Linyaari did was purify the air, which reeked of human excrement from the privy trenches. The smell was not improved by the odor of food rotting in the sun.

Abuelita and Jalonzo had made their way to the landing zone and embraced their Linyaari friends. Children clung to their shipsuits, patting them, squealing for attention, or just looking up at them with pleading eyes. They all had been through so much already, especially the younglings who had lost their parents, and now their second homes, to the terrible scourge.

"Please, Khorii, can you save some of the food?" Abuelita asked. "Without containers it goes bad so quickly. It has made many sick already."

"I'll take care of the sick," Ariin said. "Where are they?"

"Abuelita, Jalonzo, this is my twin sister, Ariin," Khorii said. "She's come to help, too."

Jalonzo grabbed Ariin's hand and pulled her toward the outer edge of the encampment. "They're here, señorita. A little ways from the others. Some feared that the plague was beginning another cycle and did not want the sick among the healthy."

By the time Neeva, Melireenya, Mother, and Father had purified the fields so that the grasses sprouted green and strong once more, the first shuttle had landed, and food was distributed among the people, who quickly removed it from any plas or metal containers. Groups of kids gathered the containers and carried them out to the barrier. Meanwhile, the adult Linyaari turned their attention to freshening the water supply, a small river flowing through the fields. When Khorii had saved what food she could, she joined Ariin among the sick people. There were over one hundred of them, but they were so sick and dirty that she didn't think it wise to put them in the river to do a mass healing, and began curing them one at a time. She and Ariin were working on the last few when one of the *Condor*'s shuttles landed. Uncle

Joh jumped down and began pulling more supplies out of the hold. "Stars! This plague thing is just the gift that keeps on giving, isn't it?" he said. "How long have you folks been out here anyway?"

"Two Standard weeks," Abuelita told him. "It is very difficult with no shelter. Many are burned painfully by the sun, but at least the monsoon season is past."

Uncle Joh handed out the last of his supplies and jumped back into the shuttle. "Big load from the *Mana* coming next," he promised.

Captain Bates piloted this one, and Hap jumped out and began dispensing supplies.

"Joh says you folks need shelter," she said. "Anybody ever do any basket weaving?"

The Linyaari joined her in leading the older children to the river, where the tallest reeds had been restored to healthy growth on previous visits. They gathered armloads of these and began weaving and teaching the techniques to everyone old enough to learn, making panels of basketry they hooked together into awnings, then shelters. All the while they worked, the shuttles came and went, leaving as soon as the supplies were dispensed so that the vessels didn't draw the tentacles into the field again.

Finally, they had completed four shelters and were sure that there were enough refugees who knew how to make them, then the Linyaari and Captain Bates stood in the landing zone to indicate their readiness to depart. Shuttles from all three ships landed—the *Balakiire*'s on autopilot, since Khaari stayed with the ship. Hap was aboard the *Mana*'s shuttle and Elviiz piloted the *Condor*'s.

The shuttles ascended with viewports turned toward the city and the passengers watched, fascinated in spite of themselves, as the inogre tentacles extended and stretched higher and farther out into the countryside, less like snakes now than the elongated tongues of frogs. This impression was heightened as the nearest tentacle receded, then whiplashed out, its tip touching the *wii-Balakiire,* wrapping around it as if to pull it down. Then it whipped back again, pulling off and away from the egg-shaped shuttle so quickly that it set it spinning. Neeva's face grinned—with teeth showing for the unseeing benefit of the inogre. "It doesn't seem to like the taste of our technology. No doubt the bioelectronics engineered by our two-horned allies is unappetizing to them."

But while their attention was on her, the tentacle lashed out again, and this time attached itself to the hull of the *Condor*'s shuttle.

chapter 19

ccelerating," Elviiz said, but though he pushed the engines until the little craft shuddered, the tentacle quickly filled the viewport with its sludging brown, and they heard the hull creak as the creature bit into it.

"Mayday, *Condor*, we are under attack," Elviiz said. Though his voice sounded as calm as Maak's, Khorii felt a rush of panic from her brother. He had suffered badly from this life-form before and did not wish another close encounter.

"Fire on them!" Uncle Joh's voice boomed through the com. "I retooled that shuttle with top-of-the-line weaponry."

"I am Linyaari!" Elviiz protested, with an agonized look at his Linyaari family.

"It eats metal for breakfast, boy," Uncle Joh bellowed again. "Don't think of it as attacking, think of it as giving it a meal. Be a philanthropist and feed the freakin' thing everything you've got!"

"Excellent point," Elviiz said, and pushed the trigger, holding it down as the missiles shot into the shuttle's captor. It shrank away from the hull to coagulate around the darting projectiles. Any explosions they might have caused were smothered in sludge that dragged them back to the surface with it.

By the time Elviiz had the shuttle back on course, the other two vessels were far above them, ready to dock in their respective ships.

Uncle Joh said a Standard word that the LAANYE translated only as "extremely rude." At the same time Hap's voice on the com said, "The *Mana*'s pulling away from us! Jaya?"

"How in the cosmos did they get past my sensors?" Uncle Joh said, among other impolite words and phrases.

"Who?" Mother asked.

"Pirates!"

"Not again!" Captain Bates sounded dismayed and annoyed. She had fostered among the pirates. "We had an agreement."

"I'll circle around, ram one up their tractor beam, and blow them to kingdom come." Uncle Joh, his mustache bristling in full battle mode, was in his element. Next to salvage and his friends, he liked fighting best and couldn't understand the Linyaari aversion to violence.

"No!" Khorii and Melireenya cried at once. "Mikaaye—" Khorii said.

"My son is aboard one of their ships," Melireenya explained.

"A Linyaari pirate?" Uncle Joh sounded justifiably baffled.

"It's kind of an exchange program, Jonas," Captain Bates explained.

"What kind?" Uncle Joh demanded.

"Kind of a quasi-hostage, quasi-training, quasi-reform program," Captain Bates replied. "Mikaaye volunteered, and Melireenya doesn't object, do you, Melireenya?"

"Only if someone tries to blow up the ship he's on,"

Melireenya said. "I think communication is in order rather than an exchange of weapons fire. Especially since all of the shuttles and the *Balakiire* are now within firing range as well and since your shuttle has fed her missiles to the beast below, Captain Becker, we are all unarmed."

Uncle Joh said a number of other rude expressions, and scowled as ferociously as RK when he attacked Khiindi. "Those fleas on the face of the galaxy sure know how to pick their moment," he said. "I got them now, you know. They've been listening in, and they uncloaked just to jeer at me. I could have seen them before if I hadn't been instructing El-viiz on the ethics of interspecies interactions."

"Oh good," Father said. *"You can relax, Melireenya. The danger from Joh is over now. He has returned to employing words of more than one syllable to express himself. We can concentrate on the threat from without now."*

"Can you thought-talk with Mikaaye from this distance, Melireenya?" Mother asked. Ship-to-ship telepathic contact was rather difficult, especially when one of the ships was running as far from the others as it could, but close family connections could often communicate over even more vast distances. *"Is he on that ship? If he is, can he tell us what their plan is?"*

As they communicated from shuttle to shuttle, the *Balakiire*'s docking hatch opened to admit the *wii-Balakiire,* and the *Condor*'s docking hatch opened to admit its shuttle.

"Hang on, gang," Uncle Joh said. "There's not room for two shuttles there, but if Hap and Captain Bates suit up, Maak will come out and attach your shuttle to our hull and pull you in."

"We will maintain surveillance in the meantime, Joh," Khaari assured him.

"Fine, while we load the shuttle, you track the pirates, and we'll track you," Uncle Joh told her.

"Do you think Jalonzo and Abuelita and the other people down there will be all right?" Khorii asked her parents.

"As long as they continue to surround themselves only with organically based materials, they'll be fine," Mother said reassuringly.

"Maybe once the inogre has eaten everything in the city it will starve to death," Ariin put in, sounding cheerful.

"That would be terrible," Father chided Ariin for her *ka*-Linyaari unkindness. *"Perhaps we should find a way to feed it."*

Ariin had no response for that, but they could all tell she was appalled by what she saw as their father's naïveté. She had not been raised, as Khorii had, among people who still remembered how Aari had been tortured by the horrible Khleevi, escaped, and lived to tell the tale. Despite the terrible things they had done to him, he had still retained his innate goodness and not let himself be twisted by the experience. To Aari, all life was valued—theoretically even his former captors. Just because the Khleevi hadn't been interested in peaceful cohabitation didn't necessarily mean this creature wasn't either.

Father simply smiled at Ariin, and said, "Since Maak had to leave the bridge to help your friends, I will go help Joh."

"We should go help the newcomers with their gear," Mother said, then smiled at Ariin. "I think in time you will come to trust your father as I do. His ideas may sometimes seem odd, but the best ideas often do."

Khorii thought Mother ought to know. She had had plenty of odd ideas of her own over the years. As a Linyaari raised by humans, she was considered even odder than Father was, but like Father, she had long ago earned the respect of more conventional Linyaari.

By the time they helped Captain Bates and Hap out of

their pressure suits and oxygen helmets and brought them to the lounge, another crisis was under way.

On the remote screen, the surface of Paloduro had been replaced by an image of the *Mana*, suspended in space except for a slender strawlike tube down which something bumpy was pouring itself, seemingly endlessly, into the ship.

"They're boarding her," Captain Bates said as she walked into the lounge. She didn't sit but watched the scene with fascination and anger. "So much for Coco's promise. He accepted Mikaaye, waited until I was gone, and . . ."

Suddenly the tube, which had been stretched more or less taut, broke loose at one end and people began floating out of it. They wore pressure suits, too, and others attempted to gather them back in.

Melireenya spoke, her face appearing beside the other images on the screen. "It's not what you think. Mikaaye says they needed the *Mana*. The 'ghosts' aboard the *Black Mariah* continued damaging her until they formed the larger creature. The taking of the *Mana* is not so much a hijacking as an evacuation. The captain had a terrible time getting everyone to go, and now it looks as if the *Black Mariah* has been—there, do you see?"

The ship had reappeared somewhat beyond the waving tube. It bulged, straining, and broke into several large pieces as they watched. Sludgy inogre oozed out between the pieces, covered them, and slowly absorbed them. Before it had finished devouring all of the visible pieces, however, parts of it froze, turning white and motionless in the vacuum of space. Finally, from within its core, it extruded one tentacle that clutched at the tube.

The last of the evacuees had been plucked from space and pulled through by a rescuer attached to a cable apparently moored to the *Mana*. As the tentacle made a final desperate lunge, it caught the free-floating end of the tube.

Almost simultaneously, the *Mana* accelerated, and the tube broke free from its hull, where it was sucked into the creature until the tentacle also hung rigid and still from its body.

"It ate too much. It ate too fast," Uncle Joh chanted, no doubt quoting one of those ancient Terran aphorisms of which he was so fond.

Ariin smiled unpleasantly, and for a change it was not aimed at Khorii or Khiindi. "I see now the wisdom of Father's kindness. Without protection from space, the creature freezes and dies."

"We cannot actually be sure it's dead," Mother said. "But unless it is thawed, rehoused, and fed again, it should be moribund for all intents and purposes."

Captain Bates rose from her seat in the lounge and headed for the bridge, saying, "Hail the *Mana* now, Joh. I want to have a couple of choice words with my clan daddy, Coco." Khorii followed. The new screens were great, but they didn't show what was happening on the bridge itself.

"This is the *Condor* calling the *Mana* and all crew and passengers," Uncle Joh was saying into the com, "Everybody okay?"

Captain Coco stood behind Jaya, his heavily ringed hands on her shoulders as if he were a kindly uncle. Every tribally beaded braid was in place, and his expression was as cool as if he lost a ship to a ravenous monster every day.

"How good of you to ask," he said suavely. "We all made the move to our new home before the destruction of our previous quarters reached—ah—critical mass. We were overcrowded anyway, which was to be expected, although the virulence of the creature that stowed away was not. We were heading for Corazon to lighten our load, but detected that it had similar problems. So fortunate for us that you happened to be waiting between us and the surface with this commodious ship. Asha, I love the décor of my new cabin."

"You can't keep the *Mana,* Coco," Captain Bates told him. "We had a deal. You know how the clans despise a welcher."

"They'll understand. The *Mana* was the only available ship large enough to hold all of our people. Even our cabin boy Mikey the Horn agreed that we had no alternative, isn't that right, lad?"

Mikaaye, looking shaken but relieved, peered around the captain, and with a feeble smile, said, "Arrrrgh."

"What's that supposed to mean?" his mother asked from the *Balakiire.*

"Occupational jargon, Melireenya," Captain Bates told her. "An all-purpose kind of answer."

"So I suppose you're going to demand that we turn over the passengers to you now, eh?" Captain Coco said, as if sneering at the very idea.

"Not really, no," Captain Bates said, giving Uncle Joh a wide-eyed look that was probably supposed to look innocent but, accompanied by a shrug, invited Uncle Joh to play along with her.

"No room," Uncle Joh said with a shrug of his own. "This look like a passenger liner to you, bub?"

"Then you don't care what we do with them? Asha, don't play games with me," Coco scolded Captain Bates. "You are very attached to these kids. You were ready to lay down your life for them when last we met."

"Wrong, Coco. I was ready to lay down your life for them," Captain Bates corrected him. "And I will do it yet if any harm comes to them. You took command of their ship, now you're responsible for them."

"What am I supposed to do with them?" he demanded. "I have women and children enough already."

"A few more shouldn't make any difference then," she said. "They're a package deal."

"Tell you what, buddy," Uncle Joh said. "We were on our way over to Dinero Grande, where the rich and powerful used to live. We're checking on a cargo for Hafiz Harakamian himself. Why don't you stick with us and see if we can't turn up a newer, fancier model than that old bucket for you and your band of merry men, women, and children? Then you can leave the *Mana* to the kids that own it, no harm done, and you haven't made an enemy of Jonas P. Becker."

Khorii didn't know what to expect from that—possibly an offer to blow them out of the sky. Fortunately, she knew the cargo ship was not heavily armed, whereas the *Condor* was always equipped with a full array of weapons salvaged from many different eras. Most of them didn't work very well, of course, since Uncle Joh spent too much time on more functional modifications for his ship, but armed combat should be avoided. The Linyaari were against it on principle, and she was against it because all of the people she cared about most were within range of ship-launched weapons. Someone could get hurt. Someone probably would get hurt since that was, to the best of her understanding, the general idea behind weapons.

"Jonas Becker, son of Theophilus Becker, of Becker Intergalactic Recycling and Salvage Enterprises, Ltd?"

"That's what it says on the side of the ship," Uncle Joh said.

"Sorry, I don't have my reading glasses on," Coco apologized. "Spoils the image."

"I got a few pair around here somewhere if you need more," Uncle Joh said. "Sounds like you've heard of our firm, huh?"

"Heard of you? You and your father are legendary among my people. Those who do not know us well believe we are only murderers, thieves, kidnappers, and brigands. This belief is not entirely without foundation, but the truth is, we foster our reputation for fearsomeness and mystery. What few people realize is that we are among the earliest and most innovative recycling experts in the universe, and much of what my generation does was taught to our people by your own honored father."

"Izzat right?" Uncle Joh asked, nonplussed. He looked to Khorii for confirmation. Khorii shrugged. She'd met the pirates but claimed no special knowledge of them.

"Indeed. He was an honored adopted elder of our clan."

"I had no idea," Uncle Joh said.

"Me, neither," Captain Bates admitted. "Must have happened before Mom and I joined them. Now that I think of it, I did hear some of the senior people, when they were looking at a particularly useless scrap of something, ask each other, 'What would Off do?' But I thought at the time they were referring to some sort of cleanser."

"You should meet my lady friend Andina," Uncle Joh told her out of the side of his mouth, "She knows all about cleansers and stuff." To Coco, he said, "So, you going to hang with us and look for some awesome salvage or what?"

"We'd be honored."

On another private com band Melireenya said, "Mikaaye is reading him, and he is sincere."

"Okay then, boys and girls, we're burnin' starlight," Uncle Joh said, using another of his strange and unusual Terran expressions that were unlike any that Khorii's other human friends employed. "Dinero Grande or bust."

Khorii and Captain Bates returned to the lounge. Mother was no longer there.

"Where did she go?" Khorii asked Ariin.

"She went to find Maak and Elviiz," Ariin said. "Did you know she can analyze the mineral and chemical content of something just by looking at it? She has determined what the sludge thing is made of, and hopes with the help of Maak and Elviiz to develop a defensive weapon that will defeat, if not destroy, it."

Khorii sighed. "And I was afraid I'd miss something if I stayed here."

Ariin looked chuffed at being one-up, but said placatingly, "You can't be everywhere at once any more than I can. Maybe that's why we're twins."

And to Khorii's surprise, when Khorii sat back down in the seat next to her sister's, Ariin gave her a brief and somewhat awkward hug.

The moment was cut short when RK jumped onto their chair backs and prowled back and forth, purring and demanding attention. Ariin pulled her arm away and stood up quickly. She was still nervous around cats.

Khorii wondered how Khiindi was and what he was doing. She missed him. Of course, she particularly missed his being her little cat, but she found she had also begun to miss Grimalkin. If he was here, he'd probably turn into Puss from the story, pounce on the inogre, and wrestle it to the ground.

With that thought, she knew she had fallen asleep and was dreaming. The real Grimalkin was far more likely to turn himself into Khiindi and hide behind her.

chapter 20

Grimalkin didn't need Pircifir's ship in order to leave Vhiliinyar. Even less did he need children to cramp his style. However, as long as he was in the post-Khorii time period, he was stuck in small cat form. The plague and its mutations unfortunately fell into that time period, and though he could attempt it, he doubted it would do any good to try to convince Odus to refrain from doing something potentially disastrous before he'd done it. Odus was not amenable to warnings. His unjustified confidence in his own genius kept him from believing anyone trying to deter him from his chosen path, least of all Grimalkin. He and Odus had never actually come to blows, but they had never been companions either. Grimalkin attributed their antipathy to what he considered to be his own empathetic nature. He always knew and cared what others thought and felt, if only to use it to manipulate them. Odus had no clue about others or an interest, other than for the purposes of scientific experiment, in obtaining one.

It wasn't that Grimalkin felt especially responsible for Odus's actions, because for a change, he'd actually had nothing to do with it other than help introduce the creature—in its most benign form—to his own people. But he was aware of the outcome as far into the future as he and the girls had traveled. Furthermore, he was enough of a time traveler to realize that it wasn't safe even for his people to toy with the entity whose ancestors had formed their homes. A creature like that might know where you live and find a way to time travel back and—who knew?—look up its predecessors and in the process destroy his race, the unicorns, and the Linyaari as well. No, he told himself, he didn't feel at all responsible, but he did think it was in his own best self-interest to put a stop to this. He just did not see how he could do it as a small cat in the same time as the youngsters occupied now.

No, he needed to stay in a time in which he could maintain humanoid form long enough to pilot a ship to the coordinates Odus had indicated, and only then, if he could not foil Odus earlier, go forth into the plague-ridden future on little cat feet. He could be a very beguiling cat. He had had lots of practice. He ought to be able to persuade someone to deactivate the freeze placed on his little feline self so he could communicate with Odus enough to deal with the problem the scientist's tinkering had created. If not, of course, especially if someone got his crono away from his comparatively helpless furry form, he, all of humanity, and possibly his own race were in deep trouble.

That didn't deter him, however. He was intimately familiar with deep trouble, having been in some degree of it one way or another for so much of his life.

The wealthy citizens of the Solojo system chose to live on Dinero Grande because it was the most beautiful of the three planets clustered closely together in its part of the system. It boasted wide, tranquil meadows, broad, clean rivers and streams, distant, gorgeous mountains, and a few small, calm seas perfect for pleasure craft.

The homes were all large estates, containing houses, stables, garages, gardens, and landing zones for the personal spacecraft residents used to obtain supplies both necessary and luxurious from Rio Boca, the import/export and intergalactic relations center of the system,

A great many of Dinero Grande's wealthiest and most illustrious citizens had been aboard the *Estrella Blanca*'s ill-fated maiden voyage. Their homes had been closed up before they left, and any staff members not attending their employers had been sent on holiday. Most of them would have gone to Corazon, where the Carnivale was under way.

In these isolated, empty homes, the plague had killed no one, and without plague-ridden bodies to grow from, the inogres did not develop either. The gardens had grown freely into tropical jungles choking the pathways and filling the fountains of the palatial homes. The tiled courtyards were pried loose and upended by unattended root systems.

Furthermore, since the creatures were tunnel-like but did not actually seem to tunnel, they had not thus far spread across the fields or through the forests to further ravage the unaffected areas.

Neeva said she knew just the place where the ships could land safely and led them to a large "country cabin" built entirely of local hardwood logs. Across a broad meadow, it faced a lake as clear and sparkling as quartz, though not nearly so inviting to inogres as real quartz would have been.

Khorii hadn't seen this part of the planet, and Ariin was completely enchanted by the loveliness of the place, which was situated and landscaped to a dramatic effect not achieved by the studied naturalness of their reterraformed Vhiliinyar.

But it was Mother who, upon seeing the passengers disgorged from the *Mana,* unstrapped herself and raced from the *Condor* even faster than Melireenya bolted from the *Balakiire.*

Mikaaye had not yet appeared in the field, but Grandsire

Rafik had! There he was, along with his wife and her sisters and some of the people Khorii recognized from her cleansing mission on Frida Moonbase.

"Captain Coco evacuated Frida!" Khorii said, amazed, and unstrapped herself to head for the meadow behind Mother and Father, who had gone after her, and Ariin, who was right behind them.

"Sonofa—pirate," Uncle Joh said. "I guess he must have. Either that's Rafik, or my old eyes are deceiving me."

"It is!" she said. "Why didn't he say so? You were about to do battle."

"Apparently it was just a lot of boyish posturing on both sides," Captain Bates said, with a pointed look at Uncle Joh. "And Coco doesn't like to admit to doing good deeds. Bad for his reputation. Keeps his name from striking terror into the hearts of people, etc. etc. I suspect your granddad's wife and sisters must belong to an affiliated clan."

"I don't know," Khorii said. "I knew they were from some kind of tribe with ties to Uncle Hafiz's and Grandsire Rafik's culture, but . . ."

"Let's go get some fresh air and say hello, shall we?" Captain Bates suggested.

Unfortunately, by the time they reached the others, reunions had been replaced with verbal firefights.

"The *Mana* is mine." Jaya, emboldened by backup from the other two ships and with her feet on the ground, took the opportunity to challenge Coco. He stood straddle-legged, arms folded across his chest in a stubborn and lordly manner, his braided beard and hair bristling and a well-practiced sneer marking his face. "I was born there, my parents died there, and I almost did, too," Jaya declared.

"It's never too late," Coco told her. "You are a slip of a wench and do not need so much room. My people do. Our ship was destroyed saving this lot—"

He waved his hands at the dazed-looking crowd of Fridans. Elviiz was passing among them, collecting names and identity numbers. This action on his part kept the clanspeople away from the refugees. They didn't want anyone outside their own clans to know their names, and they certainly didn't have ID numbers, or divulge them if they did.

"Which does not entitle you to take my ship," Jaya insisted. She only came as high as his chest, but she looked up at him with her dark eyes blazing. If she had been modified, as Elviiz had, with deployable laser beams in her eyes, Coco would have sizzled and been crisped into a pile of ashes.

"It says on the computer that it belongs to the Krishna-Murti Company," Coco said.

"Which is a wholly owned subsidiary of House Harakamian," Grandsire Rafik said. He had parted from Mother and his first meeting with Ariin to intervene. "The heads of Krishna-Murti unfortunately were on the passenger roster of the *Estrella Blanca* and their bills were not paid, so House Harakamian is the vessel's default owner. Jaya and her crew are our authorized agents. Leave her alone, Captain Coco. Park your people here, and I'm sure in gratitude for our rescue, House Harakamian will be happy to build you a brandnew ship to your exact specifications."

"A new ship?" Coco exclaimed indignantly. "The clans would disown me! My people would hate a new ship! We prefer customizing an existing craft to meet our needs."

Uncle Joh turned to Captain Bates. "You know, I'm starting to like this guy."

"There are thousands of derelicts floating through the galaxy now, adrift since their crews succumbed to the plague. We can help you retool those," Grandsire told Coco. "But the *Mana* is one of the few remaining supply ships. Now more than ever we need her to take provisions to isolated colonies or particularly hard-hit areas."

"We'll be happy to take care of the supplies for you," Coco said with a wolfish grin that showed a lot of gold-enhanced teeth.

"We'll give you all the supplies you want, our gift for your rescue of me and the colony," Grandsire said. "But we need the *Mana*."

Captain Bates spoke up. "We had a deal, Coco. And now you're being offered an even better one. I am clan, and I am Jaya's captain. She and the kids have become my clan."

Sesseli had grabbed her skirt and hugged her legs in greeting. Captain Bates reached down and waggled one of Sesseli's beaded braids at him. "See? Hijack clan, and you'll get a really bad reputation, especially when you've been made an offer any chieftain would give the gold out of his teeth to have." She turned to Rafik. "I'm sure whatever they give you, House Harakamian would be prepared to swear that you stole it or cheated them out of it."

Grandsire nodded.

Captain Coco shrugged magnanimously. "When you put it that way, I accept," he said. "As soon as we are able to 'steal' this vessel from House Harakamian, my people will abandon the *Mana*, leaving only the girl and her kiddie crew aboard. Until then, however, she's ours."

"Jaya?" Grandsire asked.

"I guess so," she said, shooting Coco a grudging glance.

"Coco, an oath on your ancestors," Captain Bates said.

"Asha, you haven't turned out well, have I mentioned that? You have become such an interfering old maid, butting in to betray your own——"

"The oath, Coco," she insisted.

He swore, and Jaya nodded, then stuck her tongue out at him.

Coco snorted and revenged himself on Captain Bates for the insult, saying, "I need to find you a husband." He sighed deeply and changed tacks, turning to Uncle Joh and saying in a distinctly oily tone, "Speaking of House Harakamian, you mentioned a cargo belonging to them that could be found on this world?"

Grandsire narrowed his eyes disapprovingly at Uncle Joh, who shrugged. "That's what the old man told me, but mostly he said he was worried about Rafik here."

Grandsire looked resigned. "I doubt the shipment made it, or survived if it did. We could take one of the shuttles to check on it."

"That would be safest," Uncle Joh agreed. "Less yummy ship stuff to attract a hungry inogre."

"In—what?" both of the other men asked.

Uncle Joh began relating the story of Puss in Boots, enhanced in his own inimitable style, as the three men returned to the *Condor* to board a shuttle.

Mother, Father, and the other Linyaari, including Khaari, had spent the time during the argument healing both clansmen and Fridans injured during the transfer. They also delivered a premature human child born to a young Fridan woman, Melissandra Ortega. Acorna Neeva Melireenya Khaari Ortega was born with birth defects that Mother and Neeva, with her recently acquired knowledge of human physiology, were able to correct.

At Mother's suggestion, Khorii preceded the others to the abandoned log mansion, looking for the blue plague dots. She didn't expect to find any, and she didn't. Once she completed her inspection, she and the other Linyaari helped the Fridans settle in. The clansmen appropriated the lounge and kitchen and camped out there and in the gardens.

Ariin knew she was supposed to be soothing and comforting people, taking care of them, being helpful, but the truth was she didn't actually know how. Nobody had cared for her in any special way for as long as she could remember except for the unicorns, and they used thought-talk and equine body language. It seemed to be necessary to use words with humans, and pat them or put your arms around them or touch them with your horn even if there didn't seem to actually be anything wrong with them. It was very awkward, and she resented it that just because she was a Linyaari, she was supposed to know how to do this stuff automatically.

A horde of ragtag children from the *Black Mariah* were fighting among themselves for the opportunity to slide down a large conference table with many chairs (soon overturned) and several large screens, like the com screens Uncle Hafiz had, except his were on a ball. An office then. One of the smaller kids who kept getting kicked off the table found the vid controls and clicked on a screen. Ariin paused to see what was on it, in case it was more interesting than wandering around looking solicitous toward a bunch of strange humans with whom she felt no connection.

Well-dressed men and women flickered across the screens in a random fashion, but one screen was devoted to a casually dressed male against a background that looked identical to the log-walled room in whose doorway she stood.

The kid flipped the controls so that sometimes the people spoke comically, in reverse, and sometimes different people appeared on the screens. All they did was talk in very serious tones about topics with which she was unfamiliar. Then, as she was turning to leave, she heard someone mention the *Estrella Blanca.* The boy clicked past it, and she entered the room, sending a strong mental push to him to stop. It was so strong that not only did he stop clicking but the kids sliding on the table, fighting under the table and fending off each other with chairs also stopped, staring at her as if she'd hit them.

"Go—" She started to say "go back," then was riveted by the face on one of the screens. "Akasa?"

"What?" the boy with the clicker said.

Ariin had no idea how or why Akasa was on a vid screen in this particular conference room on this particular planet, but she knew it was important. She said not a word to the boy. She wasn't aware of thought-talking to him or pushing him any further, but the room stayed absolutely silent, and the boy wordlessly handed over the control device. She found the symbol for reverse and the symbol to increase the audio output, and returned the screen to the place where Akasa's face first appeared.

Another person, a human male clad in white garments that were not a shipsuit but looked to be of high quality and for formal usage, appeared beside Akasa. He spoke in Spandard, the dialect of Standard spoken on worlds that were heavily influenced by a certain cultural and linguistic group from Terra, the original breeding grounds of all the humans populating the habitable landmasses in this sector of the universe. He introduced her as "La Doña Akasa."

Ariin snorted at the title, though she didn't exactly know what it meant.

Pointing to the remote control, the boy said, "Press 1 for Standard."

She did, and when Akasa spoke, it was in Standard, though that hadn't been the language she'd spoken when Ariin lived in the cell off the laboratory. "I am from a race of superior beings who live on a world not far from yours," she said. "I bring to you, the business leaders of the Solojo system, an unparalleled opportunity to invest in a magnificent venture. It will vastly improve the lives of your people and enrich you greatly."

"We are already rich, Doña Akasa," one of the other screen-framed faces told her. "And several of us, including your host, are pressed for time, as we have a ship to catch within a few hours."

She smiled, confidently, beautifully. "What I have to share

with you is so wonderful it will make you forget all about some silly trip. You'll be dying to stay at home and enjoy all of the variety you could hope for. You see—"

"Your pardon, Madame, but this is an extremely important trip to us all. Its launch initiates the maiden voyage of the *Estrella Blanca,* flagship of our proposed new luxury cruiser fleet."

Akasa said, "Even though this ship of yours can travel from one place to another, she will always look the same. These wonderful homes I am prepared to show you constantly change at the whim of the owner. From castle to cottage to country cabin, the structure, size, color, and apparent materials all alter to suit . . ." She hauled out some vids and began to run through them, but the committee wasn't paying close attention, no doubt distracted by the journey they were about to take.

Good for them, Ariin thought. *Those homes aren't some new invention—those are vids of Kubiilikaan back on Vhiliinyar. She can't sell them those!*

Her host said, "Doña Akasa, perhaps you can provide a live demonstration of this amazing technology—a sample? That way my colleagues could grasp the full importance of your product."

"A sample will be ready soon, but these prototypes clearly show—" She recomposed her face and gave them a dazzling smile. "This trip you are about to undertake. What is its ultimate destination? Perhaps it could make a stop where my prototypes are located so that you could see how marvelous they truly are?"

Her host looked pained. And a bit pale, even against the whiteness of his suit. It was not truly a change in pigmentation, Ariin realized, but a blanching around the eyes, a tightening of the mouth.

"You don't seem to understand," one of the women said

indignantly. "This voyage has been planned for years, and the passenger manifest filled with the cream of Solojo society even before the ship was completed. It is a great—"

Whatever she was about to say was overridden by another man, this one with dark, slicked-back hair and a thin mustache. His eyes looked out as if at Akasa's image. His expression was speculative, and not just regarding Akasa's business deal. It was a look Ariin had seen on Odus's face at times, except that his was somewhat subtler. "I might have room in my party. One of my traveling companions has become indisposed. I would like to see more, Doña Akasa."

"That is wonderful. I have so much more to show you," she said, with a purr worthy of Grimalkin.

chapter 21

The coordinates Odus had provided led Grimalkin to a system just beyond what had been, before the plague, Federation-patrolled space, on the far side of the Solojo system. This reinforced Grimalkin's suspicions that Odus had started the intergalactic infestation as it had first manifested among Solojo's worlds.

Picking a time for his departure had been tricky for Grimalkin. He had been quite busy right up until he was stripped of his crono and shapeshifting capabilities. He wanted a recent-model ship that could travel vast distances through space and required only a single operator. Once Grimalkin deposited Aari back in the cave on Khleevi-ridden Vhiliinyar, he timed it back to the mass exodus from the planet and, disguised as a Linyaari, traveled with Aari's people to narhii-Vhiliinyar. He graciously waited until the transfer of the populace was completed, then stole one of the smaller ships.

Thereafter, it was a race against time. He would find it very awkward if the trip to Odus's new planet took so long it ran into the time after Khorii's birth. He had no wish to be stranded in space as a small kitten.

When he saw the large red, yellow, and blue planet his kind had selected for their new home, and saw their first settlement, he understood why Odus and Akasa had been driven to try to replenish the supply of mutable-dwelling creatures. The new world was, to put it charitably, a fixer-upper.

Grimalkin landed without unintentionally sprouting a tail or pointy ears, though it was a close thing. His former agenda regarding Acorna, Aari, and their children would be catching up with him momentarily.

There was no spaceport, merely a flat place between the group of rather sad-looking buildings and a pretty blue stream. However, technicians still bustled about inspecting this and fueling that. Grimalkin found their presence reassuring.

One female feline-fancying tech saw him and rushed to greet him. "Lord Grimalkin! You've returned to us. We feared you were lost forever."

Grimalkin embraced the woman tenderly. They had had an erotic encounter at one point, and while it was probably more of an exotic erotic encounter for her than for him, he did admire the taste and discernment of those who admired him. Getting his ears scratched was nice, too.

"I'm not that easy to lose, Sona. I urgently need to speak with Odus and Akasa. Do you know where I can find them?"

"Lord Odus hasn't left the laboratory in many days. Lady Akasa is resting in her dwelling."

"What's Odus working on?" Grimalkin asked casually.

"Look around you, lord. Not to be impertinent, but I'm sure you have observed already how much less grand than Kubiilikaan this city is."

"I have noticed that these dwellings never change size, color, or shape. Why is that?"

"They're just ordinary houses, milord. The toffs thought if they left the mutable dwellings behind, they could always get bigger, grander ones, but it didn't work out that way. Lord

Odus has been trying to clone new ones from some window-sills and roofing bits we brought with us, but the shock of separation didn't set well with the creatures. They died on the journey, or at least haven't moved or changed into anything since then. He's still working with the remains, but judging from the way the laboratory quakes with the force of his rages, he doesn't seem to be having much luck."

Odus, Odus, Odus, you never did learn, did you? Grimalkin thought. "Perhaps I can be of assistance," he said. "Which one of these—hovels—is the laboratory?"

"I'll show you, milord."

She led him to two of the low stone huts and threaded her way between them. The once-pristine uniform she wore was mended and patched, but clean. There also seemed to be somewhat more of her and less of the uniform than there had been formerly.

Behind the two huts was a shed that looked to be part of the hull of a large space vessel, its top roofed with more salvaged material.

He found it hard to believe that his race had fallen so low, and what was worse, seemed to be reacting to the situation so passively.

He nodded to Sona, who bowed and left. Opening the door/hatch, he boldly stepped inside.

He stood there for some time before Odus's eyes focused enough to notice him. "Grimalkin?"

"None other. It took me a while, but I found you."

"So it seems," Odus said, and turned back to look at his work.

"The mighty have certainly fallen since moving from Kubiilikaan," Grimalkin said, goading.

"Nonsense, old cat. Temporary campaign headquarters until we can get new dwellings trained."

"It seems to me you could use better building materials, a good architect, and some workers to make plans into homes."

"Where would the fun be in that? The mutable dwellings are perfect. I'm afraid I've been wasting my time trying to be frugal and reuse these old bits and pieces, but there were some annoying insectoid aggressive aliens lurking about, and it hasn't been safe to retrieve new specimens. I understand that threat has been dealt with now, so Akasa and I are about to go on a little jaunt to collect new specimens."

"Odus," Grimalkin said, "that is not a good idea."

"Whyever not? Because it wasn't yours? You're always zipping about the multiverse in a spacecraft. What do you know of the finer points of gracious living?"

"I've seen the Khleevi and what they can do, and I've also seen the future. When you go to collect your specimens, you'll begin an intergalactic plague that will decimate mankind."

"And your point is?"

"Well—don't," Grimalkin said. "It will upset space and time and the multiverse as we know it."

"Don't be silly. Why would I want to do anything to mankind? Actually, I'm considering bringing enough specimens to market to the neighboring systems. They have plenty of lovely things to keep even Akasa happy for a while, and some of them would relish the novelty of the mutable dwellings. To keep the balance of trade on our side, we could accept goods in exchange for dispatching our technicians periodically to maintain, tune, and retrain the dwellings."

"No, no," Grimalkin said, waving his hands. "I tell you it will be a catastrophe, a disaster, a—"

"Oh, stop your caterwauling," Odus said. "Now that you're here, since you've already been to the creatures' world before you may as well come, too. We'll work out some sort of profit-sharing split."

Grimalkin had always been a fast talker, a silver-tongued

trickster, but it only worked when he could get the attention of the person he was trying to con. Odus never paid attention to any ideas that weren't his own. Going on the trip was the best he would be able to do for the moment. Perhaps when Odus saw the condition of the serpent planet, Grimalkin could talk him into leaving. After all, he could talk to him from two directions at the same time, since one of him would be on the *Pircifir* and the other on Odus's ship. He'd never done that before, but that didn't mean he couldn't, did it? Of course, before he could say much of anything, Ariin would turn him back into a cat and that would be awkward, but on the other hand, it might allow the remaining him to be more present. When there were two of him at once, however briefly, both of him were a bit punier than usual. If one of him was a cat, that might allow the larger form more substance, mightn't it? He supposed he'd find out.

He supposed wrong. Akasa entered the laboratory, gave a small, excited squeal when she saw him and a dazzling smile. She certainly was a fine-looking female. She rushed forward and threw her arms around him, as if they were amiably disposed former lovers. Actually, they had been lovers long long ago, and the parting, though not exactly amiable, had at least been accompanied by quite a lot of distance, keeping him safely out of her way until she and Odus had formed their long-standing alliance.

"Grimalkin! It's been so long!" she said. "We thought we had lost you forever. We looked for you everywhere when we moved, but you were off in space somewhere, as usual."

Odus said, "I told her not to fret. 'Bad cats always return,' I told her. And here you are. Dearest, I've invited Grimalkin to accompany us on our dwelling-acquisition mission. He was considerate enough to bring a rather nice recent-model vessel with him, though we'll need a larger one if we're to transport as much cargo as I wish."

"That will be so handy and—'historic,' I believe, is the word the little linearly limited people use—since it was you and dear departed Pircifir who discovered our dwellings originally, was it not? Of course it was."

Grimalkin said, "I can take you to pick up the ship you desire, then I'll lead you there and stand watch while you make your collections."

Odus said, "Our friend has expressed reservations about our mission, dearest. He claims that, as a result of them, some sort of nasty disease will cause a lot of bother to the humanoids. Are you sure the reason you want to fly in a separate craft isn't so you can betray us, old cat?"

Grimalkin hadn't thought of that, though it sounded like something he might have considered. The only problem was that the serpent planet was not in Federation territory, so there were no law enforcement people available there, even if such puny beings would have been able to prevail against two of his kind. "Perish the thought! I want to come so that I can help you make the transfer safely and see that whatever went wrong in the future I've experienced doesn't go wrong this time. It must have been an accident, since you are, for the most part, benevolent and use your powers to help all beings." They nodded at what they judged to be his astute evaluation. He knew that actually, they helped themselves first, and when they did do something for or to other beings, it did not necessarily have anything to do with what those beings wanted. "I was merely thinking that two vessels may be better than one. If the catastrophe that creates the disaster happens sooner rather than later, it might overtake you, and I would be there to rescue you."

"Or in case of our tragic demise and the loss of our ship, you would still have a means of escape?" Akasa asked.

"That, too, of course. One must be practical, even in the face of such tragedy," he replied.

And so they set out, and, because he was in a separate vessel, he avoided meeting himself coming and going. If he still appeared on the *Pircifir* with the children, and if his messages confused Odus and Akasa, they didn't mention it via com. They also time traveled, of course, and were to some degree accustomed to erratic appearances on the part of others. Besides, he had actually indicated he knew what they were going to do, which could only be because he had been there before.

So he took them to Vhiliinyar, where they acquired their ship, then showed them the way to the serpent planet and waited in orbit while they landed. He watched from his ship's com as his fellow Friends saw for themselves how the Khleevi had destroyed and in turn been destroyed. In spite of a brief appearance by the *Pircifir,* which blinked out quickly, presumably when Ariin wrested the crono from him and took them back to the future, Akasa and Odus collected their specimens and left the surface without further incident.

Landing once more at the primitive settlement where his people now lived, Grimalkin watched as the cargo was off-loaded and taken to Odus's laboratory for study.

Grimalkin was an explorer rather than a scientist. His catty curiosity was better satisfied by discovering new worlds and races that lacked only an infusion of his superior genes to climb several rungs up the evolutionary ladder.

But he humbled himself to take the role of Odus's most attentive laboratory assistant, and what Odus wouldn't explain to him, he asked Sona and the other technicians about.

Odus poked and prodded his specimens and found remnants of both serpent and dwelling DNA. "They appear to be different parts of the life cycle of the same being," he told Grimalkin and Akasa. "The dwellings are analogous to the shed skin of serpents of other worlds, except that they retain their own viability—rather like the severed bits of worms.

From specimens of our old dwellings, it is clear that once liberated from the elongated cylindrical form of the serpents, the new forms can and do take any shape desired—or trained into them. Unfortunately, these new specimens were altered by the invading hordes. Whereas the serpents must have tried, with much success, to kill some of the Khleevi, the other life-forms tried to absorb them, blending Khleevi amino acids with their own."

Grimalkin hovered attentively over the specimens, which lay inert and seemingly lifeless on the table.

"However, all is not lost," Odus lectured. "You of all beings know, old cat, that a bit of our own essence can improve other species."

"How in the cosmos do you intend to do that, Odus?" Akasa asked.

"All in good time, my dear. All in good time," Odus said. He coaxed the remaining life in his specimens, nursing it along and studying it.

"The creatures reproduce as snakes," Grimalkin told them. "The first one we encountered was ill because she had attempted to reabsorb her eggs when she was captured. Her effort was not successful, but the fact that she had eggs indicates that even if it has independent life, the tunnel form is only a by-product."

"You mean we have to put up with a lot of snakes writhing around before we can have our nice houses again?" Akasa asked with a little shudder. She liked to be the slinkiest creature in her vicinity. "Whatever will we do with all of them?"

"I don't know," Grimalkin said. "Take them home and help them rebuild, perhaps, or reserve an isolated section of this world as their domain. That would be handy. I have a better idea. Why don't we return to Vhiliinyar and pack up the houses that are already there? We needn't do it all at once, but surely it would be easier and safer than all this." He indicated the piles of specimens filling a slant-roofed annex attached to the laboratory. That wall had been removed to allow easier access.

"Nonsense, old cat," Odus said. "Where's the challenge in that? Where's the thrill of overcoming difficult odds?"

Grimalkin, though he admitted he might have been spending too much time in the company of the Linyaari and humans lately, thought that the oddest thing about the whole situation was Odus and his almost manic desire to do anything the hardest, most complicated way possible.

"The Council felt that Kubiilikaan was our legacy to our progeny," Akasa said. "Some rather important events in their development will occur once they discover Kubiilikaan."

Grimalkin scoffed. "I know. I was prominently involved in many of them, but I recall nothing that would be altered significantly by moving a few of the houses to make us more comfortable. I'll talk to—" he started, before remembering that the Council that convened on Vhiliinyar to banish him and freeze him in small cat form had happened in the past, and some of them might have better memories than others. "You can tell them I said so," he told Akasa.

Odus gave him a look venomous enough to be worthy of the serpents.

"Dearest, the Council also decided to leave our homes on Vhiliinyar because they were growing old. These creatures, as they have been, do die and have to be replaced. I believe there is a way around that, and that we can also circumvent or at least considerably diminish the role the serpent form plays in the life cycle of the form more valuable to us. If I can distill the essence of the serpent form into an easily transmittable nanocrobe that can be hosted by a wide variety of other forms, we won't have to deal with the snake problem."

Grimalkin was shaken from his inner whiskers to his inner tail. This was exactly how the plague began. Odus would not listen to him, and he didn't want to arouse any further hostility. He would have to destroy the research when it was beyond a point where it could be re-created.

However, that proved to be easier in thought than in deed. Odus worked, slept, ate, and even mated in the laboratory with an unusual dedication that was probably spurred by Grimalkin's opposition. He was therefore careful to be at his trickiest, always appearing interested and sometimes incredulous at Odus's results. He found them wholly credible, however, since he had seen their unintended, devastating consequences.

He stuck far closer to Akasa and Odus than he liked, waiting for an opportunity, but to his chagrin saw the experimental specimens grow livelier and livelier.

"At this stage, I wish to infuse them with something of our own vitality and longevity, so that they may be trained once more into appropriate vessels for our illustrious beings."

In Grimalkin's head, he could imagine Ariin saying something extremely rude regarding Odus's illustriousness. But this experiment was now too dangerous to continue. Grimalkin had to stop it, even if he was forced to endanger his own precious hide by doing it openly.

Akasa was saying, "Do you mean to say you intend to mate with one of those things? I don't care for that idea at all."

"Dearest, surely a radiant being such as yourself is not jealous of a mere dwelling?" he teased.

"Don't be ridiculous," she said.

"It needs only a bit of our vitality and longevity to revive as a species—or two species," Odus said. "Now then, excuse me. I have to change."

Grimalkin thought he'd put something in a beaker or in-

ject something with something else. He had not expected
this. Despite all of Odus's fiddling with their composition
and life cycle, the specimens were reviving only slowly from
the sorry state to which their battle to assimilate the Khleevi
had reduced them. In spite of their dangerous alterations, he
couldn't see that they were yet a threat to anyone. But once
infused with some of Odus's potent and all-but-immortal
DNA, they could become—and apparently had become—
much stronger. This was the critical step in their development then. The step that must not take place.

"You're not jealous, too, surely, old cat?" Odus asked.
"You want to change and take the honors as the father of
another new race?"

"Who?" Grimalkin asked, startled out of his plotting. He
had never been all that attracted to things that lacked legs.
"Me . . . ow. Meow?"

Before he could say another world, he shrank to small cat
form. He could make no more arguments to dissuade Odus,
for the cat had truly got his tongue.

Akasa upended him to pick up the crono that had out-
grown his tiny paw until it surrounded three paws and the
tip of his tail. "You won't be needing this. I remember now
why we haven't seen you in a while. The Council exiled you.
Naughty, naughty. It must be time for you to return to Vhiliinyar and be a birthing present."

riin had no idea how to use the information she'd just acquired. Did it mean Akasa was on the doomed ship and dead? It almost certainly meant, since Odus and Akasa had harvested what was left of the serpent planet species and had something to do with the creation of the plague, that Akasa had introduced the plague to Solojo. She looked healthy enough in the vid, but maybe the Friends didn't get sick and die from it but carried it instead, as Mother and Father had done.

Even Ariin's long-held grudge against Akasa and Odus was insufficient to convince her that they would have deliberately wreaked such profound disaster on so many people.

She wasn't used to confiding in people yet or asking for help, but she was the newest telepath in a family of experienced ones. As she walked away from the conference room with the vid screens, Mother, Father, Khorii, and Neeva flooded her mind with inquiries. *"What's wrong?"*

She told them. Then nothing would do but that all of them, including Maak and Elviiz, had to come and view the vid as well. Only Khorii, who had met Akasa, truly understood what it meant.

"I don't remember seeing Akasa among the bodies,"

Khorii told her. "But I didn't see everyone, I didn't know Akasa then, and people do look different when they're dead."

Maak and Elviiz were exchanging data over in a corner behind cupped hands. Elviiz said, "As you know, Khorii, I downloaded the ship's computer's files. However, my memory was almost totally destroyed by the inogres."

"That is true," Maak said. "So it's a good thing that when he recharged after we left the *Estrella Blanca,* I duplicated his memory. It is a sound parenthood principle always to know what one's children are thinking."

Ariin was very glad she was organic and not available to anyone to download. Thought-talk was invasive enough!

"And?" Father asked. "Was this woman on the *Blanca*?"

Maak had taken a moment for inward reflection, at the conclusion of which he nodded, and said, "Affirmative, Aari. For a short time at least."

"What do you mean, 'a short time'?"

"In her log, the captain noted that she was concerned about people attempting to launch their private vessels from the docking bay of the *Blanca*. One vessel registered to a Don Domingo Castillo actually did leave the *Blanca* shortly before the captain arranged the deaths of all passengers and crew to prevent a spread of the contamination she had already noted aboard her ship."

"So I was right. Akasa didn't die, but she did spread the disease to people aboard the ship."

"Not everyone, of course, but enough people to alarm the captain," Maak agreed.

"And apparently the contact she had with the man on the vid and other people she saw in person in this system also led to their becoming ill and transmitting the disease," Khorii said. "Why did she do such a thing? I thought she was rather vain and selfish, but I never got the sense that she was evil."

"The prototypes she showed them are just pictures of structures at Kubiilikaan," Khorii said. "It's the new tunnel creatures we thought might have caused the plague,"

"Obviously, there is still a great deal to learn before we can determine the etiology of this disease system and how best to neutralize it," Mother said.

Not long after their discussion, the *Condor*'s shuttle came whizzing back and set down with a shudder well away from both its mother ship and the other vessels.

"Lost cause," Uncle Joh said. "Hafiz's shipment was a huge load of premium catseye chrysoberyls, but they have made lunch for the monster that almost got the shuttle. Need to make sure none of it clung to the shuttle's hull before we park it on the ship again."

"Serves them right," Ariin said. *"Off chasing riches while we look after the refugees and I gather important information about our mission. Akasa may have been the main one to infect people, but we still need to follow those coordinates and find Odus. Much as I will hate seeing him again, he does seem to be the key to this whole thing."*

Mother replied, *"I couldn't agree more, daughter. If we're to avert further disasters, we need to keep everyone on task."*

From the *Condor* there was a rattle, a swoosh, and another rattle as RK let himself out the *Condor*'s cat door. Rather than wait for the robolift, he leaped from the hatch to the ground, no short distance.

"Good thing for you that Aari, Acorna, and their family are here, cat," Uncle Joh called to the feline first mate, who rested after impact to wash his paws. "You could have broken your legs or your darn fool cat neck with that little stunt, but you knew they were here and could fix you, didn't you?"

Ignoring the captain completely, RK headed for the shuttle, tail in the air, though his footsteps were a bit more careful than usual. Khorii couldn't help herself. That had been quite a landing, and it was a very long way. She scooped the massive brindle-coated cat upside down into her arms while he wriggled, hissed, and growled in an intensely annoyed fashion. RK's fur was so soft, yet his personality was so not. She bent her horn carefully to each paw, then flipped him over and did his spine. "There. Just in case anything was hurt but not badly enough to show right away," she said, stroking his back before he freed himself. But he twined around her ankles twice, purring in thanks, before continuing his mission.

He stalked up to the shuttle, circled it, selected a spot near the hatch, and hunkered down, hissing. Having vented his feelings verbally, he turned his back on the vehicle, lifted his tail, and, with a mighty shaking and quaking, thoroughly sprayed the offending spot.

"You allow your animal to slime your transport?" Coco demanded.

"He probably objects to pirate spoor aboard his personal property," Uncle Joh told him.

RK selected another spot and repeated his marking. It was a heroic display of feline repudiation of alien invasion as the *Condor*'s resolute protector walked the twelve-foot circumference of the vessel, stopping every two steps to back up to the ship and, with mighty quiverings of his stern, rechristen the shuttle again and again as his own. When he had completed the first round of spraying, he turned to face the offending vehicle and attempted to leap atop it. Due mostly to his own exertions, however, the hull had become excessively slippery.

Without warning, the cat flew at Uncle Joh, hitting him in the chest and climbing upward. Uncle Joh swatted him down, growling. "No, RK, I am not going to carry you around and around so you can reach the entire hull."

"If the animal was aboard my ship, he'd be in the messmate's pot by now," Coco said. RK continued growling and looking for a way to reach the shuttle's roof. Uncle Joh was careful to keep himself out of claw range.

"We must have picked up a stowaway when the inogre that ate Hafiz's treasure tried to catch us," Uncle Joh said. RK abruptly sat down and washed his underside, soiled from his exertions to secure the shuttle. Dabbing at his lacerations, Uncle Joh chuckled, and told Coco, "RK is a real stickler for passengers paying their fares, and he doesn't want anybody else damaging his stuff." His flash of humor vanished, and he ran a hand through his thinning hair. "Fraggitall. I just finished upgrading this shuttle, too. Filthy inogres gotta wreck everything."

RK looked up at him as if to say that the ship's cat, at least, was on the job and would have been more thorough still, had the captain not hindered him in the performance of his duties.

"Sorry, old man, good try, but even you don't have enough juice to cover the entire ship, not that it would do any good if you sprayed every panel inside and out."

"We just found this spot," Neeva said. She and the *Balakiire*'s crew stood near their ship, watching the proceedings. "And now your stowaway will grow and endanger the ships and the refugees."

"Nah, I'll space it," Uncle Joh said. Grumbling, "Waste of a perfectly good shuttle . . ." he ducked into the hatch, no doubt meaning to set it into space on autopilot, but RK bolted past him into the vessel.

Uncle Joh said something rude again, then called to Maak, who was walking down the path from the house where, Khorii suspected, he'd been downloading the contents of the computer files. "Stay back, buddy," Uncle Joh warned him. "Our four-legged alien invasion indicator is saying the shuttle is infested with the inogres. You'd be worse off than your boy if they got you."

"Indeed, Captain." Maak halted a prudent distance away from the suspect vehicle.

"Is anybody hailing your chest?" Uncle Joh asked, referring to the com screen Elviiz's father/creator had installed in his own thoracic cavity. "Someone was on the com screen inside the shuttle, but RK slimed it before I could see who, and now I can't make them out. He also shorted out the audio."

Maak unzipped the upper portion of his shipsuit, revealing the screen. An unfamiliar woman was speaking. She had short dark hair, large dark eyes, and was wearing a uniform that Khorii had seen somewhere but couldn't think where. Her words seemed scrambled.

"Tell me it isn't another fraggin' distress call from a long-dead ship," Captain Becker moaned. "Those used to be so much fun, and the inogres have just ruined it. The salvage business will never be the same."

But Ariin said, "No! I know her. She's a tech—one of the Friends' servants who keep things running. Her name is Sona."

They stopped talking to give their full attention to the transmission. It was quickly evident that Sona was speaking to them in real time, not in a looped and generally broadcast distress message.

While Ariin translated what Sona was saying for the others, Sesseli burst out of the mansion and ran across the broad lawn, crying, "Khorii, Khorii, there's a lady on the com in the house, and she's found your kitty!"

"Khiindi?" Khorii asked. "But he's not on Maak's screen, Sess. Where did you see him? Is this the lady?"

"They have a really big screen in the house," Sesseli said. "You can see everything inside. It looks like she's flying one of your peoples' egg ships, everything all rounded and in pretty colors and the controls made for your fingers. But the lady has regular, human-type fingers, and Khiindi is sitting in her lap."

"Will you be still?" Ariin demanded. "She's saying something about 'Lord' Grimalkin and 'Lady' Akasa."

meanwhile, Melireenya had reboarded the *Balakiire*. In a few moments Maak's chest went blank, and he said, "The transmission appears to be over. I'm afraid that I do not have that tongue in my linguistics program."

"I do and I got most of the message," Ariin said. "Although it would have been helpful if certain other people had kept quiet while I was listening. Sona said they are trying to find us—she and Grimalkin."

Uncle Joh whistled. "No wonder RK was having a cat fit," he said.

Melireenya soon rejoined them. "Sona and the cat are on their way," she said. "I provided coordinates. She did not explain her mission except to say that Lady Akasa had sent them."

A Linyaari ship nestled beside the *Balakiire* in the overgrown meadow grass. RK emerged from the shuttle's reeking interior and stalked up to the new intruder.

"Little bugger didn't care about the aliens one way or the other," Uncle Joh said. "He knew Khiindi was on the com—don't ask me how, but he knows this stuff—and was venting his extreme displeasure. Which could mean that the shuttle isn't infested. Good thing I didn't ditch it yet."

"I don't see how you could actually want to ride in it again," Captain Bates said, holding her nose.

"Easy. Maak, shut off your olfactory sensors, scrub down the shuttle, and check it for inogre-type damage. Then, Khorii, honey, if you would be kind enough to purify the air?"

"I'll do it, Joh," Father said. "Khorii should check the newcomer and her cat for signs of plague since they seem to have been in contact with the female who began it all."

"That's command thinking, that is, Aari," Uncle Joh said. "Thanks, buddy."

The Linyaari ship's hatch opened, and the strange female emerged, but not before she had been knocked backward by a catapulting Khiindi headed straight for Khorii.

"Daughter, don't let him touch you," Mother said.

"I could cut him down with my laser," Coco suggested hopefully, taking aim.

"No!" Khorii said, and ran forward to meet Khiindi, who leaped to her shoulder.

"I'm a good shot," Coco said. "I could drop the cat without hurting the girl."

"Since the cat we have nourished as our daughter's beloved pet happens to also be a shapeshifting trickster and fraud who has caused us no end of trouble, you have no idea how tempting that is to a mother, even a Linyaari one," Acorna said.

"No blue dots," Khorii called. "He's not infected." Khiindi pressed his entire furry body hard to the side of her neck, throbbing deeply with rumbling purrs. His claws kneaded her shipsuit shoulder, and a drop of cat drool rolled off his chin and onto hers.

She wiped it away and watched the female, Sona, approach. No blue dots there either. "The pilot is also clean," she called again over her cat-free shoulder.

Sona said, "Lady Akasa spoke to us via com unit, miss. We were not in physical contact with her once we left Odussia."

"Odussia?" Ariin asked, scoffing. The other observers from the field had formed a shallow crescent around Khorii and Sona. RK rode Uncle Joh's shoulder and hissed at Khiindi, who delicately turned on Khorii's shoulder to show RK his fat, fluffy tail.

"That is what Lady Akasa and Lord Odus decided to call the world the illustrious elders chose after leaving Vhiliinyar. I had been commanded to take Lord Grimalkin back to Vhiliinyar to begin his exile frozen in form as your cat, miss. I was also entrusted with Lord Grimalkin's crono and ordered to use it to return to Vhiliinyar of old, just before the exodus of the illustrious elders, and pack up Lady Akasa's old house and bring it to her.

"I fully intended to obey those commands, but not necessarily in that order. Lord Grimalkin has always been gracious and good to me, favoring me with his regard, and I felt that since I had to time travel back before his exile, I owed it to him to revisit his original form.

"Once we arrived there, he requested an additional regression, and I could not deny him. Though I lost track of him for some time, he kept his word and reappeared, returning with me to the time of the exodus.

"I finished compressing milady's house and stowing it aboard the new ship, and traveled forward in time to your birth, miss. Milord shrank and befurred himself and mewed acquiescence to his fate. Already, miss, your infant self was attempting to stroke the small, golden feline that would merge with milord's magnificent gray self as he was forced through that loop of time once more. But before I could put milord out to meet his fate, we received a hail."

"Akasa!" Ariin said, pronouncing the elder's name with accusation in every syllable. Her pupils changed shape, slitting with the depth of her anger. "She told you to find us?"

"Not precisely. She told us to return to Odussia shortly before we'd left, before Lord Grimalkin reentered his bodily exile. We were to use his crono to force Lord Odus forward into the future to see the results of his frivolous research. I have never beheld Lady Akasa in such a state." Her voice shook as she said this. "I am accustomed to seeing her in many guises, but never before have I seen her devoid of beauty or grace."

"What did she look like?" Ariin asked, this time with what Khorii felt was an unhealthy relish.

"Her eyes were sunken in her skull, their color faded and overlaid with milky spots. Her noble brow draped over them, and the skin of her face that was not deeply creased and folded was covered with red-blue lines, broken blood vessels, I suppose. Her flesh hung in wattles beneath her chin. Worst of all, her magnificent mane had been reduced to a few snowy strands poking from her skull. Even the melodious tones of her voice had been altered until it was so cracked I had difficulty understanding her orders." Sona shuddered.

"Why would she turn into an old lady?" Khorii asked aloud, puzzled.

"The disease," Ariin said.

"But she didn't appear altered in the vid," Khorii said.

"That was before she boarded the *Blanca,*" Elviiz reminded Khorii. "Possibly, although she did not immediately exhibit symptoms, as some others did not in the early stages, by the time she had infected those aboard the plague ship, her own energy was too diminished for her to maintain her young and vibrant shape. You have told me how our shapeshifting forebears never appear to age but have been alive while generations of our people have been born, lived their own comparatively long lives, and died. I suspect that their youthful appearance is itself a shape they can assume but that Akasa might have been unable to do so once the disease diminished her vitality."

"The boy's got something there," Uncle Joh said. "I know I sure felt a lot older when I was sick."

"You say this woman told you to go to another world—Odussia?" Mother asked. "How did you come to find us then?"

"We went there, as she said, lady," Sona replied. "But no matter how early we arrived, Lord Grimalkin could not seem to take Lord Odus or any of the others into the future. It was as if time was broken, or at least as if the crono was malfunctioning—even when, in desperation, I borrowed a crono from another elder, the result was the same. It was truly heartrending to behold Lord Grimalkin's efforts. Inevitably, he was prevented from stopping Lord Odus until the time came when he transformed into a cat, and I had to listen to his piteous cries, mewing his failure over and over again across many galaxies."

Khorii shook her head, and said to Ariin, "It must be the way it was with Pircifir. Once one of them dies or perhaps when some profound change happens in their lives, it can't be undone with intervention by crono, just relived."

Ariin smiled rather terribly. "I wonder if turning into an aged hag qualifies as profound in Akasa's case."

Sona said, "We must find Lady Akasa and let her know we've failed. She had intended to return to Vhiliinyar when she traveled with the doomed ship, but after seeing what happened there, and suspecting that she might have been the cause, she dared not return there. So if she still lives and is not still drifting through space in her vessel, she would have returned to Odussia. Even if she cannot recover completely from her illness, we can at least offer her the comfort of her own home. It is still aboard my ship. Even though it was already aboard when Lord Grimalkin and I returned to Odussia, because of the incessant time loop we never had the opportunity to give it to her."

"Certainly we must try to help her," Mother agreed, casting a reproving look at Ariin. "And hope she can help us put an end to the harm she and this Odus have done."

Let me get this straight," Coco said. "You lot plan to return to the planet where you think the plague and these ship-eating beasties were invented?"

"Only Sona, the cat, and the Linyaari will go dirtside," Uncle Joh told him. "Maak and Elviiz and I will stay aboard the *Condor.*"

Coco scratched, then shook his head. "And people say that our clans go looking for trouble . . . well, good luck, in any case, however . . ." he said with a speculative gleam in his eye. "Perhaps we should accompany you as well—after all, it would be a shame if something happened to you, and your ship was just left to drift."

Aari and Khornya practically had to drag Joh, hurling verbal imprecations at Coco the entire way, onto the *Condor,* he was so incensed at the pirate captain's suggestion.

chapter 23

O dussia, red and gold with veins and plains of blue-green, filled the viewscreen of Sona's ship. Khorii's family had transferred from the *Condor* to Sona's Linyaari ship over Uncle Joh's loud objections. Not even he, however, could deny that only the Linyaari were equipped to face the plague—again. However, he gained unexpected allies in the *Balakiire*'s crew, who said that they should be the ones to go instead.

"Khornya and Aari may be weakened by their prior exposure," Aunt Neeva argued. "They could be dooming themselves to permanent isolation."

"On the other hand," Elviiz countered, "although we have no evidence one way or the other, their previous infection may have conferred immunity on them that you do not have. And my sister must be among the first to go, of course, since she is able to detect the plague by sight. Our family has been divided too long already by this thing." He'd looked around at the rest of them with an expression that on a human might have suggested modesty or shyness. "I am new at feeling the emotions of others, and cannot yet thought-talk as freely as the rest of you, but I think I can safely say that I speak for us all in stating that we wish to face this danger together."

"Then we'll go, too," Neeva said.

"Me, too!" Mikaaye said, stepping past Coco to stand with Khorii's family. "I will go with Khorii. Aari is only one male, and Elviiz cannot risk his inorganic parts being destroyed again by the inogres. The females will need another male to protect them."

"You will not!" Coco commanded in an unnecessarily loud voice. "Don't forget, you are still under my command, and besides our own people, we've got the rest of this useless lot, including the crew of my new ship, to take care of. I'm going to need a healer. In fact, I could use more than one."

Melireenya surprised them all by saying softly, "Then let my son do what he thinks he must, and I will remain in his stead."

Aunt Neeva took a general reading of the emotional atmosphere, and said, "Since my sister-daughter and her family wish to go, and Melireenya's son wants to accompany them, Khaari and I will join our shipmate in tending the humans here, at least until such time as we may be needed to assist our friends in the completion of their mission."

"And my first mates and I will take Elviiz—"

"And me!" Grandsire Rafik said. "I'm not letting my daughter and her family face this without going along for backup. Gil, Calum, and Hafiz would skin me alive."

"You're my hostage!" Coco objected. "You think I'm stupid enough to let the head of House Harakamian out of my piratical clutches?"

"You think it will matter if the inogres eat up everything in the universe that has never drawn a breath?" Grandsire asked.

Coco's struggle between his sense of self-preservation and his avarice were clear to Khorii and the other Linyaari. Khorii felt Ariin give the pirate a little push. "Oh, well, it's your funeral," he said, and turned his back and strode to the house.

* * *

Khorii's parents took over piloting duties for Sona, since their hands were better suited to the controls. Staying in constant communication with the *Condor* orbiting Odussia, the Linyaari ship prepared to land in the spot where the Friends' settlement had been.

"The inogres have probably eaten all of the houses now," Ariin speculated. "All of the Friends will have died of the plague, and Akasa will be old and out in the open, exposed to the elements. I wonder if it rains a lot on Odussia? What do you think? The blue-green looks like water."

Khorii rolled her eyes at her sister's persistent *ka*-Linyaari acrimony toward the people who had raised her, after their fashion. They weren't very nice people, it was true, but they hadn't actively mistreated her in the way the child slaves Mother had freed had been mistreated, for instance.

Khorii had spent much of the journey, shortened by Uncle Joh's unconventional navigation techniques, trying to peel Khiindi off the bulkheads and prying his claws loose from everyone's shipsuits and hair. He drove everyone mad racing around and ricocheting off every surface in the ship, yowling loudly all the while. This behavior was not helped by RK's hissing and growling at him from the *Condor*'s com unit whenever Khiindi was on the bridge.

Father said, "When I learned that Grimalkin had been changed into Khiindi, I thought it a great improvement. I am not now so certain of that."

Ariin snickered and patted Father's shoulder in agreement.

Sona said, "The mighty Lord Grimalkin is frustrated by his inability to save us all from the foolishness of the other elders. He has always been the best of them," she added fondly.

"Even I would have to agree with that," Father said. "The others had no more feeling for me than they would have had for a beaker of acid. I'm sorry you had to endure the same treatment, Ariin. The brief encounter your mother had with them was not what I would call warm and nurturing either."

"That is not their way," Sona said. "Still, I shudder to think of seeing them all as I saw Lady Akasa. And I cannot help but wonder what has become of my fellow technicians. Although we are considered a lesser race—"

"By guess who," Ariin put in.

"—our fates are bound to theirs."

As they drew nearer to the landing site, Sona seemed puzzled, then surprised and relieved. "All is well, Lord Grimalkin," she addressed Khiindi. "It is better than when we left. Your fellow elders must surely be in their usual robust health, and it looks as if someone has learned or perhaps recalled something of the building trades in the meantime."

None of the structures in the small city before them changed shapes but reminded Khorii of shorter versions of the time lab. They were mostly rectangular except that the sides met in a peak at the top. This was impressive on the taller structures in Kubiilikaan, but a bit pointless when the buildings were no more than two or three stories. The elders seemed to have picked this site for its resemblance to Kubiilikaan's. As in that city, the main street led down to a vast expanse of water along which there was a broad path. Unlike in Kubiilikaan, this water was roiling and turbulent, foaming as it licked the edges of the path and littered it with seaweed and driftwood. Rocky prominences just offshore rose in wild, water-sculpted forms. Most looked larger than the city's buildings, and one had a huge smooth hole in its middle that was big enough to fly a ship through. Far beyond these was a small mountainous bit of land. From the air, Khorii noted that it was covered in trees and that a haze hung over the central peak, obscuring it.

As there had once been in old Kubiilikaan, a brightly colored pavilion occupied the middle of the cross street leading down from the center of the town, its top billowing in the wind though its flaps were furled on two sides and tied to the stakes that gave it shape. Under the colorful cover another dance floor gleamed. The elders had not stopped enjoying their balls, apparently. The disasters that affected the rest of the universe seemed to have bypassed the very place from which they had originated.

As the ship landed, the audio sensors picked up the deep and sonorous vibrations of what sounded like a gong. People dressed like Sona ran out of several doorways at once. Each of them carried a white, flat object the size of one of Hafiz's platters before him. Or possibly her. Difficult to tell from the uniforms.

They ringed the ship. Over the com unit another uniformed tech, male from the sound of his voice, said, "Unidentified Linyaari vessel, you do not have permission to land nor to disembark. You must leave at once or our enforcement technicians will take appropriate measures."

"This is Sona, Bogan. Your mate's sister Sona. I have returned with Lord Grimalkin in his frozen small cat form, his charge, Khorii, her parents, Khornya and Aari, and her twin once known to us as Narhii, but now called Ariin. Also a young male, Mikaaye, unaffiliated familially to the others but who makes noises indicating he is a prospective mate for Khorii."

Khorii shot a glance at Mikaaye, whose starclad white skin had turned the color of the exotic roses in Uncle Hafiz's garden. The back of her neck suddenly felt warm and her skin tingly. Mate? She wasn't even sure she liked Mikaaye. What had made Sona think such a thing?

Meanwhile, Bogan's face remained stern and unwelcoming. Sona said, "All are free of diseases, but we come at the summons of Lady Akasa. We also wish a word with Lord Odus regarding the scourge he loosed upon the galaxy."

Bogan said, "The Lady Akasa no longer dwells among her fellows."

"Where is she then?" Ariin demanded. "And Odus? Look here, it's all very well for you to protect yourselves, but those two have incredible—" She was going to say "crimes to answer for," but Khorii stopped her with a thought.

"Don't. That's not how to get him to tell us. Push him."

"Right," her sister thought, and her lips curled into a smile worthy of RK before he attacked something. *"Tell us where they are,"* she commanded.

Bogan said. "In her current condition, the Lady Akasa has been deemed unfit to dwell among her fellows. She lives alone on the wooded island a few miles from shore."

"And Odus?" Ariin asked.

"Lord Odus disappeared shortly before Lady Akasa left us, and returned changed. He had been working very hard on his experiments, and perhaps took a vacation among the humans and was, like the lady, damaged. Or perhaps he has taken refuge in a previous time and place and will return to us later. Without the time map that yet remains on Vhiliinyar, it is difficult to keep track of the elders." Khorii wasn't trying to read his thoughts, but his expression told her he was finding it extremely tedious even to try to keep track of them.

"I can well imagine!" Sona said, rolling her eyes sympathetically. "It was hardly an easy task, even with the map. If our mission here wasn't so extremely urgent, Bogan, I'd love to keep chatting. However, I must ask, after Lord Odus disappeared and Lady Akasa departed, what remained of his laboratory?"

"Nothing," Bogan said. "Nothing remained. That is, when the others searched the laboratory after Lady Akasa left, it had been completely emptied. All of Odus's research, the specimens, experiments, and his notes, were gone. The building was destroyed when the new edifices were erected."

"I take it the plague hasn't reached you here?" Khorii said. Of course, she wouldn't know for sure until she had a closer look, but she saw no sparkle of blue dots anywhere.

"Our races have great resistance to diseases, lady, even without the healing powers of your unicorn ancestors. And we have been careful to remain undetected by any who are not our own. That was why we were so startled to see your ship land."

"We'll need to see Akasa," Ariin said. "You won't try to stop us from visiting her island?"

Her tone was as imperious as Akasa's own, but Bogan merely shrugged. "Why not? You could even take her provisions with you and spare the boatman a journey."

All the time they'd been speaking, the so-called enforcement technicians had menaced the ship. But apparently they had a direct line to the com tower because they suddenly relaxed, most of them returned to the buildings from whence they came, and a few returned with bulging cloth bags. Sona went to the hatch and accepted these. As soon as she was seated again, they lifted off. Father took his turn at the controls, flew the versatile Linyaari vessel in low-altitude mode to the island, and set down once more.

Close to the waving fernlike trees, like an oversized exotic flower pod, sat another Linyaari ship, its hull bright with purple flowers, lime green leaves, and wavy aqua lines separated by swags of gold. Sona said, "That is her vessel."

The tech addressed the com unit again, "Lady Akasa, Lord Grimalkin and I have returned. We brought with us your dwelling, which may be of comfort to you now that you live alone."

The screen remained dark, but Akasa's voice, though somewhat quavery, was identifiable as she said, "Take it right back again. I shudder to think that I ever lived inside the treacherous thing."

"That is perfectly understandable," Mother agreed.

"Who is that, Sona?"

"There is a delegation of Linyaari folk here who would speak to you about the plague, lady."

"I do not wish to speak to anyone ever again of anything whatsoever. Go away."

"I fetched Lord Grimalkin, too, though he is still in the form of a small domestic feline."

"Good. Him you can leave. I have use of him. The vermin on this island disturb my sleep."

"No!" Khorii said. "I'm sorry if you're old now and lonely, but you brought it on yourself, infecting everybody with the plague so you could try and sell those moving houses to people. You can't have my Khiindi just to catch your nasty vermin."

"Akasa, I am Ariin," her sister said. "You know me as Nar-hii. I found my family just in time to be separated from them because of your plague. Had it not been for the Linyaari, your disease and its monster children would have destroyed all life and matter in the universe. You owe it to everyone to help us find a way to put an end to your creation once and for all. We're coming out, and you can't stop us."

As Mother murmured, "Manners, Ariin," Captain Becker's voice boomed over the feed from the *Condor*. "Attagirl, Ariin. You tell the old—gal—she's ruined the salvage business, too. If she doesn't cooperate, I'll send RK down there to make things really nasty for her."

It was an empty threat, Khorii knew. Uncle Joh could never part with RK, but she had to smile at the thought of the feline first mate treating Akasa and her belongings as he had the *Condor*'s shuttle.

Before Akasa could speak again, Ariin opened the hatch and hopped to the ground. For once, Khiindi followed her, so Khorii followed him.

"Gently, girls," Mother cautioned them. *"Can you not feel how consumed she is with grief and regret? She did not intend to cause this disaster."*

"She should have been more careful then," Ariin retorted hotly. *"They have always been this way. Act first, and regret it—if they even stop to think about it—later."*

The beach was coarse gravel, though it sparkled in the bright sunlight as if it contained hidden gems. Khiindi raced across it, hopping over tide pools and not even stopping to harass the teeming marine life within them. Clearly Akasa had not brought the plague with her to this place.

Something moved near the forest-docked ship, and the trees and brush shivered. Khiindi raced ahead, Ariin and Khorii pelting behind him. The rough stones didn't bother their hooves, though Khorii was more careful than her sister not to lodge one where it would lame her, however temporarily.

They broke into the woods behind the white flash of the underside of Khiindi's striped tail and caught a glimpse of color before the cat leaped. Ariin was right behind him and threw herself down.

"Leave me be, brat!" Akasa screeched.

Khorii reached them and helped Ariin restrain the struggling elder by embracing Akasa, pinning her arms, then laying her horn among the sparse white strands covering the woman's pink scalp. As she infused calm and healing feelings into that hard old head, Akasa relaxed, and Khiindi threaded himself between Akasa's neck and Khorii's. By that time Mother, Father, Mikaaye, and Sona had arrived. Mother and Father joined their horns to Khorii's, and soon Akasa was so relaxed that she almost fell asleep in their arms.

"Now then," Mother said softly, "why don't you tell us all about it?"

Akasa looked at the faces ringed around her, flinching

only at the hardness in Ariin's. Her eyes looked somewhat clearer and brighter than they had when Khorii first saw her.

"He ignored me!" were her first words. "I'm sorry I even mentioned the dwellings to him. At first he sought the dwelling creatures to please me, and of course for his own comfort, but when they were damaged, he became obsessed with restoring them."

"Yes," Sona said. "Lord Grimalkin and I witnessed that for ourselves. We tried to do as you told us, lady, and take Lord Odus to the future to see the end results of his work, but always Lord Grimalkin changed back into a cat before his arguments were complete, and I could not make the time device do as I wished, though it worked well enough elsewhere."

Akasa moaned. "A few things, once set in motion, cannot be undone. The time line extends only to the past, and even with the crono, there is no future. Or the future that is possible is doleful and doomed."

"As it certainly ought to be for people who murder an entire universe," Ariin said. "Why did you spread the plague? Why didn't you try to warn someone?"

"I didn't intend to," Akasa said, the creases in her face seeming to deepen and her voice shaking. "But I was not accustomed to being neglected and ignored. I tried to pretend it did not concern me and that I would find another consort, so I left him to his experiments and ignored him for three whole days to see how he liked it. I thought he would tire of his tubes and computer codes without someone to admire his handiwork, but when I finally tired of being alone myself and returned to the laboratory to confront him so he could suffer properly from my defection, he was no longer there."

"Where did he go, Akasa?" Ariin asked aloud while pushing with all she was worth mentally.

"I don't know!" Akasa wailed. "He wasn't there, but his work was. I was weary of him spending all of his time on it. Do you know he even tried to mate with one of the dwelling creatures?"

"I was there, lady, just before Lord Grimalkin changed, and we had to leave," Sona said. "I can understand how insulted you must have been."

"It didn't work, you know. Those things don't reproduce at that stage. So he found a way to blend some of his essence with the earlier stage of the creature, the one he had created to substitute for the serpent phase of the development. Before I stopped going to see him, he told me all about it and showed me slides with this creature on it and described what it was supposed to be, though frankly, I couldn't see it. I took his word for it. I have always been far more interested in behavioral sciences, as you know, Narhii, than in all of those test tubes and mathematical codes and things.

"When I found Odus gone, I decided that I would go, too. I had long ago wearied of this rustic new homeworld. I wished to return to the past on Vhiliinyar, before all of you were created, when Odus and I were happy and comfortable and everything was pretty. But such journeys, even when one has a ship to command, are costly. One needs provisions, fuel, and a few trinkets to exchange with the natives one meets along the way. So I took the holos and video representations of our homes on Vhiliinyar and his precious slides and a few vials from which they had been extracted. I did not wish to be interfered with by Odus, so I set my crono for several years in the future and flew to the planet in the Solojo system I knew to be the place he planned to interest in the creatures.

"I had no trouble convincing some quite influential and wealthy human males that I had a product that would benefit them, and after my demonstration, one was so impressed that he invited me on what was meant to be a luxury cruise. Only something went horribly wrong. First my host sickened, then all of his servants, then other people with whom he came in contact. It was messy, and smelled. I found it offensive. And then a few people died, and the trip was simply no fun any longer. By that time the ship had traveled far enough toward our own home quadrant that I could reach Vhiliinyar without further resources. I took back the things I had sold to my dead host, who certainly had no use for them, returned to my ship, and managed to escape from the docking bay just before the captain locked it down. I monitored the ship for a time. The captain was maddened by my enterprising exit from so much illness and chaos. She refused to allow anyone else to leave and in the end I fear—I very much fear—she caused their deaths."

"She did," Khorii said.

As Akasa had been speaking, Mother and Father had pulled up ferns to make a backrest for her against a tree. Sona took a packet from her shipsuit pocket that became a self-heating cup of a restorative drink and offered it to the elder. Khorii had to steady Akasa's hand as she held the drink, for it trembled as with a palsy.

"I thought it was shock making me feel unwell," Akasa said. "I do not actually recall having felt unwell prior to that although while aboard the cruiser I was not my usual ebullient self. I attributed that to the lackluster quality of my companions. However, particularly after I returned with Odus's materials to the confines of the much smaller ship, I felt increasingly ill, drained, diminished, and I found it harder and harder to maintain the routines that have always helped me look my best. I found I could not shift forms either. Then I picked up other signals concerning a terrible plague, believed to have started on the planet I visited, and I began to suspect the truth. I knew I could not return to Vhiliinyar, lest

I bring disaster there, too. That was when I contacted you, Sona. I did not know who else to turn to. As time wore on, I was reduced to the form you behold.

"Feeble and alone at last, I had no choice but to return here, but I deliberately chose this island for my landing, lest I be infected."

"You are not infected," Khorii told her, because there were no blue dots dancing around her. "Possibly you were, but your strong constitution threw off the plague, though at the cost of your youthful appearance. Maybe as you get stronger you'll start looking more like your old self again." She had no idea if this was true, but felt the old female needed a bit of hope right then. Even self-centered Akasa had finally realized at least a portion of the enormity of what she had done and was suffering as much as she was capable of suffering on behalf of others.

"Do you really think so, Narhii?" she asked, even though Ariin was there, too.

Khorii didn't correct her.

Sona said, "Lady, we came to see if you could help us find Lord Odus so he might suggest a way to destroy this creation of his. It is not, as you know, what he intended."

"I cannot help you. I spaced the materials I took from his laboratory, even the visual and holographic depictions of our homes on Vhiliinyar. I shall never be happy and whole again!"

And she began sobbing in earnest self-pity.

"You take the ship," Sona told the Linyaari. "I will remain with her and care for her until she is well enough to rejoin the others. She does look better already, thanks to your healing."

As the rest of the group left, Khorii's heart sank. Now they were back to square one, with no idea how to find the one person who might be able to help them.

chapter 24

"Two of you started this mess," Ariin harangued the elder Ancestral Friends. "Now the rest of you have to put a stop to it."

Khorii thought her twin's righteous wrath more than made up for two planets full of pacifistic Linyaari. The elders, via Bogan on the com, had wanted to refuse the second landing of Sona's vessel near their city. They thought the gentle Linyaari they seemed to consider their somewhat feebleminded offspring would acquiesce to the order and go away. They had obviously mistaken Khorii's family, her human-reared mother, her heroic father, who had endured Khleevi torture and lived, and even Mikaaye, the volunteer pirate, for what they considered the usual sort of Linyaari. Even Khorii, who had the most conventional upbringing of them all, had witnessed so much death and illness in her attempts to save the Federation-controlled sector of space that she had little sympathy and no respect remaining for the elders' finer sensibilities and what she considered to be their outright cowardice.

Her race had always held these people in awe because the legend was that they had saved the unicorn Ancestors. Now that she knew the truth behind that story, and how miserably these arrogant people had treated her sister as a helpless, ignorant child, Khorii's awe was over. And then there was Khiindi/Grimalkin, a trickster and untrustworthy at times, perhaps, but nevertheless in her opinion the best of his race and one who had been punished for trying to spare her and her family, even if it had been at Ariin's expense.

When the refusal came from Bogan, it was Mikaaye who best expressed the attitude of his shipmates. "Arrrgh, then, me fine fellow. Prepare to be boarded," he said, though it came out somewhat differently in his Linyaari accent. Father laughed, and Mikaaye said defensively, "Well, it's the traditional thing to say. Captain Coco taught me himself."

Ariin was the first out the hatch. When the enforcement techs surrounded her with shields, she looked each of them in the eyes, and said, "Makawe, Tika, Ano. Shame on you. You are the ones who have all of the real knowledge and do all of the work. How could you just sit here with these preening buffoons while they allowed the universe to die around them without lifting a finger?"

Tika lowered her shield. "Frankly, Narhii, when some of us heard of the plague and realized what Lord Odus and Lady Akasa had done, we thought we were doing the universe a service by keeping our elders from harming it any more than they already had."

Father, just behind Ariin, thought, *"That sounds like a reasonable course of action to me."*

Ariin gave a mental push hard enough to send the techs scrambling from the path of the Linyaari delegation and stalked ahead.

It took Mother to make something useful from Ariin's aggression. "Excuse me," she said sweetly to the one Ariin had addressed as Tika. "Could you tell me where we might locate the Council of Elders or someone who can call them together to speak with us? It's rather urgent. A matter of life and death actually."

Meanwhile, Ariin was giving everyone a headache with her incessant demands that the Council convene immediately.

Tika answered a personal com device, and said, with a courtly wave of her hand, "This way, honored offspring. The Council has agreed to grant you an audience."

The Council looked very august and imposing, seated as they were in a collection of ornately crafted massive chairs along the curving inner wall on the top story of the tallest building in the city. A moving ramp like the one Khorii remembered in the time device building spiraled up from the ground floor, carrying the Linyaari into the presence of the frowning elders.

Ariin bared her teeth at them in an expression that humans would consider a friendly grin, but Linyaari considered overtly hostile.

"What is it, Narhii?" the senior elder demanded. "You have chosen an inopportune time to return, if you wish to dwell with us again, and your family has not been invited."

Now it was Mother who bared her teeth. "You know very well why we've come, you—you plague-spreading kidnappers. And for your information, I would not allow any of you to come near my children or any of my family if the circumstances were not so very dire."

Father said, "You have the only uninfested planet in this sector, and you have scientists and laboratory facilities. You must help us find a way to—ah—neutralize the harm your people have done."

"We really cannot help you," said one of the females, clad in gilt robes embroidered with jewels. "Lord Odus acted independently, and he was among our more brilliant scientific minds."

"I don't believe that for a moment," Ariin said. "And anyway, what we need most from you is a lab and supplies. Our brother Elviiz and his other father Maak are more brilliant than all of you put together, even though one of the nasty creatures created by your arrogance almost killed Elviiz. But we need help now, and you owe it to us and all of your other victims."

They mumbled among themselves, shaking heads, throwing up hands, then nodding. In the end, a hawk-nosed male regarded them all with an expression Khorii had difficulty deciphering. "Finally," he said. "An offspring who takes after our side of the gene pool. Very well. But under no circumstances do you bring samples of that disease or those creatures here, nor will any of us leave, nor will you disclose our location or presence to any other beings whatsoever."

"Sure," Ariin said, "Except for Captain Becker and the crew of the *Condor,* including Elviiz and Maak."

"Shall we instruct them to land now?" Mother asked with her sweetest expression. "Orbiting can be so tiresome."

We've been talking this over," Uncle Joh said when he and the *Condor*'s crew had joined them. "And I think we've come up with a battle plan—I mean a cure, begging your pacifist pardon, princess," he added, apologizing to Mother.

The crews of both ships except for Khiindi and RK stood on the single floor of a huge hangar building where, at one end, a new time device was under construction. Techs set up equipment on long tables, including the computers Maak and Elviiz would not need, since their internal ones were more sophisticated than most unincorporated models, and Maak updated both of them often. Other techs and two of the elder scientists looked on expectantly.

"Come over here, you guys." Uncle Joh beckoned to them. "You should hear this, too." When his audience had assembled to suit him, he continued. "The thing is, we know from the trip Elviiz and the girls made and what the old lady told you—little Sona reported it all by com—that one thing that turned this—organism—mean is that they were attacked by and apparently absorbed some of the more charming qualities of our old pals, the Khleevi. Namely a bad attitude and a big appetite. We already know how to kill Khleevi, so why don't we just zap these inogres with the same sap we used before?"

"Could it possibly be that easy?" Mother wondered aloud. "The sap destroyed the carapace, and these creatures have no carapace to destroy."

"Yes, Khornya," Maak said. "But the sap also set up a virulent infection in each Khleevi on a cellular level."

"It is worth a try," Father said. "You know the sap-gathering procedure, Joh, as do Neeva and the *Balakiire*'s crew."

"Right," Uncle Joh said. "I will gather the plant botherers."

One of the techs said, "Then you may not need this facility after all?"

But Mother responded reasonably, "The sap-producing plants cover one area of a rather small planet. They produce the sap only under extreme stress. The creatures we wish to—neutralize—now cover much of many populated worlds. We will need to synthesize the sap to produce the necessary quantities."

The hawk-nosed man, whom Ariin identified to the others as Hora, had been following their conversation, and now said, "If you do not need the facilities now, you will have to come back when you have something for us to work on. We cannot tie up valuable resources—"

"And we cannot afford to waste any more time," Ariin cut in.

"Of course, we understand that time is of the essence," Hora continued smoothly. "Therefore, those of you who stay here as well as our people must be able to concentrate. You may remain and await the return of this man and his ship if he takes the female younglings with him."

"Oh, yes, you'd like that, wouldn't you?" Ariin challenged, but Father said, *"Daughter, go with your sister. Captain Becker may require your assistance since he is loaning us Maak's services. And since one gathers sap from the plants by irritating them and making them feel threatened, I believe that you, Ariin, may prove invaluable on that portion of the mission."*

Father's faith in Ariin's ability to annoy the plants was fully justified. Mikaaye decided that in case his extra male brawn was needed to compensate for the lack of Maak's, he would leave with them on the *Condor.* Of course, Grandsire Rafik was also aboard the ship, where he had remained while Maak and Elviiz went ashore with Uncle Joh.

Khorii gave him a hug when she came aboard. "I'm glad you're here," she said.

"Someone had to keep the cats from killing each other," he said. "And I feared my presence in an already tricky negotiation would complicate matters further. As it was, Maak let me know what was going on by keeping the channel on his personal com to the ship open. You did fine, by the way."

Rafik put his hand on Ariin's shoulder. She was brooding a bit at Father's suggestion that she was irritating. "You, my dear, are a jewel beyond price. You brought those stuffed shirts to the table, so to speak, and made them relinquish what you wanted. You really must spend more time with your uncle Hafiz. He could help you refine your talents and make good use of them."

Ariin brightened at his compliments, and said, "I would like to spend more time with my new uncle when all of this is over."

Khorii had heard the story of the first sap-gathering to defeat the Khleevi, and asked, "Now we'll have to gather more of our people to collect the sap?"

"We could stop and try to talk Coco into loaning us the *Balakiire* and crew," Uncle Joh said. "But then we'd have to argue with him about whether or not there was treasure involved."

Grandsire said, "Acorna was right, of course, in that no matter how many people we have aggravating the sap out of the plants, it will have to be synthesized in order to have enough. So why don't we keep our mission among ourselves and gather a sample big enough to ki"—he glanced at his granddaughters and Mikaaye—"test on one of the creatures?"

The others could see no problem with this plan. Using all of the navigational tricks in his arsenal, Uncle Joh took them to the planet where long ago the *Condor*'s crew and Mother and Father had gone to answer a distress call from a Linyaari ally. There they had accidentally discovered the plants whose sap destroyed the carapaces of the insectoid Khleevi, thereby, to make a long story short, saving the entire universe, at least for the first time.

Khorii and Mikaaye sang the song to Ariin, the one Mother and the others had used to get the cooperation of the plants. "Move gently, open wide" was all the first part of the song consisted of, but it was necessary to have the right attitude to go with the thought-words, and it took Ariin a while to calm down enough to grasp that. The next part was more complicated. "Close up, gather together, twining, tangling, plaiting."

Mother and Father kept in touch with the ship via Maak's com. When Ariin proudly sang the song for her, Mother said, "You won't need that last bit quite so much. We used that to teach the vine people to capture the Khleevi, but we don't want them to capture you. You do need to explain to them why you want sap though, and they understand smells better than sound. We finally gave them the smell of Khleevi, and they understood that and produced plenty of sap."

"We should try that again, then, perhaps," Khorii said. "We can't bring the smell of the disease or the inogres to them without risking infecting them too—though the inogres wouldn't bother them, I suppose, since they only eat inorganic things."

"Why can't the vines talk Standard like everybody else?" Uncle Joh complained. "We don't have time to go making another trip back to that place they came from to get Khleevi spoor."

"There's probably some left on Rushima, Joh, from the battle there," Father said.

"Got it," Uncle Joh said.

Collecting the spoor was tricky. It was buried at some distance from the town of Bug Gulch, but inogres oozed up and down the ravaged streets, and the faces of the people Khorii saw were frightened and looked as if they'd been that way for a long time. She wished there was time to go see Moonmay and their other friends, or even get some tips from the spectral community that routinely haunted their living counterparts on Rushima, but once they had the stinky Khleevi relic, they had to leave quickly before the *Condor* became another morsel for the inogres to devour.

"It's the most horrible smell ever!" Ariin complained.

"Don't worry," Uncle Joh said. "We can leave it for the vine people to destroy once we get the sap."

Khorii had been told that the vine world was beautiful, but her first sight of it made her catch her breath. Climbing, trailing, twisting ropes burgeoning with multicolored blossoms exhaled sweet fragrances into her nostrils, creating a beautiful patchwork of greenery dotted with exotic flowers that stretched as far as she could see.

It took the growls of the cats from the hatchway behind her to remind her that these lovely plants were also dangerous and deadly.

They thought the first part of the song at the plants, and, amazingly, the vines remembered and responded, making room around the *Condor* and its landing party.

Mother had said, "These are sentient beings, sapient beings. Treat them with respect for their intelligence, and they may reward you by making your task easier this time than ours was before."

When Uncle Joh brought out the containers, it took only a single whiff of the Khleevi spoor before the blossoms changed color, the perfume turned acrid and stinging, and cherry amber sap began rolling down the stems of the plants. They had to keep thinking the "Move gently, open wide" part to get the vines to allow them to walk among them and collect the sap they needed.

Since the smell was part of the vines' gift, the Linyaari horns didn't do much to dissipate it, and they could scarcely wait to return to the ship.

"I thought I was going to choke to death from the stink!" Ariin complained. "It made the Khleevi sample smell almost good by comparison."

"Smelled worse than my shipmates when I first joined them," Mikaaye agreed.

"There's a saying among human healers that if a cure isn't painful or distasteful, it isn't any good," Grandsire Rafik said. "With a smell like that, the sap should cure anything."

"It doesn't have to," Uncle Joh said, with a bloodthirsty glint in his eye. "All we want it to do is kill that salvage-spoiling son-of-a-pox." They capped and packed the last of the containers, and he added, "Okay, we've got some annointin' to do. Where shall we start?"

"Corazon," Khorii said. "That is a huge monster, so we can see how much of it the sap kills. Maybe if it dies altogether, Jalonzo and Abuelita can go back and gather whatever food they left behind before it attacked."

"Corazon it is," Uncle Joh said. "It's handy to the big-shot planet, too, where the lab is."

Once there, the *Condor* flew over the monster as low as it could while still dodging tentacles and dropped a payload of sap onto it where it had begun to stretch out into the field.

"Take that!" Uncle Joh said vindictively, after dropping three sap-centered torpedoes into the thing. He dusted his hands together to signify a completed mission, but the inogre did not appear to be dead or significantly changed by the sap.

"Maybe it has to eat through the shell first," Mikaaye suggested.

"I know!" Ariin said. "We should use the crono and go back in time to when the thing was smaller. Maybe then a little sap would do it more harm."

"Maybe later, kiddo, when we've decided what works. For now I think we should stop screwing around with time and try to come up with something that kills—I mean, puts these things on a reducing diet—once and for all."

Khorii looked at the screen, which still showed where the torpedoes had disappeared into the sludgy brown surface. "We can't tell much from up here. I would like to get closer and see if our gift has altered it at all."

"No way!" Uncle Joh said.

"You can't get that close to one of those things," Grandsire Rafik told her.

"It's perfectly safe," Ariin replied. "We did it with the one eating the *Estrella Blanca*—" She started to say more about the location, but Uncle Joh gave her a look. The *Blanca* had been docked on his secret asteroid. By now probably all of his most special salvage had been absorbed into the inogre.

"It only likes inorganic food, and if we go bootless, we'll be fine," Khorii agreed.

The *Condor* set them down in the field near their friends, who watched anxiously as the girls and Mikaaye approached the monster. The undulations that might have signified its respiration or circulation as well as attempts at locomotion swelled and folded in the great gray-brown expanse so that it resembled a sea of mud.

"I hate to say it, but for one of these things, it looks perfectly healthy to me," Mikaaye said.

Khorii noticed that the extension of the creature that had been confined to the road had now puddled over surrounding grass.

"It's not supposed to do that, is it?" Ariin asked, poking at the creature. It lifted, and Khorii gasped. Between the underbelly of the creature and the grass was a sea of tiny, sparkling red dots.

"Come away," she told the other two urgently. "Come away now. And Ariin, hold still while Mikaaye and I go over you with our horns. And we must warn everyone to stay as far away from here as possible."

"Why?"

Khorii wasn't surprised at the question, since she was the only one who could see the blue dots indicating the plague. "There were red dots underneath it. I hope I'm wrong, but I think it might be incubating a mutant strain of the plague."

chapter 25

Hhorii told their friends first, Abuelita, Jalonzo, and the throng of children and elders that were all that remained of the population of the once-thriving city of Corazon and the surrounding countryside. She spoke to them from a distance, for safety's sake, warning the humans not to approach the edge of the monster and that they needed to move their encampment as far from it as they could. Still, she saw the lines in Abuelita's kind face deepen and a bleakness come into her eyes. Some of the people reflexively crossed themselves in remembrance of old religious beliefs from Terran times.

"Are we lost then, after all?" one boy asked her. "Will it all be over soon?"

"Not if we can help it," she said, that being all the assurance she could offer.

Then she joined the others in the ship, where Uncle Joh and Grandsire Rafik were already engaging com relays as far as they could reach into populated areas all over the galaxy, warning people of the new threat and asking them to report new illnesses or changes of any sort in the voracious creatures devouring their homes as the plague had already devoured their families.

Khorii felt ill in a way that she knew had nothing to do with the red dots. They had all fought so hard to try to rescue people and help them get on with their lives, despite the grief and pain they'd already been through. And now it began to look as if it was all for naught.

Grandsire Rafik pulled her into a hug. "It will be okay, little one. Hafiz is already telling your people to prepare to return and help us through another one if necessary."

"They may not be able to help," she said. "This is a different strain, I can tell by the indicators. What if we can't find a way to stop it?"

Khiindi inserted his hard, furry head under her limp hand and forced her to pet him.

The sap didn't work," Uncle Joh said.

"We think that may be because it is an organic substance, Joh," Father said. "Once we synthesize it so it is wholly inorganic, if may be better absorbed by the creature and have greater effect."

They all stood in the hangarlike building while the sap was decanted and examined by the techs and elder scientists.

"Also, Odus used a viral vector to give the proteins he simulated from the serpent creatures the ability to infect different species and serve as a reproductive base for the creatures," Hora said. He looked less arrogant and slightly more anxious about the problem than he had before.

"Why the frag didn't you stop him from doing a fool thing like that?" Uncle Joh demanded.

Hora shrugged. "We did not wish to be forced to deal with all of those serpents. Odus seemed to know what he was doing."

"Well, you found out that was a crock, didn't you?" Uncle Joh said. Even his usual energy had been replaced by a tone of bitter regret.

"We have been constructing an antiviral agent, a salt," Father said. "A mineral rather than biological form. With the synthesized sap, it may be able to stop the creatures from spreading."

"The problem is the way they're changing," Khorii said. "The very thing that made Odus and Akasa want them to begin with is letting them create this new form. It's starting the life cycle over again according to the way Odus set it up, and who knows whether your salts will kill everything it can become?"

"Odus did say he was going to impart some of his own vigor to the thing," one of the female scientists said in a maddeningly admiring tone.

Although it seemed to take forever for the new formula to be synthesized in sufficient quantities to use on the massive monster covering the remains of Corazon, in truth the process was far shorter than it would have been anywhere else in the universe. The scientist Friends might not have been very clever about blending themselves with the Ancestors, and they might have been downright dangerous trying to mutate another life-form, but, fortunately, making formulas to kill things was something at which they excelled.

When the *Condor* released its first "feeding tubes," as Uncle Joh had dubbed his sap-and-antiviral-salt-cocktail-filled torpedoes, they watched breathlessly on the new telescopic zoom the captain had hooked up to one of the com screens.

Three metal tubes hit the sludge, were sucked in, then exploded, which they knew because the sludge suddenly expanded with a globby splash that made more ripples in it than usual.

They cheered and hugged each other as first darker places, then definite holes, appeared in the mass, spreading and deepening until they could see broken tree trunks and strips of dirt that had previously been covered. The three holes widened and deepened until they connected.

Khorii, Ariin, and Mikaaye jumped up and down, hugging each other so hard it hurt, and Ariin was pushing in a most *ka*-Linyaari fashion. *"Die, murderous monster, die."*

Grandsire Rafik watched the screen with a veiled, neutral expression that reminded Khorii of Uncle Hafiz about to close a business deal, but his posture was so watchful that had he a tail, he would have looked like RK or Khiindi stalking prey.

In fact, RK and Khiindi sat, for once not fighting with each other, on the backs of the command chairs, crouched and tails lashing, whiskers twitching, ears pricked forward as if waiting to hear cries of distress from the miles of monster before they pounced on it to finish it off.

Then the sludge seeped back over the strips of dirt separating it from the tree trunks and began creeping over the trunks from another direction. In a separate area, a wooden fence exposed by the second hole was slowly covered and gradually, although there was an unmistakable dip in the surface of the creature, the hole refilled itself.

The *Condor* retreated; the crew's collective moan of dismay, both heartfelt and verbalized, was so loud the people huddled in the fields below might have heard it.

Is that all you got?" Captain Becker asked when the *Condor* had landed on Odussia and all of the crew, even the cats, had joined Mother, Father, Elviiz, and Maak in the hangarlike laboratory. The elder scientists shrugged.

"It didn't work?" Mother asked.

"Almost, but not good enough," Uncle Joh told her. "I think we hurt it, but it healed itself while we flew over it waiting for it to die."

"It's that vigor of Odus's," the female scientist said with

what, on a less-august being, might have been a giggle.

The hawk-nosed elder took off his lab robe and flung it to one side for a tech to pick up. "Well then, I think even Narhii can see that we've done the best we can, and everything you asked, to undo this thing. But as Nasia said, Odus was behind this, purely with the best intentions and, as usual, ended up doing things entirely too thoroughly. Now if you'll excuse us, we have a ball to prepare for this evening."

Ariin gave Khorii a look that said, as clearly as thought-talk, "you see what these people are like now."

The adults were all clearly thinking the same thing, but also felt it was futile trying to get any further concessions out of such callous beings.

Khorii could think of one more thing she wanted, however. "You're just going to run off and say, 'oops, too bad about humanity. Sorry, but we have to go to a dance'? You know, the only good thing I can think of that any of you did was to give me my cat, Khiindi, and even he came to me because you punished one of your own for being better than the rest. Maybe you can never ever make up for this plague, but the least you could do is turn Khiindi back into Grimalkin. Maybe he could find a way to help us if he had his original powers back because at least he cares."

"An interesting viewpoint," Hora said. "But this sort of thing—when one of us is killed or altered in a profound way—cannot be undone. I see that you have illegally obtained a crono from somewhere. I suggest that all of you return to an earlier, happier time for your race and allow Grimalkin to return to the time before he became entangled with your family. He can be himself then. In this time, however, he will live out a feline lifetime and go the way of mortal flesh. That will release him from cat form though what he'll become after that I really couldn't say. His case is unique."

He began walking away. One of the techs said, indicating rows and rows of gourdlike containers, "What shall we do with all this if it doesn't work, milord?"

"Load it aboard the *Condor*," Uncle Joh said. "Maybe we can't kill that big beastie with it, but it might make more of an impression on some of the smaller critters. It's worth a try at least."

He shot a look at the backs of the retreating lords and ladies that should have done to them what the sap bombs tended to do to the creatures. But they were oblivious, and Hora just waved his hand in assent.

The last of the containers had been sealed in the cargo hold when the com unit came on.

Khorii cringed, fearing it was word from some of their friends that more people had fallen ill to the new strain of plague.

But it was only Sona.

"We saw you land," Sona said. "How went the mission?"

Mother, in the copilot's seat, gave her the dismal news.

"I'm very sad to hear that," she said. "However, since you're here, Lady Akasa would like you to return to her island and give her another treatment with your horns. She is much improved since your last show of solicitude and hopes that if you give her more of the same, she might even feel well enough to rejoin her fellows, perhaps in time to attend the upcoming ball."

Mother gave an uncharacteristic low growl. *"And to think I used to like dancing,"* she told the family and Mikaaye. But to Sona she said, *"I suppose we could, especially if she has no objection to us telling her what we did and perhaps trying to think of any further lines of action we could pursue."*

Sona smiled. "She might object privately to me, but she'll do it. Her hair has grown back since you were here, and her skin is smoother."

"We do not promise to be able to restore youth," Mother warned.

"The elders are a special race with unusual vi—"

"Don't tell me. Vitality, vigor, and longevity." Mother sighed, and said sweetly, "We'll do what we can, and if she thinks it helps her, then that fact alone may make her feel better."

They flew back to the island and landed on the beach.

"Look there," Ariin said, pointing to a familiar edifice rising almost as tall as the ship and spreading across the entrance to the woods, its windows shining, its sills and door-frame gleaming with bright colors. "Looks like she changed her mind about her house."

But that was not exactly the case.

Sona met them outside the hatch of Akasa's purloined Linyaari vessel. "Akasa is inside," she said.

"Isn't the house ready yet?" Ariin asked.

"She still refuses to live in it, but if I am not to have my own ship or the companionship of my own kind, I decided I would like somewhere comfortable to live instead, so I am going to tailor it to my own taste. It isn't one of the diseased ones, after all."

She looked at the delegation. Uncle Joh, Grandsire, the two cats, and five Linyaari.

"It may be a bit cramped in there. Perhaps the humans, the created humans, and the cats could wait in my house? I've prepared refreshments for all species, hoping to see you again. Though truly, I hoped you'd be leaving because your mission was a success."

"That makes—one, two, three, four, five—nine of us," Uncle Joh said. "Counting the cats."

Khorii entered with the others and greeted Akasa, who did indeed look better. Her white hair was now wavy and shining, and her skin was less lined, her eyes brighter. Recalling the group of her own friends huddled and frightened in the field outside Corazon, Khorii found she couldn't enjoy the effects of her healing on this arrogant woman who had been so instrumental in causing the death and suffering of others.

Nor did she have the inclination to challenge her, as Ariin did. And, in the confines of the ship, there wasn't room for five horns to—well, horn in closely enough to do healing.

"Excuse me. I am suddenly famished," she murmured aloud for Sona's and Akasa's sake rather than her family's. "I think I'll go out and graze for a while."

She didn't really want to graze, but she didn't want to go inside the mutable dwelling either.

As it turned out, she didn't have to. Khiindi came flying out of the door with RK and Elviiz hot on his tail. "Khiindi, bad cat!" Elviiz scolded. "Stealing is antisocial behavior."

"Leave him alone, Elviiz," Khorii said crossly, and knelt to pick up the former elder who would always be her kitty now. He had something short, cylindrical, and metallic clenched carefully in his jaws. The moment she opened her palm he uncharacteristically opened his mouth and dropped the item.

"Hmmm," she said, turning it over. Khiindi growled a warning. "I don't think this is just some shiny object he decided to pilfer. Look at him. His ears are back, and all the fur along his spine is bristling, and his tail is fluffed. And he isn't even looking at RK. Whatever it is, this thing is dangerous."

aak was about to take Khindii's shiny prey from Khorii when the ship's hatch opened and Ariin emerged, followed by Mother and Sona. Father and Mikaaye supported a wobbly but ambulatory Akasa between them.

"Khiindi found something in Akasa's old house," Khorii told her family and Mikaaye. *"He seems to think it is dangerous, but he wanted me to have it. I think maybe it is his Grimalkin self that took the thing instead of just Khiindi playing with a shiny object."*

"Show me," her parents said together.

Khiindi continued to growl and bristle as Khorii carried it to them and at an urgent hiss from the cat, she laid the thing gently into her father's outstretched hand. His other arm and hand were taken up with Akasa, who saw the thing and frowned. "I haven't seen that in a while," she said in a voice close to her old one. "I'd forgotten I still had it. No! No! Be careful. Don't point it at me, or I'll never recover from this state I'm in."

"Why would that be?" Ariin asked, plucking it from Father's hand.

"Careful, Narhii! Be careful handling that."

"But why, milady? What is it? What was it doing in your

house if it was so dangerous, and why would Khiindi bring it to my sister?"

"He probably thinks she can return him to his Grimalkin form with it, but of course she can't. It can only freeze forms. It cannot unfreeze them."

"Is that a fact?" Uncle Joh asked. "This is the thing you people used to turn old Grimalkin into Khorii's kitty, is it?"

"Yes, have I not said so?"

"How does it work?"

"Joh, are you thinking what I am thinking?" Father asked, which was not fair since he wasn't letting any of the rest of the family know what he was thinking.

"I think so," Uncle Joh replied. "Well, lady, we ain't any of us getting younger while we're waiting on you, and some people could be dying. Can this thing help us or not?"

"I'm sure I couldn't say," she replied. "I'm not accustomed to dealing with your sort of problems."

Ariin said, "We don't need her to find out. Sona knows the last time Grimalkin was himself. We can set the crono for then and ask him why he brought it out."

"No," Akasa said. "No. I might have to go through that terrible ordeal again. I suppose if Grimalkin, even in cat form, thinks this object might be of use to you in undoing what Odus began"—Khorii noticed Akasa took none of the blame on herself—"then it might be. If you point it—no, other end around—and press the trigger on the head of it, it has the ability to tighten molecular structure. Our people share with the creatures that made our houses a loose molecular structure that allows us to shift shapes easily. This condenses the form, compresses it into a smaller, more closely connected being that cannot alter its shape, at least no more than normal growth patterns. A small cat was the smallest of Grimalkin's many shapes, so that is what he became."

"So, maybe if we use this on the creature, we could condense it back into a muddy spot in the road?" Uncle Joh said. "It's worth a try."

The *Condor* carried two more passengers on its next run over Corazon. Sona and Akasa rode with them. This time they did not fly over the creature, but set down in the field, on the far side of the encampment.

Jalonzo jogged out to meet them, followed by several of their other friends. "You have brought your abuelita, Capitan José'?" he asked Becker.

"No, no, she's not my grandma," Uncle Joh said.

Mother quickly explained the situation to Jalonzo.

"But it is too far for her to walk to the creature," he said, and before the Linyaari or Maak or Elviiz could do so themselves, he swept Akasa into his arms and began jogging with her toward the creature.

"Come, children, they may need us," Mother called.

"Wait for us, Jalonzo," Mikaaye cried, running to catch up.

"Maak, you, Elviiz, and me, back on the bird," Uncle Joh said, running back to the *Condor* as Khorii and her family galloped after Jalonzo and Mikaaye.

They arrived in time to see Akasa raise a hand that at first trembled, but then, with the imperious assurance Ariin knew so well, aimed the shining cylinder at the nearest portion of the undulating, sludgy mass of the monstrous inogre.

Khorii fully expected disappointment again, despite the feeling she had had since Khiindi first brought her the object that it could be the key they needed.

She had not expected the immediate and dramatic shrinking of the creature as it retreated farther and farther toward the center of the city from which it had spread. Jalonzo started to charge in after it with Akasa in his arms but Father stopped him, shaking his head, and took her from him.

The *Condor* flew in a circle over the city, dropping "feeding tubes" into the mass ahead of Father's advance with Akasa. Perhaps that was why Khorii saw no more red dots.

In the end, they were back in a patch of grass measuring the length and breadth of a city block. This was the town square, and the graveyard, Khorii realized with a start. The carefully placed markers had disappeared, but beside the square, in the middle of what used to be a street, the last of the inogre congealed into a vibrating, brown-colored mass. When it had become as small as it seemed likely to, Akasa lowered her hand, Father lowered Akasa to the ground, and everyone gathered around the mass.

"It looks like a face," Mikaaye said.

"It looks like Odus," Ariin and Akasa said together.

The last bit of the Corazon inogre was killed by one small application of the viral, salt, and, synthesized, sap mixture from the *Condor's* arsenal.

Uncle Joh, having delivered the final blow to the thing, shook his head, and said, "Too bad there's only one of those gizmos. We could use thousands, but I bet those fancy pants on Boss World wouldn't make more of them for a little thing like saving the universe."

"They don't have to," Mother said. "They didn't make that one. Grimalkin invented it, and later modified the device, enhancing it with the catseyes. He used it to freeze the mutable acid beings on a hostile planet. It's a long story. But it was a created thing. If we need more advice on how to modify them for this purpose than the elders are willing to give us, we can still resort to time travel, I suppose."

There was no need for that, although in the last push to rid the universe of the final effects of Odus's experiments, the Linyaari fleet and all of the weary volunteers who had only recently returned home were called out again. Since the creature was not an independent race, but an artificially produced menace, Linyaari ethics were not compromised by combating it.

The catseye chrysoberyls required to fuel the devices were mostly obtained from Hafiz's stores. Only the smallest ones were used, and when more of that size were needed, the Makahomians willingly supplied them.

As the universe once more grew as safe as it ever had been for mankind, for commerce, salvagers and pirates included, Khorii's family, the *Balakiire,* and the *Condor* headed back to MOO. Jaya and the *Mana* were under a new, long-term contract from House Harakamian to begin mass supply runs to worlds that had suffered from the plague and its aftereffects.

Uncle Joh, Maak, and RK stopped off on MOO to discuss an "interesting business proposition" Uncle Hafiz had for them.

Khorii's family and Mikaaye joined the *Balakiire*'s crew and at last arrived home.

Before Mikaaye followed his mother and the rest of her crew to their pavilions, he squeezed Khorii's hand. *"If you find a bouquet at your tent flap some morning, it's meant for you, Khorii,"* he told her. For one of the very few times in her life so far, she was left speechless.

They traveled to their old quarantine area, in the heart of the Ancestral grazing grounds, and wearily entered the family pavilion.

However, no sooner had they taken to their mats than Khiindi jumped onto Ariin, pawing at the crono she still wore around her wrist.

Ariin glared at him, but Khorii slipped off the crono she had taken from Pircifir and held it out to her cat. "I will miss you, Khiindi kitty, but you've earned your freedom, and if you want to live in the past, where you can be Grimalkin, then I will gladly do without you," she said.

But he didn't take it from her. Instead he nudged her hand until it rested on Ariin, then walked to Mother's pallet and Father's and finally, somewhat hesitantly, Elviiz's. All the time he meowed in a very bossy and irritating fashion, as if ordering them about.

"I think he wants us touching," Khorii said. "He wants us together so we can all time travel with him."

"Oh, no," Father groaned. "Not tonight. Grimalkin, I just want to be home."

"It seems important, Aari," Mother said, and took his hand and Ariin's. Father took Elviiz's hand, and he took Khorii's free hand, the one that wasn't touching Ariin. They formed a tight circle, with Elviiz in the middle and Khiindi on his shoulders, with his whiskers against Khorii's cheek and his tail brushing Father's. Khorii held up the hand she'd joined with Ariin's for the cat to choose his time.

The pavilion blurred and disappeared so that they stood in an open meadow with the sea shining in the distance and down the shore, an early and comparatively unimpressive version of Kubiilikaan. Khiindi was no more. Grimalkin stood behind Elviiz.

"When are we and what is this all about?" Father asked. "If this is another trick . . ."

Grimalkin smiled and shook his head. "This is no trick, my friend and grandson. But since you have all endured rude treatment at the hands of my race as they pursued the origins of your race, I thought you deserved to see what those origins are. Khorii, I may return to you from time to time to have my ears scratched as only you can, but you gave me leave to go, and I wish to take it here with your original Ancestor and many times great-granddam, my true lifemate, Halili. Don't laugh, Aari. You and I know I have helped found many races, but yours is the most interesting, and Halili is the mate I love best. Fortunately for you, but inconveniently for me, she is not feline. Now pardon me while I change."

Khorii's family stood together as they watched Grimalkin's body lengthen into the sleek, fleet form of an Ancestor, and he galloped away into the meadow, meeting up with another beautiful, snow-white unicorn that was part of a small herd. They nuzzled each other's necks, then the herd galloped off over the hills. Grimalkin's mate rushed to race with them, and the mischievous erstwhile feline reared once, pawing the air with his hooves as if actually saying good-bye, before running over the hill to join his new family.

Glossary of Terms and Proper Names in the Acorna Universe

aagroni—Linyaari name for a vocation that is a combination of ecologist, agriculturalist, botanist, and biologist. *Aagroni* are responsible for terraforming new planets for settlement as well as maintaining the well-being of populated planets.

Aari—a Linyaari of the Nyaarya clan, captured by the Khleevi during the invasion of Vhiliinyar, tortured, and left for dead on the abandoned planet. He's Maati's older brother. Aari survived and was rescued and restored to his people by Jonas Becker and Roadkill. But Aari's differences, the physical and psychological scars left behind by his adventures, make it difficult for him to fit in among the Linyaari.

Aarkiiyi—member of the Linyaari survey team on Vhiliinyar.

Aarlii—a Linyaari survey team member, firstborn daughter of Captain Yaniriin.

Abuelita—grandmother to Jalonzo Allende.

Acorna—a unicorn-like humanoid discovered as an infant by three human miners—Calum, Gill, and Rafik. She has the power to heal and purify with her horn. Her uniqueness has already shaken up the human galaxy, especially the planet Kezdet. She's now fully grown and changing the lives of her own people, as well. Among her own people, she is known as Kornya.

Akasa—One of the Ancestral Friends who raised and experimented on "Narhii," better known as Ariin, Khorii's twin.

Al y Cassidro, Dr. Phador—headmaster and dean of the mining engineering school at Maganos Moonbase.

Ali Baba—Aziza's ship.

Allende, Jalonzo—a young genius from the planet Paloduro.

Ancestors—unicorn-like sentient species, precursor race to the Linyaari. Also known as *ki-lin*.

Ancestral Friends—an ancient shape-changing and spacefaring race responsible for saving the unicorns (or Ancestors) from Old Terra, and using them to create the Linyaari race on Vhiliinyar.

Ancestral Hosts—*see* Ancestral Friends.

Andina—owner of the cleaning concession on MOO, and sometimes lady companion to Captain Becker.

Annunciata—a victim of the space plague on the planet Paloduro, whose form was appropriated by the Ghosts.

Aridimi Desert—a vast, barren desert on the Makahomian planet, site of a hidden Temple and a sacred lake.

Aridimis—people from the Makahomian Aridimi desert.

Arrinye—Ariin for short, Khorii's twin sister, stolen from Acorna while still a tiny embryo, and raised by the Ancestral Friends in a different time and place under the name Narhii.

Attendant—Linyaari who have been selected for the task of caring for the Ancestors.

avvi—Linyaari word for "daddy."

Aziza Amunpul—head of a troupe of dancers and thieves, who, after being reformed, becomes Hafiz's chief security officer on MOO.

Balakiire—the Linyaari spaceship commanded by Acorna's aunt Neeva.

Basic—shorthand for Standard Galactic, the language used throughout human-settled space.

Bates, Asha—teacher on the Maganos Moonbase, then temporary captain of the supply ship *Mana* after its original crew was killed by the plague.

Becker—*see* Jonas Becker.

Boca Rio—a planet in the Solojo star system.

Bogan—An Ancestral Friend in charge of security.

Bulaybub Felidar sach Pilau ardo Agorah—a Makahomian Temple priest, better known by his real name—Tagoth. A priest who supports modernizing the Makahomian way of life, he was a favorite of Nadhari Kando, before her departure from the planet. He has a close relationship in his young relative, Miw-Sher.

Calla Kaczmarek —the psychologist and psychology/sociology instructor on Maganos Moonbase.

Calum Baird—one of three miners who discovered Acorna and raised her.

chrysoberyl—a precious catseye gemstone available in large supply and great size on the planet of Makahomia, but also, very rarely and in smaller sizes, throughout the known universe. The stones are considered sacred on Makahomia, and are guarded by the priest class and the Temples. Throughout the rest of the universe, they are used in the mining and terraforming industries.

Cleda—one of Coco's pirate band.

Coco—leader of the pirates that Marl Fidd tries to enlist in his efforts to kidnap Khorii and use her to purify the riches on other deserted worlds.

Commodore Crezhale—an officer in the Federation Health Service.

Concepcion Mendez—a grandmother on the planet Paloduro, mother to Annunciata, who died in the plague, and grandmother to Elena, who survived it.

Condor—Jonas Becker's salvage ship, heavily modified to incorporate various "found" items Becker has come across in his space voyages.

Crow—Becker's shuttle, used to go between the *Condor* and places in which the *Condor* is unable to land.

Declan "Gill" Giloglie—one of three human miners who discovered Acorna and raised her.

Delores M. Grimwald—Captain of the ship *La Estrella Blanca,* deceased. She sacrificed herself and everyone on her ship to avoid spreading the space plague.

Delszaki Li—once the richest man on Kezdet, opposed to child exploitation, made many political enemies. He lived his life paralyzed, floating in an antigravity chair. Clever and devious, he both hijacked and rescued Acorna and gave her a cause—saving the children of Kezdet. He became her adopted father. Li's death was a source of tremendous sadness to all but his enemies.

Dinan—Temple priest and doctor in Hissim.

Dinero Grande—a world in the Solojo star system.

Domestic Goddess—Andina's spaceship.

Dsu Macostut—Federation officer, Lieutenant Commander of the Federation base on Makahomia.

Edacki Ganoosh—corrupt Kezdet count, uncle of Kisla Manjari.

Egstynkeraht—A planet supporting several forms of sulfur-based sentient life.

Elena—a youngster who survived the space plague on the planet Paloduro.

Elviiz—Maak's son, a Linyaari childlike android, given as a wedding/birth gift to Acorna and Aari. According to Maak, the android is named for an ancient Terran king, and is often called Viiz for short.

enye-ghanyii—Linyaari time unit, small portion of *ghaanye*.

Estrella Blanca—Also known as the *White Star*, a pleasure spacecraft that was where Acorna, Aari, Khorii, Jonas Becker, and Khiindi first encountered the plague. It was a ghost ship after Captain Delores Grimwald killed the crew and passengers to prevent the plague from spreading.

Fagad—Temple priest in the Aridimi desert, who spied for Mulzar Edu Kando.

Felihari—one of the Makavitian Rain Forest tribes on Makahomia.

Feriila—Acorna's mother.

Fiicki—Linyaari communications officer on Vhiliinyar expedition.

Fiirki Miilkar—a Linyaari animal specialist.

Fiiryi—a Linyaari.

fraaki—Linyaari word for fish.

Frida—A moon in the Solojo system.

Friends—also known as Ancestral Friends. A shape-changing and spacefaring race responsible for saving the unicorns from Old Terra and using them to create the Linyaari race on Vhiliinyar.

Gaali—highest peak on Vhiliinyar, never scaled by the Linyaari people. The official marker for Vhiliinyar's date line, anchoring the meridian line that sets the end of the old day and the beginning of the new day across the planet as it rotates Our Star at the center of the solar system. With nearby peaks Zaami and Kaahi, the high mountains are a mystical place for most Linyaari.

ghaanye (pl. ghaanyi)—a Linyaari year.

gheraalye malivii—Linyaari for navigation officer.

gheraalye ve-khanyii—Linyaari for senior communications officer.

Ghost—a deadly alien life-form with the ability to take on the forms of the dead of other species and cultures, which feed on the higher forms of inorganic matter produced by those other cultures.

giirange—office of toast-master in a Linyaari social organization.

Grimalkin—an Ancestral Friend who has become entangled with Aari and Acorna and their children in their voyages through time. He even impersonated Aari for a while. He was punished for his impudence by his people, who trapped him in the body of a cat and took away his machinery for time travel and time control. He has become Khorii's boon companion—she calls him Khiindi. He is the key to a number of secrets that none of the humans or Linyaari are privy to, including the fate of Khorii's formerly lost twin, Ariin.

GSS—Gravitation Stabilization System.

haarha liirni—Linyaari term for advanced education, usually pursued during adulthood while on sabbatical from a previous calling.

Hafiz Harakamian—Rafik's uncle, head of the interstellar financial empire of House Harakamian, a passionate collector of rarities from throughout the galaxy and a devotee of the old-fashioned sport of horseracing. Although basically crooked enough to hide behind a spiral staircase, he is genuinely fond of Rafik and Acorna.

Hap Hellstrom—a student on Maganos Moonbase, and one of Khorii's best friends. He crewed on the *Mana*.

Highmagister HaGurdy—the Ancestral Friend in charge of the Hosts on old Vhiliinyar.

Hissim—the biggest city on Makahomia, home of the largest Temple.

Hraaya—an Ancestor.

Hrronye—Melireenya's lifemate.

Hruffli—an Ancestor stallion, mate of Nrihiiye.

Hrunvrun—the first Linyaari Ancestral attendant.

Iiiliira—a Linyaari ship.

Iirtye—chief *aagroni* for narhii-Vhiliinyar.

Ikwaskwan—self-styled leader of the Kilumbembese Red Bracelets. Depending on circumstances and who he is trying to impress, he is known as either "General Ikwaskwan" or "Admiral Ikwaskwan," though both ranks are self-assigned. Entered into devious dealings with Edacki Ganoosh that led to his downfall.

Inogre—a name coined for the inorganic-matter-eating entities also known as ghosts.

Jaya—captain-in-training on the *Mana*.

Johnny Greene—an old friend of Calum, Rafik, and Gill; joined the Starfarers when he was fired after Amalgamated Mining's takeover of MME.

Jonas Becker—interplanetary salvage artist; alias space junkman. Captain of the *Condor*. CEO of Becker Interplanetary Recycling and Salvage Enterprises Ltd., a one-man, one-cat salvage firm Jonas inherited from his adopted father. Jonas spent his early youth on a labor farm on the planet Kezdet before he was adopted.

Judit Kendoro—assistant to psychiatrist Alton Forelle at Amalgamated Mining, saved Acorna from certain death. Later fell in love with Gill and joined with him to help care for the children employed in Delszaki Li's Maganos mining operation.

Kaahi—a high mountain peak on Vhiliinyar.

Kaalmi Vroniiyi—leader of the Linyaari Council, which made the decision to restore the ruined planet Vhiliinyar, with Hafiz's help and support, to a state that would once again support the Linyaari and all the life-forms native to the planet.

Kaarlye—the father of Aari, Maati, and Laarye. A member of the Nyaarya clan, and life-bonded to Miiri.

ka-**Linyaari**—something against all Linyaari beliefs, something not Linyaari.

Karina—a plumply beautiful wannabe psychic with a small shred of actual talent and a large fondness for profit. Married to Hafiz Harakamian. This is her first marriage, his second.

Kashirian Steppes—Makahomian region that produces the best fighters.

Kashirians—Makahomians from the Kashirian Steppes.

kava—a coffeelike hot drink produced from roasted ground beans.

KEN—a line of general-purpose male androids, some with customized specializations, differentiated among their owners by number, for example—KEN637.

Kezdet—a backwoods planet with a labor system based on child exploitation. Currently in economic turmoil because that system was broken by Delszaki Li and Acorna.

Khaari—senior Linyaari navigator on the *Balakiire.*

Khiindi—He is supposedly Khorii's cat, one of RK's offspring. He is, however, much more than that. He is actually Grimalkin, an Ancestral Friend who got into more mischief than his shape-shifting people approved of. They trapped him in the body of a cat and gave him to Khorii, as penance for his harm to her family and also to allow Grimalkin time to work out his destiny.

Khleevi—name given by Acorna's people to the space-borne enemies who have attacked them without mercy.

Khoriilya—Acorna and Aari's oldest child, a daughter, known as Khorii for short.

kii—a Linyaari time measurement roughly equivalent to an hour of Standard Time.

ki-lin—Oriental term for unicorn, also a name sometimes associated with Acorna.

Kilumbemba Empire—an entire society that raises and exports mercenaries for hire—the Red Bracelets.

Kisla Manjari—anorexic and snobbish young woman, raised as daughter of Baron Manjari; shattered when through Acorna's efforts to help the children of Kezdet her father is ruined and the truth of her lowly birth is revealed.

Kubiilikaan—the legendary first city on Vhiliinyar, founded by the Ancestral Hosts.

Kubiilikhan—capital city of narhii-Vhiliinyar, named after Kubiilikaan, the legendary first city on Vhiliinyar, founded by the Ancestral Hosts.

LAANYE—sleep learning device invented by the Linyaari that can, from a small sample of any foreign language, teach the wearer the new language overnight.

Laarye—Maati and Aari's brother. He died on Vhiliinyar during the Khleevi invasion. He was trapped in an accident in a cave far distant from the spaceport during the evacuation, and was badly injured. Aari stayed behind to rescue and heal him, but was captured by the Khleevi and tortured before he could accomplish his mission. Laarye died before Aari could escape and return. Time travel has brought him back to life.

LaBoue—the planet where Hafiz Harakamian makes his head-quarters.

lalli—Linyaari word for "mother."

Likilekakua—one of Khorii's poopuu friends on Maganos Moon-base.

lilaala—a flowering vine native to Vhiliinyar used by early Lin-yaari to make paper.

Linyaari—Acorna's people.

Liriili—former *viizaar* of narhii-Vhiliinyar, member of the clan Riivye.

LoiLoiKua—a water planet in the human Federation, with human-descended inhabitants that have become fully water-dwelling. Khorii first met people from LoiLoiKua at the school at Maganos, where they were known as pool pupils, or poopuus.

Lukia of the Lights—a protective saint, identified by some chil-dren of Kezdet with Acorna.

Ma'aowri 3—a planet populated by catlike beings.

Maarni—a Linyaari folklorist, mate to Yiitir.

Maati—a young Linyaari girl of the Nyaarya clan who lost most of her family during the Khleevi invasion. Aari's younger sister.

MacKenZ—also known as Mac or Mack, a very useful and adapt-able unit of the KEN line of androids, now in the service of Cap-tain Becker. The android was formerly owned by Kisla Manjari, and came into the captain's service after it tried to kill him on Kisla's orders. Becker's knack for dealing with salvage enabled him to reprogram the android to make the KEN unit both loyal to him and eager to please. The reprogramming had interesting side effects on the android's personality, though, leaving Mack much quirkier than is usually the case for androids.

madigadi—a berrylike fruit whose juice is a popular beverage.

Maganos—one of the three moons of Kezdet, base for Delszaki Li's mining operation and child rehabilitation project.

Makahomia—war-torn home planet of RK and Nadhari Kando.

Makahomian Temple Cat—cats on the planet Makahomia, bred from ancient Cat God stock to protect and defend the Cat God's Temples. They are—for cats—large, fiercely loyal, remarkably intelligent, and dangerous when crossed.

Makavitian Rain Forest—a tropical area of the planet Makahomia, populated by various warring jungle tribes.

Mana—a supply ship whose crew and former owners died in the plague with the exception of Jaya, the captain-in-training, now captained by Asha Bates and a crew of young survivors.

Manjari—a baron in the Kezdet aristocracy, and a key person in the organization and protection of Kezdet's child-labor racket, in which he was known by the code name "Piper." He murdered his wife and then committed suicide when his identity was revealed and his organization destroyed.

Marl Fidd—a student on Maganos Moonbase, later a committed criminal and pirate. A true cad.

Martin Dehoney—famous astro-architect who designed Maganos Moonbase; the coveted Dehoney Prize was named after him.

Melireenya—Linyaari communications specialist on the *Balakiire,* bonded to Hrronye. Their son is Mikaaye.

Mercy Kendoro—younger sister of Pal and Judit Kendoro, saved from a life of bonded labor by Judit's efforts, she worked as a spy for the Child Liberation League in the offices of Kezdet Guardians of the Peace until the child-labor system was destroyed.

Miiri—mother of Aari, Laarye, and Maati. A member of the Nyaarya clan, lifebonded to Kaarlye.

Mikaaye—Melireenya's and Hrronya's son. He worked on narhii-Vhiliinyar with his father helping shape a new and less exclusive Linyaari society, then joined Khorii, along with other Linyaari, as they all worked together to eradicate the galactic plague. He almost lost his life on Rushima as he and Khorii fought the Ghosts.

mitanyaakhi—generic Linyaari term meaning a very large number.

Miw-Sher—a Makahomian Keeper of the sacred Temple cats. Her name means "Kitten" in Makahomian.

MME—Gill, Calum, and Rafik's original mining company. Swallowed by the ruthless, conscienceless, and bureaucratic Amalgamated Mining.

Mog-Gim Plateau—an arid area on the planet Makahomia near the Federation spaceport.

Mokilau—a LoiLoiKuan elder.

MOO, or Moon of Opportunity—Hafiz's artificial planet, and home base for the Vhiliinyar terraforming operation.

Moonmay Marsden—a plucky Rushima settler child, very accurate with her shotgun. With her brother Percy and their cousin Fleagle, the Marsden family helped Khorii and the company from the *Mana* bury their dead.

Morniika—Linyaari Ancestor mare and Neicaair's mate.

Mulzar (feminine form: Mulzarah)—the Mog-Gimin title taken by the high priest who is also the warlord of the Plateau.

Mulzar Edu Kando sach Pilau dom Mog-Gim—High Priest of Hissim and the Aridimi Plateau, on the planet Makahomia.

Naadiina—also known as Grandam, one of the oldest Linyaari, host to both Maati and Acorna on narhii-Vhiliinyar, died to give her people the opportunity to save both of their planets.

Naarye—Linyaari techno-artisan in charge of final fit-out of spaceships.

naazhoni—the Linyaari word for someone who is a bit unstable.

Nadhari Kando—formerly Delszaki Li's personal bodyguard, rumored to have been an officer in the Red Bracelets earlier in her career, then a security officer in charge of MOO, then the guard for the leader on her home planet of Makahomia.

Nanahomea—a LoiLoiKuan elder, grandmother to Likilekakua, one of Khorii's poopuu friends.

narhii—Linyaari word for new.

Narhii—the name given by the Ancestral Friends to Khorii's twin sister, later renamed Ariinye, who was stolen from Acorna's womb while still an embryo.

narhii-Vhiliinyar—the planet settled by the Linyaari after Vhiliinyar, their original homeworld, was destroyed by the Khleevi.

Neeva—Acorna's aunt and Linyaari envoy on the *Balakiire,* bonded to Virii.

Neicaair—a Linyaari Ancestor stallion.

Neo-Hadithian—an ultraconservative, fanatical religious sect.

Ngaen Xong Hoa—a Kieaanese scientist who invented a planetary weather control system. He sought asylum on the *Haven* because he feared the warring governments on his planet would misuse his research. A mutineer faction on the *Haven* used the system to reduce the planet Rushima to ruins. The mutineers were tossed into space, and Dr. Hoa has since restored Rushima and now works for Hafiz.

Nheifaarir—the egg-shaped spacecraft assigned to Maati's family, often used by Maati and Thariinye.

Niciirye—Grandam Naadiina's husband, dead and buried on Vhiliinyar.

Niikaavri—Acorna's *G*randmother, a member of the clan Geeyiinah, and a spaceship designer by trade. Also, as *Niikaavre,* the name of the spaceship used by Maati and Thariinye.

Nirii—a planetary trading partner of the Linyaari, populated by bovinelike two-horned sentients, known as Niriians, technologically advanced, able to communicate telepathically, and phlegmatic in temperament.

Nisa—one of Coco's pirate band, a friend of Captain Bates.

Nrihiiye—an Ancestor mare, mate of Hruffli.

nyiiri—the Linyaari word for unmitigated gall, sheer effrontery, or other form of misplaced bravado.

Odus—one of the Ancestral Friends who raised and experimented on "Narhii," better known as Ariin, Khorii's twin.

Odussia—the new homeworld of the Ancestral Friends.

Our Star—Linyaari name for the star that centers their solar system.

Paazo River—a major geographical feature on the Linyaari homeworld, Vhiliinyar.

pahaantiyir—a large catlike animal once found on Vhiliinyar.

Paloduro—a planet in the Solojo star system, infested by the space plague.

Pandora—Count Edacki Ganoosh's personal spaceship, used to track and pursue Hafiz's ship *Shahrazad* as it speeds after Acorna on her journey to narhii-Vhiliinyar. Later confiscated and used by Hafiz for his own purposes.

Pauli—one of Coco's pirate band.

Pebar—an intergalactic circus carney who exploits Khorii as part of his new act.

Petit—one of Coco's pirate band.

Phador—*see* Al y Cassidro, Dr. Phador.

piiyi—a Niriian biotechnology-based information storage and retrieval system. The biological component resembles a very rancid cheese.

Pircifir—an Ancestral Friend.

Poopuus—a term for water-dwelling students from LoiLoiKua used on Maganos Moonbase, an abbreviation from the words "pool pupils."

Praxos—a swampy planet near Makahomia used by the Federation to train Makahomian recruits.

PU#10—Human name for the vine planet, with its sentient plant inhabitants, where the Khleevi-killing sap was found.

Raealacaldae—the corrupt Federation head of LoiLoiKua, who died after poisoning the waters of the planet. His palace on the dry land of the planet remains, and has been inhabited by the Ghosts.

Rafik Nadezda—one of three miners who discovered Acorna and raised her.

Red Bracelets—Kilumbembese mercenaries; arguably the toughest and nastiest fighting force in known space.

Rio Boca—a planet in the Solojo star system.

Roadkill—otherwise known as RK. A Makahomian Temple Cat, the only survivor of a space wreck, he was rescued and adopted by Jonas Becker, and is honorary first mate of the *Condor*. He is often (and erroneously) thought to be the father of Khorii's cat Khiindi.

Roc—Rafik's shuttle ship.

Rushima—a planet with an agriculturally based economy invaded by the Khleevi, and saved by Acorna. After the galactic plague and the Ghosts made things miserable there again, it was saved by Khorii and Mikaaye.

Scaradine MacDonald—captain of the *Arkansas Traveler* spaceship, and galactic freight hauler.

Sesseli—a curly-headed blond student on Maganos Moonbase with very strong telepathy, she is the first person to spot the Ghosts.

Shahrazad—Hafiz's personal spaceship, a luxury cruiser.

Shoshisha—a student on the Maganos Moonbase.

sii-**Linyaari**—a legendary race of aquatic Linyaari-like beings developed by the Ancestral Friends.

Siiaaryi Maartri—a Linyaari Survey ship.

Sileg—an intergalactic circus carney who exploits Khorii as part of his new act.

Sinbad—Rafik's spaceship.

Sita Ram—a protective goddess, identified with Acorna by the mining children on Kezdet.

Smythe-Wesson—a former Red Bracelet officer, Win Mythe-Wesson briefly served as Hafiz's head of security on MOO before his larcenous urges overcame him.

Solojo—a star system in the human galaxy, one of the first infected with the space plague.

Spandard—A variant dialect of Standard Galactic Basic, once known as Spanish.

Standard Galactic Basic—the language used throughout the human-settled galaxy, also known simply as "Basic."

stiil—Linyaari word for a pencil-like writing implement.

Taankaril—*visedhaanye ferilii* of the Gamma sector of Linyaari space.

Tagoth—*see* Bulaybub.

techno-artisan—Linyaari specialist who designs, engineers, or manufactures goods.

Thariinye—a handsome and conceited young spacefaring Linyaari from clan Renyilaaghe.

Theophilus Becker—Jonas Becker's father, a salvage man and astrophysicist with a fondness for exploring uncharted wormholes.

thiilir (pl. *thilirii*)—small arboreal mammals of the Linyaari home-world.

thiilsis—grass species native to Vhiliinyar.

Toruna—a Niriian female, who sought help from Acorna and the Linyaari when her home planet was invaded by the Khleevi.

Twexa—an Ancestral Friend.

Twi Osiam—planetary site of a major financial and trade center.

twilit—small, pestiferous insect on the Linyaari home planet.

Uhuru—one of the various names of the ship owned jointly by Gill, Calum, and Rafik.

Vaanye—Acorna's father.

viizaar—a high political office in the Linyaari system, roughly equivalent to president or prime minister.

Virii—Neeva's spouse.

visedhaanye ferilii—Linyaari term corresponding roughly to "Envoy Extraordinary."

Vriiniia Watiir—sacred healing lake on Vhiliinyar, defiled by the Khleevi.

Wahanamoian Blossom of Sleep—poppylike flowers whose pollens, when ground, are a very powerful sedative.

White Star—see *Estrella Blanca*.

wii—a Linyaari prefix meaning small.

yaazi—Linyaari term for beloved.

Yaniriin—a Linyaari Survey Ship captain.

Yiitir—history teacher at the Linyaari academy, and Chief Keeper of the Linyaari Stories. Lifemate to Maarni.

Yukata Batsu—Uncle Hafiz's chief competitor on LaBoue.

Zaami—a high mountain peak on the Linyaari homeworld.

Zanegar—second-generation Starfarer.

BRIEF NOTES ON
THE LINYAARI LANGUAGE

By Margaret Ball

As Anne McCaffrey's collaborator in transcribing the first two tales of Acorna, I was delighted to find that the second of these books provided an opportunity to sharpen my long-unused skills in linguistic fieldwork. Many years ago, when the government gave out scholarships with gay abandon and the cost of living (and attending graduate school) was virtually nil, I got a Ph.D. in linguistics for no better reason than that (a) the government was willing to pay, (b) it gave me an excuse to spend a couple of years doing fieldwork in Africa, and (c) there weren't any real jobs going for eighteen-year-old girls with a B.A. in math and a minor in Germanic languages. (This was back during the Upper Pleistocene era, when the Help Wanted ads were still divided into Male and Female.)

So there were all those years spent doing things like transcribing tonal Oriental languages on staff paper (the Field Methods instructor was Not Amused) and tape-recording Swahili women at weddings, and then I got the degree and wandered off to play with computers and never had any use for the stuff again . . . until Acorna's people appeared on the scene. It required a sharp ear and some facility for linguistic analysis to make sense of the subtle sound-changes with which their language signaled syntactic changes; I quite enjoyed the challenge.

The notes appended here represent my first and necessarily tentative analysis of certain patterns in Linyaari phonemics and morphophonemics. If there is any inconsistency between this analysis and the Linyaari speech patterns recorded in the later adventures of Acorna, please remember that I was working from a very limited database and, what is perhaps worse, attempting to analyze a decidedly nonhuman language with the aid of the only paradigms I had, twentieth-century linguistic models developed exclusively from human language. The result is very likely as inaccurate as were the first attempts to describe English syntax by forcing it into the mold of Latin, if not worse. My colleague, Elizabeth Ann Scarborough, has by now added her own notes to the small corpus of Linyaari names and utterances, and it may well be that in the next decade there will be enough data available to publish a truly definitive dictionary and grammar of Linyaari, an undertaking that will surely be of inestimable value, not only to those members of our race who are involved in diplomatic and trade relations with this people, but also to everyone interested in the study of language.

Notes on the Linyaari Language

1. A doubled vowel indicates stress: **aavi, abaanye, khleevi.**

2. Stress is used as an indicator of syntactic function: in nouns stress is on the penultimate syllable, in adjectives on the last syllable, in verbs on the first.

3. Intervocalic *n* is always palatalized.

4. Noun plurals are formed by adding a final vowel, usually -i: one **Liinyar**, two **Linyaari**. Note that this causes a change in the stressed syllable (from **LI-nyar** to **Li-NYA-ri**) and hence a change in the pattern of doubled vowels.

For nouns whose singular form ends in a vowel, the plural is formed by dropping the original vowel and adding -i: **ghaanye, ghaanyi**. Here the number of syllables remains the same, therefore no stress/spelling change is required.

5. Adjectives can be formed from nouns by adding a final -ii (again, dropping the original final vowel if one exists): maalive, malivii; Liinyar, Linyarii. Again, the change in stress means that the doubled vowels in the penultimate syllable of the noun disappear.

6. For nouns denoting a class or species, such as Liinyar, the noun itself can be used as an adjective when the meaning is simply to denote a member of the class, rather than the usual adjective meaning of "having the qualities of this class"— thus, of the characters in ACORNA, only Acorna herself could be described as "a **Liinyar** girl" but Judit, although human, would certainly be described as "a **Linyarii** girl," or "a just-as-civilized-as-a-real-member-of-the-People" girl.

7. Verbs can be formed from nouns by adding a prefix constructed by [first consonant of noun] + ii + nye: **faalar**—grief; **fiinyefalar**—to grieve.

8. The participle is formed from the verb by adding a suffix -an or -en: **thiinyethilel**—to destroy, **thiinyethilelen**—destroyed. No stress change is involved because the participle is perceived as a verb form and therefore stress remains on the first syllable:

enye-ghanyii—time unit, small portion of a year
  (**ghaanye**)

fiinyefalaran—mourning, mourned

ghaanyie—a Linyaari year, equivalent to about 1 1/3
  earth years

gheraalye malivii—Navigation Officer

gheraalye ve-khanyii—Senior Communications
  Specialist

Khleevi—originally, a small vicious carrion-feeding
  animal with a poisonous bite; now used by the
  Linyaari to denote the invaders who destroyed their
  homeworld.

khleevi—barbarous, uncivilized, vicious without reason

Liinyar—member of the People

linyaari—civilized; like a Liinyar

mitanyaakhi—large number (slang—like our "zillions")

narhii—new

thiilel—destruction

thiilir, thiliiri—small arboreal mammals of the Linyaari
  homeworld

visedhaanye ferilii—Envoy Extraordinary